I0668319

Tsunami Crimes

by

Chrys Fey

Disaster Crimes, Book 3

Tsunami Crimes

Cover Art by *Kim Mendoza*

The Wild Rose Press, Inc.
PO Box 708
Adams Basin, NY 14410-0708
Visit us at www.thewildrosepress.com

Publishing History
First Crimson Rose Edition, 2017
Print ISBN 978-1-5092-1237-8
Digital ISBN 978-1-5092-1238-5

Disaster Crimes, Book 3
Published in the United States of America

A blast of wind

slammed into Beth's back, knocking her forward. Mist swooped around her. The smell of salt tingled her nostrils. She turned to see a wall of water surging toward them. Cars were whisked away as if they were toys, and palm trees were flattened. People were screaming and running past them, but Beth was paralyzed with fright. The wave reached far above the buildings it engulfed. It was massive. Incredible. Terrifying.

Tsunami!

The word blazed through Beth's mind. Even though she knew what it was, it was too impossible to believe. A tsunami couldn't strike on her honeymoon. A tsunami couldn't wash her away. The thought was crazy, something that could happen in dreams or fiction. Too impossible for real life, and yet, it was happening.

Donovan pulled Beth to him.

She grasped his arms. Fear of the wave, of not telling him she loved him, and not having a life with him beyond their wedding rippled through her, tearing her insides to shreds with long, curved talons. Water washed over her feet and flowed up her shins. She sucked in a breath a millisecond before the wave plowed into her, tossing her backward, knocking her down, and yanking her from Donovan's hold. Her body slid along the black pavement. The feel of her skin peeling away made her grit her teeth. Then the water lifted her and sent her rolling. She fought against the sheer power of it as she would fight off an attacker, but this wave was fiercer than any opponent she had ever faced.

Praise for Chrys Fey

"*HURRICANE CRIMES* is a pure delight. It is a romance first and a suspense novella second, but both are combined in a perfect formula for a wonderful afternoon's reading."

~*Readers' Favorite*

~*~

"*SEISMIC CRIMES* is an action-packed novel that contains a little bit of everything. There's the suspense of a crime-fighting story, the adventure of surviving natural disasters, and the passion of romance."

~*Sherry Ellis, author*

~*~

"Get set for action, suspense, and edge-of-your-seat danger with Chrys Fey's *TSUNAMI CRIMES*. Couldn't put this book down."

~*Diane Burton, author of the Alex O'Hara PI series*

~*~

"The Disaster Crimes series has the potential to be a terrific series that is spellbinding and have readers on the edge of their seats."

~*InD'tale Magazine*

Dedication

To all impacted by tsunamis.

~*~

Thanks to Diane Burton, beta reader extraordinaire;
Lori Graham, my editor,
for being the best editor I could ever ask for;
and Kim Mendoza
for creating wonderful covers for my series.

Chapter One

The water stretched to the horizon and blended into the sky, tricking the eye into believing the ocean went on forever. Looking out at the distant ocean could make a person feel microscopic, which was what Donovan liked most about surfing. Salty air touched his skin as he straddled his surfboard and waited for a wave. He took a lung-filling breath of air and glanced at Beth, who balanced on a surfboard beside him. She wore orange board shorts and a black wet shirt. The surfboard beneath her was yellow with a pattern of Hawaiian flowers down the middle. Her hands hovered over the water's surface. Gentle waves lapped over her fingers. She looked like a serene goddess, a modern-day Venus with wet hair and pineapple sex wax on her board.

During the past year, he had taught Beth to surf. She tackled the waves with vigor. The first time she stood on the board, her eyes were bright with excitement. She was a quick learner and wasn't afraid to wipeout. Soon, she had the skill of someone who had surfed for years. Donovan couldn't wait to take her surfing in Hawaii during their honeymoon.

Looking away from Beth, he stared across the water. In the distance, a wave took shape. "This one is yours."

"All right, don't go anywhere." Smirking, she

maneuvered her board around and paddled as the wave grew in size. When the wave lifted her up, she popped to her feet, performed the short drop, and rode the wave to the end.

Donovan smiled as pride rippled through him. "She's ready."

He swung his board around and let the waves push him to the shore where Beth waited. Carrying his board under his arm, with grains of sand sticking to his feet, he walked alongside Beth to the Cocoa Beach Pier. At the end of the pier, he wrapped his arms around her. The sun was setting behind them, scoring the sky with streaks of yellow, orange, and pink. Waves splashed against the barnacle spotted wood, creating a wet gurgling sound.

With Beth in his arms, he enjoyed the scenery, the smell of salt water, and the misty breeze. In two weeks, he'd be doing this same thing on another beach halfway across the world. He was excited to start their lives together as husband and wife, to start their journey of married life.

"Two more weeks," he whispered in Beth's ear.

She snuggled her head into the curve of his neck. "I know."

"Are you scared?"

She turned in his arms. "No, I'm happy and nervous but not scared." She frowned. "Are you?"

He smoothed the drying hair from her face. "Far from it." Touching his lips to hers, he tasted the saltiness of the ocean. "I can't wait to make you mine."

"I believe you said I was *yours* when you locked me in that jail cell."

Donovan thought back to their stay with the police

thanks to the flood Hurricane Sabrina had left. There were five other men, police officers but men nonetheless, trapped in that building. He wasn't taking any chances with the woman he loved, so when she went to sleep, he locked her in a jail cell.

"I did say that, but it'll be official on our wedding day."

Beth pressed her lips to his. "It's been official since the first time we made love."

He cupped her chin with his fingers and gazed into her brown eyes. "You know what I mean."

"I do."

He smiled at her word choice. "You're not supposed to say that yet."

Her laughter filled his ears, drowning out the roar of the tumbling waves. "I'll be saying it again in two weeks. That's a promise."

The sun sank below the horizon, the sky darkened, and Donovan's stomach grumbled. After a long day of surfing, he could use sustenance, and there was one meal he preferred following a visit to the beach. "Do you want pizza?"

Beth put a hand on her stomach. "Hell yeah. I'm starving."

****

After devouring pizza and showering, Beth stepped into the living room wearing a bathrobe. Donovan moved toward her. His hands itched to undo the tie and part the sides. Fondling her body and kissing her warm skin would be the dessert to top off the day. His mouth watered. His heart rate quickened.

A few paces from her, a knock sounded at the door. He growled, "Whoever that is, I'm going to punch 'em." He peered through the peephole. With a laugh, he flashed his teeth at Beth. "It's Thorn."

She shook her head. "Don't punch him. He's your best man."

Thorn was a detective who flirted with Beth to purposefully tick him off. If that wasn't reason enough to punch him, this was one.

"Doesn't make it any less tempting," Donovan said. His gaze swept over Beth.

Her hair was wet, and the sash barely held the robe together. "Don't give Thorn any ideas. Please put on some clothes."

Beth rolled her eyes but closed herself into the bedroom, hopefully to put on a turtleneck.

Donovan opened the door. "Hey, Thorn."

"Hey, sorry to disturb you and the Mrs." He stepped into their apartment, smelling a little like gunpowder.

Donovan shut the door. "Don't ever let Beth hear you call her that."

Thorn snorted. "Do you think I have a death wish?" Despite his nonchalant words, his gaze scanned the area. Donovan assumed he did it to make sure Beth wasn't in earshot.

He smirked. "What can I do for you, Thorn? Do you want coffee?"

"No, I'm fine. I need to talk to Beth, though."

As if she knew Thorn requested her presence, Beth emerged from the bedroom wearing a black T-shirt and purple pajama pants. Black socks even covered her feet. She gave Donovan a look that said, "Happy?"

Very.

"Hey, Thorn." She gave him a hug. "It's been a

long time."

"I've been buried in work," he said with an apologetic smile.

"You'll be able to get time off for the wedding, right?"

"Are you kidding? I wouldn't miss that for the world."

She smiled. "Good. I heard you wanted to talk to me. What's up?"

Thorn slipped his right hand into his pocket. "I have something I need to ask you." He waved his other hand at the dining room table. "Can we sit?"

Beth glanced at Donovan. He supposed he looked as curious as she did.

Thorn took the seat across from Beth, and Donovan sat next to her.

"Normally, I'd only speak to you about this, Beth, but I know Donovan would find out and would likely kill me for not telling him, too."

Donovan arched a brow. "I already don't like the sound of this."

Thorn's gaze flicked to him then settled on Beth. "You did a phenomenal job when you went undercover in Viper's house. You blended in, took care of yourself, and helped us not only to get information on Buck's location, but you also aided in taking down a houseful of drug dealers. What you did was equivalent to what a person with a shield would do, and you did it without a weapon." He took a breath before continuing. "Police officers and detectives often use civilian operatives to do undercover work. These civilian operatives tend to be people we know and trust. I know and trust you."

Silence fell over the table.

Beth spoke first. "You want me to be your civilian operative?"

Thorn nodded. "I have a case I want to close, but to do that I need to nab a man who brutalizes prostitutes. Even kills them. He's done it eight times already, and I need to get him before he does it again. Except, I can't use a cop. He'll be able to spot them from a block away. I need you."

"Isn't that entrapment?"

"We won't be tempting him into doing anything he doesn't already do. We know where he hunts for the prostitutes he picks up. It's hard for anyone but these women to get close to him, so that's where you come in. We're hoping he'll take the bait."

"And we already know I can play the role of a hooker," Beth added.

Donovan couldn't forget his anger when she had lured Buck with the promise of sex into the underground parking garage of a San Francisco hotel. He hated the idea then when she had only been his girlfriend. Now she was his fiancée. And he wanted to beat the shit out of Thorn for suggesting it.

He clenched his hands on top of the table. "No way will my fiancée be bait for a man who beats up prostitutes."

"She won't be alone, Donovan. I'll have men in disguises all over the area, and I'll be there watching her back. All she needs to do is distract him by getting him to agree on sex acts. When he's engrossed in her, we'll move in."

"I don't care if you'll have SWAT on standby."

Beth put her hand on his arm. "Donovan, I could do this—"

He glanced at her. The fact she was considering what Thorn asked of her infuriated him. Heat spread throughout his body, searing him. "We need to talk about this. Thorn you need to leave."

Thorn got up without another word.

Donovan stalked him to the door and slammed it at his back, throwing the chain and snapping the bolt into place.

"Seriously, Donovan? What was that about?"

He rotated to Beth. Her fists were planted on her hips. Her brows furrowed. "I'm not allowing you—"

Beth cut him off. "Allowing me? You're not my father."

"No, but I'm going to be your husband," he shot back.

"And you think that means you have the right to make decisions for me? I am strong and smart. I can handle this, and you know it. Besides that, I made an oath to help abused women. I didn't omit hookers from that vow. If I have to go undercover to make sure no more are beaten or killed, I will." She spun on her heel and marched toward the bedroom. "I'm calling Thorn."

Donovan raked his hands through his hair "Beth, wait."

She turned back to him and crossed her arms.

He sighed when he saw her stance. She was aggravated and had every right to be. He had snapped at her and tried to control her. That wasn't his way. He stepped up to her and took her arms in his hands so he could look in her eyes. "In two weeks, you're going to be my wife. I don't want some lowlife to take you away from me before you get to walk down that aisle. The thought of you going undercover again scares me."

Her eyes softened. "No one will take me away from you." She let out a slow breath. "You know how you were determined to find your brother's killer at all costs?"

"Yes, but it's not the same thing."

"But our motivation is the same. I want to… No, I *have* to help Thorn get this guy. If you're worried about me being in danger out there, I was in far more danger when I was in Viper's house."

Donovan let go of her wrists and turned away. "Thanks for that," he muttered. He had agreed to let Beth go undercover in a notorious drug dealer's house. Watching her walk away from Thorn's car, he had felt as though she was walking into a lion's den. Listening to Viper talk to her, courtesy of the wire she had worn, had made him want to strangle the bastard with his bare hands, but hearing the fear in her voice as she ran for safety had made his heart seize. Never again, he had told himself. *Never again.*

"After seeing the effect your encounter with Viper had on you, I vowed I'd never put you in another situation like that."

Beth put her hands on either side of his face. "That wasn't your fault, and I'm not going to be in a house full of criminals this time."

"No, you're just going to be luring one to you."

Her hands fell from his face. Shoulders slumped, she dropped onto the edge of the bed as if he had defeated her. He hated seeing her like that.

He lowered onto his knees in front of her. "I'm sorry, Beth, I just can't watch you do that. I don't ever want you to be in danger again."

She laid her hand against his cheek. "I understand."

She looked away; then after a moment, she turned back to him. "What if you were there?"

Her question caught him off guard. "What?"

"What if you were a few yards away? Disguised and working as one of Thorn's men?"

Donovan shook his head, still not liking the idea, but he knew outright objecting wouldn't work with Beth. "I'll think about it."

Chapter Two

Beth woke with one sock on; the other one was tangled in the comforter. She pulled off the lone sock and chucked it into the laundry hamper. Donovan was sound asleep on his side of the bed. The fact she was awake before him was a rare occurrence.

At the dining room table with a bowl of cereal, she thought about their argument. Donovan had agreed to think about her going undercover again, and she knew that meant he'd have to come to terms with her being close to a criminal and in potential harm. Neither of those would be easy for him to overcome.

His words came back to her. His outright refusal, as if she were a child, had set her back straight. Although his words had been controlling, they came from a good place. Donovan would never abuse her in any shape or form; she knew that. He was a good man who loved her deeply. She also knew he could be a bit stubborn and rash, but she could recognize that his reaction yesterday came from a blend of love and fear. Putting herself in his shoes, she would've had the same response.

Deciding to give him time to think about it, she looked over her wedding checklist. The big day was getting closer, and there were still a lot of things she had to do, like pick up her dress and their marriage license. Bringing the spoon of granola to her mouth, she fantasized about their wedding. She knew what Donovan's suit looked like, but her imagination lacked the twinkle in his violet eyes, the strong lines of his limbs beneath the fabric of his jacket, and the way his hair would be combed across his forehead. Picturing him standing in front of her as she walked toward him made her stomach flutter like hummingbird wings.

Halfway through the bowl, her cell phone buzzed. *Thorn.* Her finger hovered over the green icon as she considered whether answering would be considered cheating on Donovan, especially since he had been so angry after Thorn's visit.

Nonsense! Thorn's our friend.

She answered the call before it could roll to voicemail. "Hey, Thorn."

"Hey, Beth." He exhaled. "I'm sorry if my visit last night caused a fight. Are the two of you still engaged?"

Beth smiled. "Yes."

"Is the wedding still on?"

"Yes, and you're still the best man."

"But the two of you fought, didn't you?"

"Of course, we did." She picked up her bowl and carried it into the kitchen. "He said he'd think about it if he could be there, disguised as one of your team members. Would that complicate things?"

There was silence as Thorn mulled it over.

"It's doable," he finally said. "As long as he doesn't do something stupid, like storm across the street to deliver an ass-kicking if the guy lays a finger on you."

"That would be bad." Beth turned from the sink to see Donovan studying her a few feet away. Tingles snaked up her body at the power of his stare. "I think he'll behave himself."

"That's easy for you to say," Thorn said.

Beth moved toward Donovan. She stopped in front of him. "No, it's not. I know what he's like."

Donovan quirked a brow.

"Thorn, is there another reason for this call other than to apologize for ruining my marriage before it could start?"

Donovan tilted his head. Worry flitted across his face.

"He's standing right there, isn't he? Well, put me on speaker. This is for him, too."

Beth hit the speaker icon. "Okay, Thorn, we're ready."

"I want the two of you to come to the hospital at noon today. I want you to talk to the latest victim of the man I'm trying to capture."

Beth peered at Donovan and hoped her eyes showed how much she wanted to talk to the woman, if she could do nothing else.

Donovan took the phone from her hand. "We'll be there," he said and ended the call. He set the phone on the counter. "Our marriage ended last night?"

Silent panic reflected in his eyes. Seeing that reaction made her panic, too; she hadn't meant to cause that. She laid a hand on his chest, hoping to ease his stress. "No, but Thorn thought it might have come close." She looped her arms around his neck. "The only reason I would ever leave you is if you cheated on me or hit me."

Donovan framed her face with his hands and peered deep into her eyes. "I would never do those things."

She nodded. "I know. You're a good man, a thousand times better than the men I dated before you."

"You wouldn't happen to have a list of those other men, would you? I'd like to have a word with each of them."

Beth squinted at him. She recalled how he latched onto her ex-fiancé's name like a dog after a juicy bone. As far as she knew, nothing came out of that, but that didn't mean she would reveal her old boyfriends' identities for Donovan's amusement.

"Not happening," she said. "And you don't have to worry about any of them anyway. You're the only man in my life." She put her arms around his waist. "Well, other than Thorn."

Donovan pinched her butt, making her jump. "One of these days, I'm going to punch him."

She laughed. "No, you're not." She leaned back. "What about me?"

He frowned. "What about you?"

"I see how women look at you. You're six feet of delicious man flesh. Women drool after you in the produce section, *and* you told me you had a bunch of girls in your past."

"I didn't say it like that."

"No, you said you took them all over Michigan to get into their pants. My point is…you're not getting a list of my ex-boyfriends unless you give me a list in return." She patted his arm and sashayed out of the kitchen.

Two can play this game.

****

At noon, Beth and Donovan arrived at the hospital where Thorn's witness had been admitted last night.

Beth glanced around the waiting room. Mothers tried to soothe their children. Elderly scooted around with walkers, and teenagers were plugged into their devices. People filled out forms, got coffee, and asked nurses how much longer they'd have to wait. One man held an icepack to his head.

Thorn stood near the front desk with his back against the wall and his arms and legs crossed. He pushed himself off the wall and walked over to them. "I'm glad you came." His gaze connected with Donovan.

Beth watched them have a non-verbal conversation. She imagined it consisted of manly grunts and chest bumping. When it was over, Thorn nodded and led them to the elevators.

Beth kept her laughter at bay. *Men. They really are their own species.*

She followed Thorn onto the fourth floor, down a corridor, and to a room. Outside the door, he faced them. "Her name is April Sanchez. I have to warn you…she's badly beaten. She was brought in yesterday morning. She has a broken arm and sutures on her cheek."

Beth nodded.

Thorn opened the door, and she followed him. A white curtain shielded half of the room. Beth stepped around it and froze. Thorn was wrong. The woman laid out on the hospital bed hadn't been beaten; she had been pulverized. Her face was puffed to the size of a volleyball. Her eyes were purple. Stitches cinched together a three-inch gash on her left cheek in the shape of a crescent moon. Bruises dotted her neck, an indication someone had choked her. Her black hair lay flat against her scalp, and her arm was in a cast and sling.

Beth had visited her students in the hospital after violent situations numerous times. She had even seen her own reflection with hideous injuries staring back at her, but nothing quite as horrific as this. Her breath fled from her lungs. Shock rippled through her.

Beth felt Donovan's hand on her back. A question was behind the touch. *Are you okay?* She took a step toward the hospital bed as Thorn put his hand on the woman's right shoulder. The woman jumped and tried to flail in defense.

He lifted his hand. "I'm sorry, April. It's Detective Thorn."

She was breathing fast when she stared at him through slits in her eyelids. "Hi," she rasped.

"I have a couple here who want to know what happened. They're not cops, but they may assist in capturing Ramirez."

From beneath thick, dark eyelids, April's gaze shifted to them.

"I'm Beth, and this is Donovan," she said.

"Hi." April's voice was so soft it tore Beth's heart.

"We're deeply sorry about what happened to you. We won't be here long. We know you need to rest."

Thorn moved a chair next to the bed and indicated for Beth to sit. "April, tell them what you remember about the other day."

"And please take your time," Beth said.

April licked her inflated lips. "It was a slow day. I was tired and already ate through the mini bag of corn chips I keep in my purse. My feet were killing me, too." She pointed a finger at the six-inch heels sitting on the table in the corner. White fuzz lined the toes. The heels were transparent, and the strap around the ankle glittered.

Beth nodded. "Yeah, those will do it."

April's lips twitched with a smile that was too painful to journey to its full length. "I was about to leave when a big ass, tricked-out Hummer pulled up to me. It was all black and chrome with sweet rims and tinted windows. If you're like me, you look at the vehicles and what the men are wearing to determine if they have money or not. And this guy oozed money. He was wearing a Rolex, a silver chain, and he had diamonds the size of M&Ms in his ears. It was clear he had money, and I felt like I found a diamond mine." She shifted and winced. "When I got in the Hummer, he asked me if I had any toys in my bag. I told him I had fuzzy handcuffs, oils, and nipple clamps. That made him happy, because he smiled." She shivered at the memory. "He took me to a crappy motel. I was disappointed, but so often I'm taken to one of those joints that I got over it. The moment he locked the door, he spun around and punched me. I tried to fight back, but he was too strong. I must've gone unconscious because the next thing I knew I was handcuffed to the bed."

She stopped there. When she spoke again, her voice was a whisper. "He raped me." Her gaze flipped to Beth, pinning her in place with that four-letter word. "I was screaming for help, but no one came." Tears squeezed from under her thick eyelids. "After he finished, he cut my cheek and told me I was his. Then he beat me some more. Thorn said a cleaning woman found me. Now here I am." She didn't have to say more, because the evidence of that beating was painted all over her body in hideous red and purple marks.

Beth put her hand over April's. "Guys…" She looked from Donovan to Thorn. "Can you give us a minute?"

They closed the door behind them.

"I wanted the guys out of the room so we could talk privately." She paused, waiting for April to meet her gaze. "I'm not judging you, or what you do, but I'm a self-defense instructor. If you decide to stay in this line of work, I want you to come to my classes, so I can teach you how to defend yourself from other men who think they can take advantage of you."

"I can't afford it. I hooked so I could pay my rent and buy food."

Beth shook her head. "All your lessons will be free."

"You'd do that for me?"

"Yes."

April blinked at her. "Why?"

"Because I made a vow to help women find their inner strength after my high school friend was raped and murdered. It can happen to any one of us, regardless of our professions. And I see a fighter in you. Don't let this monster stifle that fighter. Saying he owns you is a fear tactic. Don't listen to it. *You* own yourself. Even when you sell sex, no one owns you. Remember that."

April's hand flexed on Beth's a fraction of a second before falling limp. "Thank you."

Beth pulled out one of her business cards. "When your arm heals, please come see me. And…" Beth hesitated. She didn't want to say anything to offend

April, but she wanted to help her out of this situation. "My best friend's name is Leighton. She owns a fashion boutique, and she might be looking for some help." She scribbled Leighton's name and number on the back of her card and slipped it into April's hand. "You can give her a call if you want."

"Okay." April's response was reluctant.

"Take care."

Beth softly closed the door. She couldn't be sure if April would come to her studio for lessons or call Leighton for a job, but she hoped the woman would and that's all she could do. It was in April's hands now.

As she walked down the hall, her mind whirled with a dozen thoughts.

He raped her, branded her, beat her.

Hummer, Rolex, diamonds.

Crescent moon cut…stitches…scar.

Scarred forever; a reminder of his cruelty.

Hookers are his prizes, his toys, his trash.

The sound of her name being called out didn't stop her racing feet.

"Babe, where are you going?" Donovan's voice.

"Beth, are you okay?" Thorn's voice.

Her knees shook. She caught the windowsill to keep herself from falling.

"Beth?"

The sound of two pairs of shoes running toward her beat against her eardrums as images flashed in her mind—puffy eyes, purple bruises, strangulation marks. Dried blood and cut flesh. The red, irritated, bloody slit in April's check with the black stitches. The way the cut stretched as April talked made her stomach roll. She clamped a hand over her mouth.

Supportive arms looped around her. "Beth, talk to me."

She focused on breathing while letting the two male figures flanking her bring her strength. "I'm fine."

"No, you're not," Donovan said.

"If this was too much for you, I'm sorry," Thorn said.

She took a deep breath and tried to clear the morbid display from her vision. "No, you're not, Thorn. You wanted us to have a reaction so we'd agree to help."

"Not like this." Thorn's hand touched her arm. "Are you okay?"

"Fine."

Feeling more stable, she turned to Thorn. Worry reflected in his green eyes. She knew he'd never intentionally hurt her, but he wanted her to be affected by April, a victim. And she was.

"The man who did that is a sick son-of-a-bitch." She looked him in the eye. "You better catch him."

****

When it was time for her first class, Beth was ready to blow off some steam. She wore gray cotton pants and a teal workout top with her hair in a ponytail. All the equipment was out, and she was looking forward to pummeling her assistant, who would be fully protected, of course, but that didn't mean she wouldn't enjoy it. She would.

Corissa, the young woman who manned the front desk, wasn't there yet, so Beth stared at the wall in the back of the studio. The wall was white, while the rest were purple, with black signatures of all the people who had ever set foot on the blue mat. She recalled when the wall was a clean slate with only her signature in the middle. After five years, there were countless signatures. Would April's be the next one on it? Beth hoped so.

The phone at the front desk rang, drawing Beth away from the wall. She answered it. "Good afternoon. You've reached The Fighting Chance. This is Beth speaking. How may I help you?"

There was a pause on the other end, and then, "Did you think we forgot about you, Beth?" The man's chuckle was menacing. "We didn't."

Chapter Three

While Donovan practiced stunts in his monster truck, he had missed a call from Beth. He checked his voicemail. She had tried to sound nonchalant when she asked him to come to her studio before she locked up for the night, but he detected a little shake in her voice. Since she had purchased her older, used compact sedan, Donovan retired from his duty of dropping her off and picking her up from work. He was curious as to why she wanted him there when she was capable of driving home, and he wanted to know why she sounded frazzled. He called back, but Corissa said she was in the middle of her class, so he rushed over.

Twenty minutes to closing, he parked in front of The Fighting Chance. The sun glared off the windows, sending spears of light into his eyes. He hopped onto the sidewalk and ducked inside.

Corissa sat at the front desk with her head buried in a psychology book. She grasped a highlighter in her hand; a stack of flashcards sat at her elbow. Donovan folded his arms over the white counter between two purple orchids. "How's it going, Corissa?"

She looked at him with exhausted eyes. "Mid-terms are coming." Her words made mid-terms sound like a horde of flesh-eating zombies.

"You'll do great," he assured her. "And when you become a psychologist, I'll be your first patient." He winked at her.

She laughed. "Donovan, you and I both know you're not in this book." She tapped her finger on the page she had been reading.

Donovan grinned. "Maybe not." He turned toward the blue mat where Beth talked to a few of her students. "How was Beth when you came in this morning?"

Corissa glanced toward her boss. "You didn't hear this from me," she whispered, "but she was jumpy. I tried to ask her if something was wrong, but she shook my question off as if I hadn't spoken. Whatever was bugging her, I think she took it out on Dave. She wailed on him, poor guy."

Donovan fought hard not to smirk at that. Dave liked to flirt with Beth, and Donovan had wanted to teach him a lesson on several occasions.

I hope he's limping.

As Beth's students left, her gaze connected with his. The smile she gave him was one of relief. Her shoulders lowered as she exhaled.

"Corissa, we'll close the shop," Beth called out. "Go home and study."

"Fine by me." Corissa slapped her psychology book shut and hefted her backpack off the floor. A gentle jingle sounded when she left.

Donovan whisked the deadbolt, locking the door. He went to Beth and stopped her on her way back from the supply closet. "How were your classes?"

"Good. I'll put this stuff away, and then we can leave." She walked past him as if he was nothing more than an obstacle. She picked up an armful of boxing gloves and headgear and was moving past him again when he blocked her path. He took the equipment from her arms.

"Donovan, I have to put that away."

"And you will." He deposited them on the floor. "After."

She crossed her arms, obviously irritated.

Is she mad at me for not letting her go undercover? After what I saw that guy did to April, how could I agree?

Corissa's words came back to him.

If she's looking for someone to fight, it might as well be me. He went to the storage closet, found two helmets, the black and neon green gloves Beth gave to him for Christmas, and the purple pair Beth preferred.

Beth was still standing where he left her. He held her gloves out to her. "Now's your chance to hit me."

Beth considered him. Then she snatched the gloves from him and stuffed her hands into them.

His lips quirked. At the edge of the mat, he kicked off his shoes and removed his shirt. In the middle of the mat, Beth waited with her hands on her hips. He stopped a couple of feet from her. "Are you ready?"

She lifted her hands to either side of her face and lowered her body into a fighting stance. "Are you?"

He barely had time to mimic her position before Beth jabbed out with her fists. He blocked the blows. She advanced on him, pushing him back. Determination was bright in her eyes. Her breathing was deep, lifting her chest. The movement pulled his gaze to her breasts and the pale scar stretching across her chest. The glimpse nearly awarded him with a punch to the face. He bent backward, narrowly missing Beth's purple glove.

He popped back up as she landed a spinning back

fist to his jaw. She took a step back with a smirk on her face.

Donovan worked his jaw back and forth. The hit hadn't been hard, but it had rattled him. "Are you *trying* to hurt me?"

She innocently lifted her gloved hands. "This was your idea."

"So it was."

He blocked more of her jabs and sent his own that she blocked in return. It didn't take long before he was sweating. The sound of their padded gloves thumping into each other filled the studio. Beth bobbed and weaved to avoid his hits, but one connected with her left shoulder. She retaliated with a sequence of punches. When she mixed in uppercuts with jabs and used her legs to distract him, she was able to score another hit to the side of his head.

He shook his head as if to erase the punch. Deciding to end their fight, he looked for an opportunity to take her down. When one opened up, he took it. His foot swept her legs out from under her. As she fell, he caught her and cushioned her fall with his body. Then he rolled so she was beneath him. Before she could attempt to throw him off, he dipped his head and brought his lips to her neck.

Beth's body went still under his, as if his mouth on her skin shocked her. His lips trailed down her neck to her chest. He licked the end of her scar, savoring the saltiness on his tongue. His mouth moved to her breasts, and he sucked gently on the swell peeking over the neckline of her top.

A soft moan left her lips. "Foul," she panted. "You're cheating."

He lifted his head and grinned. "I call this winning."

Beth shifted beneath him. In the next second, her fist collided with his gut. The hit wasn't as strong as it would've been if she was fighting off an attacker, but it still dislodged his breath. As he dropped, she escaped from beneath him. When he rolled over, Beth was ripping off her gloves. She tossed them to the side and crouched, ready.

His brow lifted. Intrigued. *She wants to wrestle? This could be fun.*

He stripped off his gloves and engaged Beth in a little dance as they circled each other, looking for an opening to strike. He made a move first and took her down. On the mat, they rolled and twisted. Their bodies bumped into each other, sending electric charges throughout Donovan's body. Every time he gained an advantage on Beth, she'd perform a maneuver to switch their positions. She growled in his ear, a sound that invigorated him. He enjoyed putting his hands on her slick body as they snaked around each other; the positions they got stuck in were a lot of fun, too. Several times, his face was near her breasts or between her legs. He started to employ a few illegal techniques to win, like teasing her nipples through her top with his mouth and trailing a finger along the crotch of her pants. Her growls became moans, and her fighting became more aggressive. More sexual.

Their wrestling had turned into foreplay, a game Donovan thoroughly enjoyed. Each time their bodies rubbed together, it was as if they were in bed, tangled in a match of lovemaking. His hands sought her curves. He locked his legs around her, flipped her into the air, and pinned her beneath him. He was grinning down at her when he noticed tears in her eyes. His grin faded. His heart hitched.

Fear rattled his core. *What did I do?*

He released her. "Did I hurt you?" She tried to turn away, but he caught her face in his hands and turned her head back. "Did I hurt you?"

"No." Her voice shook with the emotion trapped in her throat.

He pulled her into a sitting position and caressed her arms. "You're that mad at me?"

She swiped away her tears as she shook her head.

"What did I do?" He couldn't stand the thought of causing Beth to cry. He never wanted to do that. Ever.

Beth dropped her head onto his shoulder. Her hands clutched his arm, and her body shook as she cried. "It's not you," she finally said. "You didn't do anything."

"Then what is it? Please talk me."

She took in a shuddering breath and leaned back. Her eyes were red and tear-lined. "We were wrestling, and I started to think about April. I saw it all in my head, everything that monster did to her. I felt her fear. All of a sudden, I was overcome by it. I'm sorry."

Donovan wiped her tears away with his thumbs. "Don't apologize." He kissed her flushed cheek. "Is that why you're aggravated? I thought you were mad at me."

She shook her head. "I was mad at him. And I was scared. I'm sorry for taking it out on you."

He shrugged. "It's what I'm here for. If you need to vent, feel free to hit me upside my head."

Beth smiled at that as he hoped she would.

"What about on the phone? You sounded shaky in your voicemail."

Beth lowered her gaze. She had a habit of breaking eye contact when she didn't want to say something. It wasn't a good sign.

"I got a call."

Donovan stopped breathing. The first time she had said those words was the day they came back from California and a man had threatened her. He recalled her exact words. *He said we pissed off the wrong people and they're coming for us.*

He clenched his hands into fists. "What did they say?" He couldn't keep the anger from his voice.

"'Did you think we forgot about you, Beth?'" Her gaze lifted, penetrating him like daggers. "'We didn't.'"

Chills curled around his spine, followed by a wave of lava that rushed through his veins. He hated that they were harassing Beth. If they would call him, he'd be more than happy to hear their threats and issue a few of his own. But calling Beth enraged him.

"Beth…" He delicately held her chin with his fingers. "You're safe with me. Whoever they are, they're not going to hurt you. Not if I have anything to say about it. We'll find out who they are and get them, just as we got Chewy, Buck, and Jackson Storm."

In the first takedown, Beth had killed a corrupt cop. In the second, they had both come out of it battered and beaten. And in the last, Beth almost had been Jackson's hostage.

"Well, maybe not like those other times." He slid his hands up and down her arms. "I'll make you a promise, if you can promise me something."

Beth sniffed. "What?"

"You'll help Thorn get Ramirez, and I'll help Thorn find the assholes who are harassing you. Deal?" Donovan stared into her eyes, never breaking eye contact. He wanted her to know he was serious. Dead serious.

It's time this ends. Once and for all.

Beth nodded. "Deal."

Chapter Four

When Donovan left to practice for his next monster truck show, Beth called her friend, Leighton Ford, to go shopping with her. Leighton flounced out of her apartment in a short skirt and high heels. Her blonde hair bounced with each step. She hopped into Beth's car, filling the space with the smell of her sandalwood perfume. Why Beth and Leighton were friends was a mystery. They met in the self-defense class Beth took as a teen, and that was all they had in common. They had attended different high schools. Not even their interests, personalities, or cup sizes were the same. Beth was a perky B and Leighton was a voluptuous D. But they had bonded as teens, nonetheless, and that friendship had lasted.

Leighton pouted her bubblegum-pink lips. "No Donovan?"

"You don't want Donovan with us while we shop for…what we're shopping for."

"Which is?"

Beth glanced at her friend before backing out of the driveway. "You can't repeat what I'm going to tell you."

Leighton batted her thick, black lashes. "I'm intrigued."

Beth shot her a look.

"I swear I won't repeat a word." She crossed her

heart and held up two fingers.

Beth told Leighton about being Thorn's civilian operative and her mission to bring down a man who brutalizes prostitutes.

"So, we're buying weapons?"

Beth grimaced at what she was about to say. "No, I need a disguise and...props."

Leighton laughed and clapped her hands. "You mean a hooker's outfit and sex toys! This is going to be so much fun."

Beth did not feel her enthusiasm. She pulled in front of a store called *Virgin No More* with pink trim and sexy lingerie in the window. A sign advertised whips, edible panties, and a wide selection of vibrators.

The air inside the shop was scented with roses and vanilla. A woman stood behind a black counter. White silhouettes of men and women tangled in various sex positions covered the surface.

"Hello, ladies. Would you like an aphrodisiac to enhance your shopping experience?" She waved her hand at a silver tray where sliced figs and pieces of dark chocolate tempted customers.

"No, thanks," Beth said.

"Are you two a couple? We have a sale on strap-ons."

Beth's jaw unhinged in embarrassed horror.

Leighton giggled and hip bumped her. "She thinks we're lesbians. No, we're not a couple. Beth is engaged to a fine male specimen. And, although I haven't personally seen it, he no doubt has a meat sword that would put all your dildos to shame."

Beth gaped at her friend. "Shut. Up." She peeked at the woman behind the counter whose blush matched her unnatural Crayon-red hair. "We're just going to look around." She grabbed Leighton's arm and pulled her toward the clothing section. "The next time you bring up my fiancés *meat sword*, I'll deck you."

"Don't be embarrassed, honey, own it." Leighton moved to a rack. "What exactly are we looking for? French maid costumes or street hooker getups?"

"I was hoping for sexy, not trashy."

"Gotcha."

They hunted through several racks before settling on an outfit Beth felt could lure men to her with their tongues hanging out of their mouths but wouldn't reveal any of her goodies if she had to make a run for it. Then they went to the sex toy section.

"Did you have anything in mind?"

"Well, April had handcuffs with her, so I figured I should, too."

Together, they faced a wall displaying many different handcuffs. Some were colored—red, pink, black. Some were in the shape of hearts, and some were adorned with feathers. Beth looked at them with wide eyes. *Handcuffs have come a long way from apprehending bad guys. A long, long way.*

"There's the durable cuffs." Leighton pointed at the thick cuffs in a rainbow of colors. "And the kinky cuffs." She indicated the rows of fuzzy cuffs. "Then there's the cuffs for sensitive people." Those cuffs were wrapped in rubber and other soft materials to protect fragile skin.

"I guess I'll go with kink."

Leighton nodded. "Nice choice. Do any catch your fancy?"

Beth stared at the wall. Leopard print, hot pink and

glittered fuzz, even ostrich and peacock feathers. The choices were daunting. "How the hell am I supposed to choose?"

"Imagine using them on Donovan." Leighton winked. "Or him using them on you."

Leighton had a good idea; Beth would be able to select one if she imagined Donovan and her playing with them. It was a thought that gave her tingles. She peered back at the wall and pictured Donovan leaning over her in bed. The lights were off. His chest bare. His hands moved to the headboard to cuff one of her wrists to the post. Her gaze landed on a pair of cuffs with violet fuzz, the same color as Donovan's eyes. The most she planned on doing with them while undercover was giving Ramirez a glimpse of them in her purse. They wouldn't be tainted by touching his skin, so she knew they were the ones she had to get. She reached up and showed the chosen pair to Leighton.

"You're good." Leighton took down a second pair.

"What's that for?"

"Honey, you need two to cuff each wrist to a bedpost."

"Oh."

They moved to the shelves with little trinkets used for foreplay. Beth passed the clamps and picked up a small, black, bullet-shaped device the size of her thumb. "What's this?"

Grinning, Leighton snatched the object from Beth's palm, fiddled with it, and then gave it back.

Beth's hand vibrated. She dropped it as if it had turned into a cockroach. It buzzed on the floor. Beth felt like stomping on it.

"What in the world is that thing?"

Leighton picked it up and held it between her thumb and forefinger. "This little doohickey is a vibrating butt plug."

Beth cringed. "Yeah, don't need that. Next."

After three hours of shopping, Beth returned home with three bags, which she intended to hide under the bed before Donovan could see them. No such luck, though. He was in the living room when she walked through the door.

"Hey, you're home early," she said.

"Yeah, my run-through went smooth. I see you went shopping." When his eyes lowered to the bags, she tried to hide them behind her legs. "Do those bags say *Virgin No More*?"

Crap! I should've put everything into Walmart bags. "Umm…"

"You bought the outfit you're going to wear undercover, didn't you? Show me." He stole the bags from her hands.

Heart pounding, she followed him to the table. "I thought of you when I picked out everything."

Donovan set the bags on the table and turned to her. His eyes glimmered with heat. "That doesn't make me feel better about what you bought."

"I meant that I thought about you killing me if I wore anything too revealing."

"Baby, you wearing a white T-shirt around this guy would be too revealing."

She rolled her eyes.

From the first bag, he pulled out a tiny pair of leather shorts with two gold chains dangling off the front. "I figured shorts would be the most reasonable option."

He arched a brow at her, clearly not liking that they were hoochie shorts. Next, he brought out a red crop top by the straps. He lifted it to his face and inspected the ribbons that made the top look like a corset. "Small, isn't it?" By the tone of his voice, she knew he wasn't happy.

"It'll show a bit of skin on my midriff."

"And a lot of cleavage."

"I don't have a lot of cleavage," she corrected.

His gaze cut through her like violet daggers. Her statement didn't help her cause.

He set the top aside and reached for the second bag. From this one, he brought out a pair of red shoes with three-inch heels. They glittered like ruby slippers. Beth thought they were cute and lethal with those spikes. If she had to fight back, a kick to the stomach could puncture a kidney.

Donovan set them aside without a comment.

She swallowed. *Is that good or bad?*

He pulled the last bag to him.

Beth winced.

He peeked inside. Then his head snapped up.

She shrugged.

He dipped his hand inside the bag and lifted out the handcuffs with a curled finger. He dangled them in the air. A silent question hung between them.

"April had a pair, and Ramirez knew that," she said. "I think he likes it when the women provide their own restraints that he can later use on them when he…" Her words faded. She didn't have to say what he did to them. The image was imprinted on both their minds. "But I picked those out for you."

"For me?"

Beth nodded. "Don't you remember saying bondage with me would be fun and you'd enjoy being my submissive?" He had said it in California while recovering from fractured ribs.

The corner of Donovan's mouth tilted up.

Seductive delight fluttered through Beth. *He remembers.*

He set the cuffs down and brought out a bottle of oil. Eyeing her, he waited for an explanation.

"Again, April said she had oil. I thought having a few things in my bag would solidify my cover, but I thought you and I could have fun with them." Blood rushed to her cheeks. "It heats on contact and is cherry flavored."

Donovan licked his lips. Whether on purpose or involuntary, she didn't know, but heat flooded between her legs. No oil necessary. He continued to search inside the bag. The next toy had him grinning when he faced Beth. He had a tiny vibrator stuck on his finger. "I don't think I can let you use this one on your own."

"I wasn't going to," she said.

Donovan's grin widened. The last item was a blindfold. "This will come in handy."

Beth's mouth went dry. "Do you approve?"

He dipped his hands into his pockets. "The outfit is sexier than I had hoped, but you'll only wear it once. As for everything else." He paused to look at the tools in question. "I approve."

****

The next day, Beth stood in the bathroom in her hooker's costume. She had slicked baby oil over her legs to make them glisten and strapped the heels to her feet, which did wonders to her legs. Her height went from five-foot-eight to six-foot-one, the same height as Donovan. The itty-bitty shorts molded to her curves and stopped short of her butt. The crop-top thrust up her boobs, as if announcing, "Hey, check out the girls!" And a strip of tan skin peeked out from beneath the top. She had brightened her lips with red lipstick, dressed her eyes with half a tube of mascara, a ton of liner, and layers of dark eyeshadow. Not even her hair looked the same. She had fluffed it beyond recognition.

Staring in the mirror, she felt especially slutty.

A knock on the door made her jump. She tugged on her shorts. "Yeah?"

"It's me." Donovan's voice came through the closed door. "How are you doing?"

"Good. I'm almost done."

"Can I come in?"

The thought of him seeing her like this had her heart rate picking up speed. "Sure."

The door eased open, and Donovan stood in the doorway. Frozen. She nervously glanced at him to see his stare pinned to her body. He didn't appear to be breathing. When she thought he'd pass out, his chest heaved. He stepped into the bathroom and closed the door behind him. His arms snaked around her hips and tugged her flush to his body.

"I don't want any other man to see you dressed like this." His voice was rough, and his eyes were the color of onyx. He swept aside the hair from her shoulder. His mouth found the skin below her ear. Then he lifted his head and whispered, "I want to be the only one to see this side of you."

"Donovan, I have to do this."

"I know." He kissed her bare shoulder. "I know."

"I was finishing up. Stop distracting me." She nudged him aside and picked up a makeup sponge.

"I think you have enough makeup on."

"I need to cover up this ugly scar. No man would find it attractive."

Donovan caught her wrist as she brought the sponge to her chest. She was about to retort when he turned her and framed her face in his hands. "This scar is a part of you, and I find it incredibly sexy. If you only knew how often I think about licking it."

Beth's knees weakened. She lowered her hand to the counter to steady herself.

"And, as I recall, my opinion is the one that matters." He pulled the makeup sponge from her fingers. "I'll do it."

She turned her head to the mirror to watch him. When she expected him to bring his hand to her chest, he dipped his head. He kissed the corner of her scar, but didn't stop with one; he trailed kisses from one end to the other. Her breath hitched. Could he feel her heart vibrating against his lips?

Her eyelids fluttered. She clutched the soft fabric of his shirt.

With each kiss he planted on her imperfection, she felt adored. What he was doing was more romantic than anything he could ever say to make her feel beautiful. Tears pressed against the backs of her eyelids. The scar Donovan lavished attention on marked the day they met and the day they fell in love. Although Beth hated how it looked, it held memories. It was sentimental, and she liked it more and more with each second Donovan's lips were on it.

Without another word, Donovan dabbed the

makeup onto her skin.

She opened her eyes. In the mirror, she saw his attention affixed to his task, as if it was the most important thing in the world. When he finished, he dropped the sponge onto the counter and met her gaze.

"Thank you," she whispered.

"Just remember that our scars tell our story."

She nodded. "I know." She reached up to trace the small scar above his brow. "I love your scars, too."

He kissed her forehead. "Are you ready?"

"More than ready to get this asshole."

Donovan led her out of the bathroom to the living room where Thorn waited. Thorn turned when Beth's heels clacked against the tile. His jaw dropped. "Damn!"

"Thorn, if you say one more word, so help me, I will kick your ass."

Donovan's warning had Thorn lifting his hands in surrender. He picked up a jacket from the table and held it out to Beth. "Here. You should cover up until we get to the location."

Beth slipped on the jacket and zipped it. It hid her scant clothing, making her look and feel as though she was naked beneath it. Teetering on her heels, she kept a hand on the bottom of the jacket as she hurried down the stairs and into Thorn's car.

Thorn drove to a rundown part of Orange County where the buildings were abandoned and condemned. You could find drug deals going down in alleys and hookers posted at every corner. Beth glanced at the hookers they passed. They were frumpy, dirty, and looked as hard as the pavement they pounded. Seeing the neighborhood where she had to be, which was far from friendly, filled Beth with anxiety.

Her heartbeat throbbed in her neck, threatening to choke her.

I can do this. I pretended to want to sell my body once. I can do it again. Except, last time she was in a crowded restaurant, not on a street corner.

Thorn pulled his car behind a building and shut off the engine. He shifted in his seat. "Okay, Beth. The street corner we want you to be at is right on the other side of this building. It's the same corner where he picked up April. All you have to do is walk down the alley and onto the sidewalk. We have an undercover cop disguised as a homeless person across the street. We also have three squad vehicles close by that can get to you in minutes."

"That makes me feel better," she admitted.

"Donovan and I will be here, too. You're wired, so we can all hear you. Your safe word is *deal*. The moment you need us or make a deal with him, we'll be there."

"Thanks." She knew they wouldn't let anything happen to her, but that didn't stop her from feeling as though she had swallowed a storm of butterflies. "When Ramirez stops to talk to me, why can't you rush in and arrest him? You already know what he did to April and the others."

"The problem is we need him to stop long enough for us to sneak up on him, which is why you're here. A cop had tried to catch him once before, but the moment Ramirez saw the car, he sped out of there. The cop lost him. We don't want him to initiate a high-speed chase, so we need you to distract him. If you play your part well, he won't be suspicious as he would if a cop was undercover.

"We'll wait for him to agree on sex acts, and then we'll make our move. Even when we come, keep your cover. I'll handcuff you while reading you your rights and bring you back here. He won't ever know you were working with us."

He lifted the photo of Ramirez so she could get a good look at his features once more. Ramirez was a big man at six-feet-five with arms like canons. He had black hair, a latte tan, and dark, bottomless eyes. "Ramirez is your objective. Don't worry about any other car that stops. Brush them off. Be on the lookout for that Hummer and make sure it's Ramirez behind the wheel."

"Doesn't sound too hard." Beth paused to take a deep breath and then met Thorn's watchful stare. "Now?"

He nodded.

Taking a deep breath, she opened the car door and stepped out into the sunlight. Donovan was at the edge of the seat when she turned. She stripped off the jacket and handed it to him. He draped it across his lap, reached up, and trapped her shoulders with his hands, pulling her to him. He stamped her mouth with his. "Be careful."

"I will." She looked between him and Thorn. "I'm counting on you boys to have my back, so play nice while I'm gone."

Walking away from the safety of Thorn's car, from Donovan's arms, took all her courage. Her knees shook as if her cartilage was made of gelatin. She moved around a puddle of dirty water with a rainbow sheen reflecting off the surface. With each step she took, her heart rate rose. She gripped her hands into fists and forced herself to take slow, deep breaths.

All you have to do is identify Ramirez and stall him by getting him to agree on sex acts. That's it. You've been through worse. She thought about being trapped in Viper's house, surrounded by criminals and weapons, suffocating on marijuana smoke. The fear then had been poison in her veins.

She stepped onto the sidewalk. Sunlight broke through the clouds, spotlighting her on the concrete. The street was calm and quiet, deceptively so. With a glance down the road, she saw a purple Cadillac parked in front of a building. Another car, a rusted piece of crap, was next to it. Two men stood between the cars, exchanging drugs for money. Farther down the road, a woman wearing white pants leaned her shoulder against a stop sign. Beth turned her back on them and walked toward the intersection.

Her heels clicked against the sidewalk. The chains hanging off her shorts bounced with each step she took. They clanked into each other, creating a musical announcement that she was coming.

She looked at the building to her right, the same building that hid Thorn and Donovan. The sign had been eaten by the elements, but she could make out some of the faded letters that advertised the old brick structure as a factory. Many of the windows had been broken. Large, jagged shards stuck out of the frames. Some were large, probably from bricks, but she noticed a few little holes the size of bullets.

The rumble of a vehicle coming toward her had her spine jerking straight. She maintained her stride. A gold car slowed and crept along beside her. "Hey, girl, how much for me to smack that ass?"

Disgust rippled through her. She coolly glanced at the car. The little twerp grinning at her had yellowed, chipped teeth. "You couldn't possibly have enough money to smack this ass. Why don't you keep on driving? The next girl you see will gladly bend over for you."

The car drove on, much to her relief. She walked over several cigar mouthpieces and cigarette butts crumpled on the sidewalk. Her gaze strayed across the street, landing on a man slumped on the ground. A shopping cart sat next to him piled high with black garbage bags and blankets. He wore a knit cap on his head and several layers of worn clothing. If Thorn hadn't told her an undercover agent was disguised as a homeless person, she never would've been able to tell.

She stopped at the intersection. The lights hanging overhead were lifeless. Minutes slowly ticked by, as if time didn't exist in this part of the city. *Must be why all the hookers here look a hundred years old.* She started to pace back and forth, hoping to speed up the time with her strides.

On her way back to the corner, a black sedan rolled through the intersection. She thought it was going to drive past her when it suddenly stopped on the opposite side of the road with a squeal of tires. She could feel eyes on her. Her heart pounded against her chest. Her feet wanted to sink into the concrete, but she forced herself to take another step, which brought her closer to the sedan.

They said Ramirez drives a Hummer. But if this is him, you have to bait him. You're supposed to be a hooker. There's a potential client right there. Act the part!

Facing the sedan, she put her hand on her hip, lifted a shoulder seductively, and crooked her finger at the driver hidden behind thick tint. The window rolled down a crack. She couldn't see anyone in the darkness of the vehicle. Then something thrust through the opening and clicked. She ducked, thinking it was a gun. A bullet didn't dive into her chest, though.

As quickly as the sedan came, it floored out of there. Beth looked after it, catching a *V* and a *W* in the license plate before it swerved around a corner. "I don't know what the fuck that was," she said as if Thorn and Donovan were beside her. "A black sedan. A black sedan stopped and rolled down its window. I thought it was a gun, but it was a camera. Someone took a picture of me." Her heart pounded so fast she felt like vomiting.

In the silence that followed her frightened speech, she heard Donovan telling her it was okay, she was okay. Even though he wasn't there, she sensed his presence.

She looked toward the undercover agent across the street. He was on his feet, obviously rattled by what happened, too. Their gazes connected briefly. She gave him a slight nod. He gave her the tiniest of nods back and resumed his position on the ground.

As she got her breathing back to normal, another car stopped in front of her. This one was a sports car. A man smiled out at her. He wore a suit and tie. "I have a meeting in an hour. I could use a blow job to take the pressure off."

Beth arched a brow. *Men are disgusting.*

"Sorry. I ate a hamburger five minutes ago. I'm

full."

As the sports car left, she sensed the officers listening to her wire laughing.

Twenty minutes later, her feet hurt, and she was bored out of her mind. She was about to suggest trying another time when the deep roar of an engine sounded. She didn't dare turn but leaned against the concrete post.

The rumble of the vehicle grew closer. Out of the corner of her eye, she saw a black and chrome bumper. She tilted her head to it. The Hummer was massive. She couldn't even catch a glimpse of the driver.

The passenger's side window slid down. She sauntered over to it, wishing her nerves would settle. Although she wore three-inch heels, she still couldn't see into the cab. She had to step onto the running board and duck toward the window. Sitting in the driver's seat, with one hand draped over the steering wheel, was a massive man built with layers of muscle. He had a big, diamond Rolex on his tan wrist. A silver chain rested on his chest. His black hair brushed the collar of his T-shirt. If he wasn't so big, he would've been classified as a pretty boy. Beth imagined that's what hookers found attractive about him.

"Hey, big daddy, what can I do for you?"

"I'd like to employ your services for the next hour." His voice was so deep it vibrated the air between them.

Beth grinned. "Employ my services? I like that. I'd be happy to let you be my boss. What's my assignment, sir?"

"Why don't you hop in?" His dark eyes pinned her in place. They were like a deep, black abyss.

Panic rushed through her. Thorn had never said anything about getting into Ramirez's Hummer, or how to avoid it. Hookers hop right into cars, but she couldn't do that. Nor could she leave. She still had a job to do. *I need him to agree on acts. Shit!*

She fought to keep the horror from reflecting on her face. Her mouth twitched with the strain. Wishing Thorn could whisper advice; she reached out and found the door handle. It shocked her fingers, as if with a warning. She jumped and stifled a curse. She put her hand back on the handle. The door clicked open. She pushed it wide and perched on the side with her feet still on the running board. "I don't like to go anywhere unless I know what's expected of me. I like to get in the mood during the drive, if you know what I mean."

The corner of Ramirez's mouth tilted up. Beth couldn't help but notice how sensual his mouth was. She banished that thought with the image of April's battered face.

"Looking at you, I wouldn't mind a buffet," he said.

"A buffet, huh? So, you want intercourse and oral sex. Would I be giving or receiving?"

His eyes trailed down her body and settled on her lap. "Both."

That single word sent Beth's stomach whirling. Her intestines felt as though they were slick with crude oil. "I see." She shifted her bag onto her lap. "And what about the level of intensity? We can do this soft-and-sweet or hot-and-nasty, but if you want to get rough, it's extra."

"I like to get a little rough."

A little? You like to beat and kill the women you

pick up. Her hand inched inside her purse. "Mm. I don't think I'd mind getting spanked by you. What do you say we do all that for two hundred?"

His eyes raked over her. He licked his lips. How he did it, as if she was a T-bone steak and he wanted to gnaw on the bone, gave her chills. "How about four hundred?"

Beth arched a brow. *He must like white meat.* "Really? Well, you've got yourself a deal." She prayed everyone listening heard that. She distracted him with her offers. Now, she wanted to get the hell out of there.

"Close the door," Ramirez said.

Her gaze ticked back and forth, searching the road for signs of her cavalry, but no one was coming. *Where the hell are they?* She reached slowly for the door handle. Her fingers were an inch from it when Ramirez grabbed her other wrist.

She froze.

His grip was bruising. He tugged her hand out of her bag. "What is this?"

In her hand, she clutched the bottle of oil. "It's intimate oil. I was going to ask if you'd like to use it."

He inspected the bottle. "I'm allergic to cherry."

"That's too bad." She pouted her lips and thought about pouring it down his throat.

He released her.

She put the bottle back in her bag. Her fingers brushed the cold metal of a handcuff. Before she could question where her backup was, she took it out and slapped it on Ramirez's wrist. She did it so fast he didn't realize what was happening until the other cuff was attached to the steering wheel. He jerked his hand as if he wanted to snap the chain in half.

"You fucking bitch!"

When he reached for her with his other hand, she threw herself out of the Hummer. Her feet slammed onto the concrete, sending lightning bolts up her heels to her knees. The second she was safely on the sidewalk, she started to run. A gun sounded and glass shot out from the back of the Hummer. Beth yelped and ducked. Her gaze flew to the undercover agent as he ripped his semi-automatic from its hiding place and charged toward the Hummer. Vehicles poured into the intersection from all directions with screaming tires. Shouts for Ramirez to drop the gun and put his hands in the air reached her, but she didn't stop running. She flew around the corner, into the alley, and slammed into Donovan.

His arms came around her. "I've got you. You're okay."

She held onto him as her knees quaked. No words came to her. She couldn't even reassure him she was fine. In his arms, she could feel his ragged breathing, and she knew he must have run to her. His heart banged against his chest, colliding with hers. He had been just as scared.

"Come on." With a supportive arm around her waist, he led her back to the car. He helped her put on her jacket and, when her hands trembled too badly to zip it, he brushed her hands aside to do it himself. She sat in the back of Thorn's car while waiting for him to come back. When he came up to the car five minutes later, she jumped to her feet and shoved him back two steps.

"Where the hell were you? I trusted you to have my back!"

"I'm sorry, Beth." Sweat glistened on his forehead. His green eyes were wide. "There was a glitch with your wire. Your voice came in and out. We didn't know what was going on, but when we heard you say *deal,* we all sprang into action. I tried to get to you as fast as I could. You have to believe me, I wouldn't have put you in additional danger."

His voice shook, and his eyes pleaded with her to believe him.

Tears stung her eyes. She got into the car without another word.

The ride back to their apartment was quiet. She went upstairs without a goodbye and went straight to the bedroom.

Donovan followed her up. "Beth."

She looked over her shoulder at Donovan.

"Thorn was frantic when your wire wasn't working. He was on his radio, demanding his team to move in immediately, but the undercover agent whispered you were in the Hummer and would be in the line of fire. When your voice came through and we heard you say *deal,* Thorn was out of the car before I was. He was screaming into his radio while running around the side of the building. He wanted to get to you as fast as possible. I went the other way in case you ran that way. Thorn did everything I would've done."

Hearing Donovan back up Thorn made her regret her words. The hurt in Thorn's eyes came back to her. "I was scared and angry," she whispered.

"I know. We all were." He took her arms. "But you did a great job."

She looked down at her red heels. "I'll call him later to apologize."

"That'd be good."

Until then, she wanted nothing more than to take a scalding shower to wash away the lusting gazes she had felt on her. She stripped out of her clothes, stepped under the scalding water, and scrubbed her body, imagining the fantasies the men had conjured of her washing down the drain. When she felt clean, she dressed in cotton pajamas and crawled onto the couch next to Donovan. He linked his arms around her, kissed her temple, and gave her everything she needed— security, warmth, and comfort. She absorbed his love for the rest of the day.

****

While having her morning cup of coffee, Beth called Thorn.

"Beth?" Thorn's voice sounded cautious and strained, as if he were preparing for her to chew him up and spit him out.

"That's all wrong," she said. "You're not supposed to answer your phone saying my name. You should say, 'This is Detective Thorn.'"

"I'll make a note of that."

Her effort at creating light conversation failed. She winced. "Thorn, I'm sorry for what I said to you yesterday. It wasn't your fault my wire wasn't working. Donovan told me how frantic you were. I was shaken up, but I shouldn't have accused you of not having my back. Aside from Donovan, you're the only other person I wholeheartedly trust with my life."

"Thanks." Relief emitted off his voice like radio waves. "Don't tell Donovan I said this but...I love you. Like a sister," he clarified, "but love is love."

She warmed at his words. "I love you, too, Thorn.

And, for the record, I wouldn't mind being your civilian operative again. I would just have to convince Donovan."

Thorn chuckled. "You're the best civilian operative in all of Florida."

She smiled. "What about Ramirez? Any news on him?"

"Well, what you did helped us to nab him. He couldn't get away, especially not while handcuffed to the steering wheel." Laughter was in his voice. "And he's been charged with assault and murder. He's not getting out."

Beth sighed. "Good."

Chapter Five

Donovan walked beside an electrical fence topped with tangled barbed wire and entered a prison. Thorn escorted him into the bowels of the building. None of the officers stopped them or so much as glanced at Donovan. With Thorn leading the way, he was invisible.

Neither of them said a word until they paused at a door in the middle of the maze. "Are you sure about this?" Thorn asked Donovan.

"If they were threatening me, I wouldn't give a damn, but they're harassing Beth. Yes, I'm sure."

Thorn nodded and opened the door to an interrogation room. Donovan stepped in, and his gaze landed on the dirty cop in a blue jumpsuit with his hands and feet shackled. His hair had grown shabbier, and his beard thicker. His eyes had sunk into hollows, and his skin was as pale as glue, but Donovan recognized the face of the man he had hunted for months—David Buckland, his brother's murderer.

Donovan and Thorn took a seat across from him.

A slow smile stretched the tight skin on Buck's face. He let out a laugh. "Ryan Goldwyn's little brother is my first visitor? That's comical."

"I'm not visiting you, Buck," Donovan spat. "I'm here to get answers."

"Oh, yeah?" Buck leaned back, as if this was going

to be entertaining.

"Beth's been receiving threatening phone calls from members of your ring."

"Really? How fascinating." Buck sneered with yellowed teeth.

Donovan felt like punching Buck until his teeth fell from his gums. He gripped his hands into white-knuckled fists. "Who are the other men you worked with?"

"I've been locked up for over a year. I don't remember any of their names."

"You remembered mine."

Buck leaned forward. The chains jingled. "That's because I have two regrets. Just two regrets for the forty years I've been alive, and both regrets involve you. When you obsess over something, you don't forget the names of the people centered in it." He leaned closer. "First, I regret not killing you the second I saw you in your brother's doorway. Chewy and I should've grabbed you, hauled you in, and killed you next to your brother. We could've made it look like two brothers beat themselves to death."

The image of his brother's dead body floated in Donovan's mind.

"My second regret is not killing you and your girl in California when I had the chance. I should've punched her to death. Then I should've picked up that rock and impaled your skull with it. If I had done that, I'd be a free man."

Donovan's chest heaved. "Tell me their names, or so help me…" His growl faded. He didn't think he should say what he intended to do with Thorn there. Even though he was a friend, Thorn was still a law enforcement officer.

Thorn sat forward. "Buck, we're not going to sit here and fuck around with you. I'm not going to promise shit because you made your bed. You're going to stay behind bars for the rest of your sentence. You'll get out when you're eighty. *Maybe*. Regardless, you're going to be here for a long time, but I can offer you privileges and a few luxuries to make your situation tolerable if you help us out. If you don't..." Thorn's lips spread into a sneer. "I'll tell every man in this prison, who's here because of you, that you're an inmate. And I'll tell the guards to turn a blind eye when you get your ass beat. You think you have allies here? Think again. You killed a respectable man of the shield. The officers here hate your fucking guts. They wouldn't care if you got stuck with a contraband blade. And I may provide that blade to Travis Gordon. You remember him, don't you?"

Donovan glanced at Buck. His white face turned nearly transparent with fear. Donovan didn't recognize the name Travis Gordon, but Buck obviously did.

"I can make sure a blade gets passed to him with the order to kill you. I'm sure he'll be more than happy to do it."

Buck's Adam's apple bobbed. "I knew the officers and dealers in this county, and you already have them. If someone is threatening you, they're from out of town, and I wouldn't know their names. You'd have to ask Jackson Storm."

Thorn nodded. "I'll see what I can do about a few privileges."

Outside the interrogation room, Donovan turned to Thorn. "Get me in to see him."

"Donovan—"

"Get. Me. In."

Thorn rocked back on his heels. "All right. Come on."

Donovan followed Thorn into maximum security lockup. Guards were posted on the roof with semi-automatic guns in their hands as they kept a watchful eye on the grounds. More guards stood ready at the prison's exits. After walking through a metal detector, Donovan and Thorn entered the building. Every few yards, though, they had to be cleared by a security guard before they could go through another door. Donovan stood silently while Thorn requested to see Jackson Storm. After thirty minutes, an officer led them to a secure room. A metal chair sat in front of a metal loop in the concrete floor. Two other chairs were positioned a few feet away. Donovan and Thorn sat in those chairs.

Two officers led Jackson into the room. The clank of the chains restraining him echoed in the room. The officers forced Jackson into the chair and latched the chains to the loop in the concrete. With a nod to Thorn, the officers left.

Jackson grinned. His gaze settled on Thorn. "One."

He looked at Donovan. "Two."

Then he turned his head to the empty place beside Donovan. "Three."

He tilted his head. "Where's your girl? Is she at home? Safe and sound?"

Donovan's jaw clenched. "She's none of your concern."

One corner of Jackson's mouth lifted. The other corner of his mouth took longer to join it. His smile was one of psychotic delight. His head fell back in laughter. "None of my concern? You're wrong about that. I had such plans for her in California. I was going to start by cutting off her fingers and toes. I wanted to box them up and send you one each day. Twenty digits, that's twenty days of torment. I wanted you to feel sick over seeing a piece of your woman inside a box. I wanted you to know she suffered, and I wanted you to know it was your fault. To prolong her agony, I was going to carve out her uterus. After that, she wouldn't be alive much longer, so I would've sliced off her breasts and left her to bleed to death. I planned on dumping her body where someone would quickly find her."

Donovan couldn't stop himself from imagining Beth—beautiful, strong Beth—mutilated at the hands of Jackson Storm. His stomach rolled with bile. He pushed it down and shot to his feet.

Thorn intercepted his charge and pushed him back. "Donovan, he's baiting you on purpose. Stop."

The sound of Jackson's chuckles echoed throughout the small, sparse room.

Donovan's glare flashed to him.

Jackson stared at him with eyes that glittered with madness. "Don't think I didn't have plans for you, son. I was going to gut you and remove your organs…while you were still alive and kicking, might I add. Then I was going to pack you full of cocaine, stuff you in a coffin, and send you off on a ship." His sneer grew. "You were going to help me illegally ship drugs overseas. I figured that would be the most fitting death for the brother of an Internal Affairs investigator."

Donovan seethed. A red haze covered his vision. His heart throbbed painfully at every pulse point. If

Thorn hadn't been restraining him, Donovan would've launched himself at Jackson with his fists flying.

"I'm disappointed I can't do any of those things," Jackson said, "but that's what's so great about having so many people willing to kill for me."

Thorn pushed Donovan aside. "Who? I want names."

Jackson turned to Thorn. "Why should I give you names? You have no leverage with me, Detective. There's nothing I want. And why would I snitch on men who are loyal to me and are keeping my business alive?"

"What do you gain from that?"

"I gain the satisfaction that I can cause havoc even while in maximum lockup."

Donovan surged forward. "Your men have been threatening Beth, and I'm done with it."

"If all they've been doing is threatening her, you're lucky. I put a kill order out on the two of you."

Donovan's chest tightened. "Then take it back."

"Can't. Once a kill order goes out, it's out forever. Besides, I don't want to. You have an unknowable amount of killers after you, son. The two of you will be dead, sooner or later."

Donovan stomped out of the building. Frustration and fear rolled through him like two crashing waves. He didn't stop until he got to his truck. Breathing heavily, he wanted to throw his fist through the driver's side window, but that would only give him a bloody fist and a window repair bill. He faced Thorn who had parked next to him. "What can we do?"

Thorn shook his head and looked off into the distance as if waiting for an answer from the Almighty.

His head lowered, and his green-eyed gaze met Donovan's. "I don't like this, but I don't know if there's anything we can do, other than to put you two into hiding."

"We're not going to hide."

Thorn sighed. "I'll talk to Chief Cormac."

Donovan unlocked his truck and paused with his hand on the top of the door. "Wait. Who's Travis Gordon?"

"A man you don't mess with, and Buck arrested him after shooting Travis's girlfriend twice in the chest, killing her. Travis has had a craving for Buck's blood ever since."

"And you would've slipped him a blade?"

"I would've done what was necessary." Thorn didn't have to say anymore for Donovan to know he would've found a way to get that blade to Travis. "For both of your sakes, be careful."

Donovan acknowledged Thorn's warning with a nod before climbing into his truck. During the drive home, Jackson's words came back to haunt him. *Twenty digits…twenty days…carve out her uterus…slice off her breasts.* His hands tightened on the steering wheel. The realization Jackson had come close to executing his plan knotted Donovan's stomach with a dozen fisherman's knots. If he and Thorn hadn't gone back upstairs when they did, they wouldn't have seen Jackson yanking Beth out of the hotel room, with her arms bound and a strip of duct tape stamped over her mouth. Seeing her like that—a prisoner to an infamous killer—shot Donovan's heart to his throat. The three of them were able to stop Jackson. Eventually. It took a pen, a knife, a car, and a punch to the face to finally cripple him. They thought his threat ended when Jackson was locked up.

They were wrong.

Donovan swallowed hard. Beth was in danger. Jackson's men could still execute his murderous plan, or they could kill her in an even worse way. His foot pressed down on the gas pedal. *No way in hell will I let them take her away from me!* His vow was a fierce thought that bounced against his temples, threatening a migraine. Despite his oath, he was determined to get home, to make sure Beth was still there…safe and sound.

He took the stairs two at a time and rushed into their apartment. "Beth?" He quickly locked the door and checked the kitchen.

"Beth?" He hurried into the empty living room. "Beth!" He spun around when the bedroom door opened.

Beth walked out with her hand to her chest. "What? What's wrong?"

Donovan's feet ate up the space between them. He yanked her close to his body.

She embraced him in return. Her hand rubbed his back. "Did you have a bad day?"

His heart raced. *You have no idea, baby.* And he didn't want her to know. He kissed her as if he hadn't seen her in a decade. Her mouth responded to him, letting him draw the things he needed from her— reassurance, strength, and love. He pulled back to press his lips to her left eye, the eye that had swelled shut and transformed with hideous colors when Buck had cracked his fist into her face. He dipped his head to the tank top she wore and kissed the soft skin at the top of her breasts. Taking her hands into his, he kissed her fingers. Then he dropped to his knees to do the same to her bare toes.

"Donovan—"

He reared up onto his knees, lifted her shirt, and planted a final kiss below her navel. With his love for Beth bursting inside him, mixing with the horror of what Jackson said, he wrapped his arms around her legs and laid his cheek against her stomach.

Beth's hands cupped the back of his head, and her fingers combed through his hair.

"Donovan, what's wrong?"

He squeezed his eyes shut and tightened his hold on her. "I'm just glad you're here."

"Where else would I be?"

Six feet under. That thought came faster than he liked. He got up, driving his thoughts back, and pulled Beth toward the couch where he lay with her in his arms.

Chapter Six

Beth filled her cup to the rim with coffee, milk, and sugar and thought about her task for the day—Mission: Wedding Dress. The seamstress altered it, and now, it waited for her to bring it home.

Months ago, when she first walked into the bridal boutique, she was overwhelmed by the white-out of wedding dresses. Silk, lace, tulle, satin, and velvet. Sweetheart necklines, strapless, off-the-shoulder, ankle-length, and A-line. The choices were daunting. Leighton went with her, but she didn't make it any easier. She kept finding the biggest, most outrageous dresses and pushing Beth to try them on for fun. Beth didn't want a dress with a long train or full skirt that made her feel like a cake topper. She wanted something simple that reflected her sportiness but made her feel beautiful. And she sure as hell didn't want a white dress or a veil.

After she told the sales women what she had in mind for the hundredth time, she finally found a dress that didn't make her cringe or feel like an imposter pretending to be a virgin. Now when she thought of her dress, she smiled and couldn't wait to put it on for the real thing.

Draining her coffee, she set the cup in the sink and picked up her keys to leave.

"Where are you running off to?"

She slung her bag over her shoulder and glanced at Donovan as he set aside the newspaper. "I have an errand to run. It won't take long."

"I'll come with you."

She held up her hands. "No! I'm getting my dress. You can't see it."

He rose from the couch and collected his cell phone. "I'll stay in the car."

"I don't want you jinxing anything by even being near it."

Donovan stood in front of her with eyebrows bunched together. "Since when are you superstitious?"

"Since now." She smiled. "Be a good groom and wait for your bride to come back with her dress. It won't take long."

He sighed and gave her a parting kiss. "Okay, be careful.

Beth paused. She was going to ask what she had to be careful about then figured it was a general request anyone would give a loved one.

"You be careful, too." She kissed him in return. "I'll be back in an hour."

Two women were inside the bridal boutique looking for the dress of their dreams when Beth arrived. The women they came equipped with for support and opinions cooed over every dress. Beth slipped past them, offering smiles to be kind, but quickly turned away before they could suck her into their wedding orbits. She stepped up to the front desk.

"Hello, I'm picking up my dress. Kennedy, Beth."

The woman's carnation pink fingernails tapped the keyboard. Then she went into the back room and returned with a white garment bag. Beth followed her to a changing room where she stripped out of her jeans and T-shirt and shimmied the dress over her hips. The seamstress zipped the dress up her back. Atop a small platform, Beth studied her reflection in the wall of mirrors.

Her makeup was minimal and her hair was in an impatient bun, but the dress radically changed her appearance. Pleasure swelled inside her. *I look like a bride. Who would've thought?*

"So how does it feel?" the seamstress asked.

Beth shook her head in wonder. She angled her body this way and that to see as much as she could. "It's perfect. Exactly what I wanted. It fits like a glove, but I can still breathe."

The sounds of the women fawning over the brides-to-be entered the viewing room. A sudden and painful longing for her mom hit Beth in the gut with such force the air left her lungs. Tears instantly clogged her throat and coated her eyes. It felt as though someone had taken a corkscrew to her heart.

She stumbled off the platform and hurried into the dressing room with silk tangling around her legs. Her hands shook as she took off the dress and put on her clothes. After paying for her dress, she sped out of the boutique and through the parking lot to her car. She gently laid the garment bag across the backseat and then slammed herself into the driver's seat. That was where she shattered. The tears she had been holding back leaked from her eyes as if a dam had broken. Her body shook with her sobs. They were so strong that the car rocked. The sounds crashing against her eardrums didn't sound human, couldn't possibly be coming from her. Her fingers fumbled with her keys until she got the right one in the ignition and started the engine. She turned the radio volume up, not caring what song was playing, and collapsed onto the steering wheel.

She wished her mother could've been there to help her pick out her dress and to handle the pesky little details of wedding planning. Her mom wouldn't be wearing a pretty dress and sitting in the front row. Her dad wouldn't be looking dashing in a suit and walking her down the aisle. There wouldn't be a rose for her mother during the ceremony or a father-daughter dance at the reception.

Although Donovan's mom and grandma would be there, her parents wouldn't be.

In the years since the brain tumor took her mom's life, and heartbreak promptly took her dad's life, she had healed as much as any child could, but their absence weighed heavily on her now.

She leaned back and gripped the steering wheel in her hands as she fought to control the onslaught of tears. Her lips quivered, her body quaked, and more tears zipped down her cheeks. She let them come until she was empty. Hiccupping with emotion, she dug through her purse for a tissue and mopped her face. She tossed the tissue to the floor on the passenger's side and took a few deep breaths before putting the car in gear and leaving the parking lot. Her chest continued to palpitate with sorrow as she drove, but she kept the tears at bay.

The light ahead turned yellow. She slowed and came to a stop at the white line. Buildings rose high around her. While leaning her head back, with her hands on the steering wheel, she concentrated on her breathing. Her gaze strayed to the rearview mirror and the black vehicle behind her. She looked away, but the sound of an engine revving had her gaze flicking back to the mirror.

Her spine snapped straight, and her hands became ice on the wheel. The car behind her was a black sedan with heavily tinted windows. The sedan she saw when she was undercover as a streetwalker flashed in her mind.

When the light changed to green, she eased her foot onto the gas pedal. She had to force herself not to stomp it to the floor.

"Calm down," she told herself.

Countless sedans with tinted windows traveled the roads of Florida. She couldn't know for sure if this sedan was the same one as before.

She glanced in the rearview mirror again. Two dark shapes lurked behind the windshield of the sedan. Their features were blackened by shadows. Her mouth went dry. All the moisture in her body went to her palms. She tore her stare from the sedan and looked straight ahead. Her foot slowly lowered on the gas pedal. The engine's roar became louder as the car picked up speed.

With a peek at the rearview, she calculated there was about two cars' lengths between her and the sedan. A sigh fluttered from her lips. Her body was relaxing into the seat when the sedan rushed forward. Its tires ate up the asphalt and plowed into the rear of her car. She launched forward with the force of the impact. She let out a cry and gripped the steering wheel. The car fishtailed. She was fighting to control it when the sedan crashed into her again. Her foot hadn't let up on the gas pedal, and she had no intention of stopping.

Pulse throbbing in her neck, she raced through a

yellow light, swerved the car into the inner lane, shot around a slow car, and made a fast right turn into traffic. Angry drivers sent their horns blaring, but it didn't faze her because the sedan was gaining. Hands shaking, she slapped the knob on the radio to turn it off, snatched up her cell phone from the center console, and jabbed speed dial number one. She activated speakerphone before dropping the phone into her lap. Ringing filled the inside of her car. The sound grated on her already frayed nerves.

"Answer, answer, answer," she chanted as if her plea could be heard through the rings and touch the ears of the person she needed.

"You better not be calling to say you're skipping out on me a week before the wedding." Donovan's teasing voice relieved her, but it couldn't distill her fear.

"D-Donovan…" Her voice wobbled. "A sedan is following me. It hit me twice. I can't lose it…I don't know what to do." Her words came out in a breathless rush.

"Where are you?" His voice was surprisingly calm but deep with aggression.

She glanced into the rearview to see the sedan drawing nearer. She jerked the wheel and floored it onto the on-ramp. Her foot didn't flinch off the gas pedal as she maneuvered onto the highway and pushed the car to eighty. "I'm on the turnpike," she said through gritted teeth.

"How far are you from home?"

"A couple of exits."

"When you get off at our exit, head straight to the police station. I'm on my way."

"Okay."

With the sedan on her tail, she urged the car forward. She moved past all the cars that seemed to be immobile and made it to the Orlando exit faster than ever before. She punched the brake when she came to a red light. The sedan crept so close she couldn't see the front bumper. Her heart rate accelerated. Even in the city, the driver wasn't going to let up.

"Beth, you need to talk to me."

She jumped at the sound of Donovan's voice, having forgotten about the phone in her lap. "Sorry. I'm at a red light. The sedan is riding my bumper."

"Baby, do whatever you have to do to lose him."

She nodded as her hands tightened on the steering wheel. His order gave her strength. "I will."

The light turned green. As soon as the cars in front of her moved, she shot forward and weaved in and out of cars in both lanes. At that point, she didn't care if the drivers called the cops on her, or if she passed one on the road, because the sedan was on her ass. She had witnesses and proof in the form of damage to her car.

After flying through an intersection, the sedan squeezed into the other lane and zoomed up beside her. She tried outrunning it, but the sedan angled toward her car and rammed into the side of the front bumper, forcing her off the road. She cursed as her car jumped over the curb, sliced through bushes, and landed on a sheet of asphalt so hard she bounced in her seat. Her shoulder bashed into the car door.

"Ow. Son-of-a-bitch!"

"Talk to me!"

"They ran me off the road into a parking lot. I'm okay. I'm still driving." She would never stop. No matter what they did, she wouldn't stop driving.

She drove through the parking lot. The sedan followed her. With a quick jerk of the wheel, she turned down an aisle. The peal of tires had her head whipping to the right to see the sedan flooring it down the next aisle over. It was level with her car as if they were racing. Getting to the end of the parking lot wouldn't help her, though. It would trap her. She stomped on the brake, yanked the stick shift into reverse, and jabbed the gas pedal. The car flew backward. By the time her chasers realized what she was doing, she was already at the start of the aisle. The police station was twenty minutes away, and she didn't want to get back on the main road where she could easily be spotted, so she cut across the road to a side street and spent a good five minutes making random left and right turns until there was no sign of the sedan.

She slowed the car to a stop. "I lost them. I don't see them anywhere."

"Good job, baby. Now please go to the police station. I'm almost there."

"Okay. I'll be there in twenty minutes."

When she pulled up to the station, Donovan was pacing on the sidewalk. She parked next to his truck. Immediately upon stepping out of the car, Donovan was at her side. He pulled her to him in a tight embrace. She held onto him. The adrenaline and energy she had behind the wheel vanished from her body the instant she saw Donovan waiting for her. Her throat constricted. Tears pressed wetly against her eyes.

"Are you hurt?" Donovan asked with his face buried in her neck.

She shook her head, not trusting herself to speak

without bawling. He drew back and cupped her face with his hands. The warmth of his palms seeped into her pores, comforting her. The wall of tears over her eyes grew thicker at the sight of his concerned face, his lowered eyebrows, and imploring eyes. She took a shuddering breath.

"I'm okay," she managed. "Just shaky." He kissed her forehead and the sweet contact made her chin wobble.

"You're sure you weren't followed?" His gaze scanned the street.

She looked, too. "Pretty positive. I couldn't stop checking the rearview mirror on my way here. It would be easy to spot them now."

He lifted her hands and checked them. She wasn't sure what he was looking for, but she knew wrist injuries from holding onto steering wheels were common in car accidents. After a moment, he studied her face from forehead to chin. "Did you hit your head? Did the seatbelt catch you?"

She squeezed his hands. "I swear I'm okay. I might need a new car, though." Although she tried to sound flippant, her voice was small.

Donovan didn't point out the tremble in her voice or how it cracked, for which she was grateful. Instead, he examined the car with her—a gash in the side above the front left tire, mangled backend, and crumpled trunk.

"You go through a lot of cars, Beth."

"Hey, this wasn't my fault, and my other car was a piece of crap. But I'm not the one who ran into a tree."

Donovan gave a small chuckle. "I'm never going to live that down, am I?"

She smiled. "Never."

Donovan took her hand and led her into the station. Thorn waited for them inside. As soon as he saw Beth, he launched forward and pulled her into a hug.

"Are you okay?"

"Yes, I'm fine." She patted Thorn's back.

He held her at arm's length. "Are you sure?" He looked her up and down and turned her in a full circle.

When she was facing him again, she said, "Do you want to do a strip search to be sure?"

Thorn's worried experience transformed into a grin. His gaze flicked to her right where she knew Donovan stood just a step behind. "Okay," he said.

"No." Donovan stepped forward. "Not happening."

Thorn sighed. "Killjoy."

Although Thorn was their friend and a jokester, he put on his detective mask the second they sat down and he picked up a pen. "Beth, tell me what happened."

She went through everything from the moment she spotted the sedan behind her to when she lost it. Her trembling had stopped, and she was able to speak without her voice cracking.

Thorn completed a crash report and took notes based on what she saw in the hopes of catching the men who tormented her. "Were you able to catch a license plate number?"

She shook her head. "The sedan never got in front of me. If it is the same sedan I saw when I was undercover, though, I was able to make out a *V* and a *W*. I know that won't help much, but the front is banged up from their assault on my car, so that has to be a big identifier." She doubted they would drive the sedan again, though. Not with the evidence of their crime all over their front bumper.

"And you couldn't see the driver?"

"No. The windows were too dark. All I know is there were at least two. I have no clue if anyone sat in the back or not. They appeared to be average height, and by their build, I am confident in saying they were men."

Thorn jotted down her words. "Can you tell me anything about the vehicle other than a black sedan? That's not much to go by."

She shrugged apologetically. "I don't know much about cars."

"Maybe you noticed something but don't realize it. Close your eyes and look through the rearview mirror again. What do you see?"

She did as Thorn instructed. The car was on the larger side and had made a meal out of her compact car. She saw the pitch-black windows, the sleek black paint, and the chrome lines of the grill. In the middle of the sparkling grill, she had caught a glimpse of the car's logo just before the sedan had zoomed up. With her eyes closed, she drew a symbol that looked like three shields in red, white, and blue. She passed it to Thorn.

"A Buick?" He nodded as he studied her drawing. "That might help."

Beth still felt bad for not having more information. It was like in San Francisco when she hadn't gotten a good look at Jackson Storm when Buck was talking to him. If she had, they would've known who they were up against sooner.

Thorn walked them back to her car and wrote down what he saw with his own eyes. When he finished, he set the report on top of the car and stepped back in disbelief.

"Damn." He looked at Beth in such a way that she had to look away. "How did you manage to drive while they were doing this?"

She shrugged and kept her gaze on the asphalt. "I just did. I knew I couldn't stop, couldn't let them get me. If I crashed into something, I had a feeling they would've dragged me out of the car and forced me into theirs." She looked up then. "I have no idea why I felt that way, but it was strong."

The two men glanced at each other.

After silence stretched for a moment, Thorn embraced Beth. "You need to be extra careful from now on. If possible, don't go anywhere alone."

Beth nodded, but she resented the fact she couldn't live her life without fearing someone was after her. Who was doing this and why? What did they have to gain?

Thorn left to file the report, and Donovan called a tow truck to transport her car back to their apartment. Beth insisted it was still drivable, but Donovan didn't want her behind the wheel, which she figured was for the best, as her hands were still unsteady.

When neither of the back doors would budge, Donovan had to smash the back side window with a rock. With the glass gone, Beth reached in and retrieved the garment bag. She hugged it to her chest. "At least they didn't ruin my dress. If they so much as put a tear in it, I'll be going out there myself to hunt down their asses."

"With me riding shotgun," Donovan added.

Three hours later, Beth returned from the ER. She was cleared of all accident-related injuries, but they prescribed her muscle relaxants as a precaution for spasms.

After talking to her insurance company, she ventured downstairs to get the mail. Bills, junk mail, two magazines, and a manila envelope filled their small cubby. She brought the mail back to their apartment, dropped it on the counter, and began going through them one-by-one, saving the manila envelope for last. The return address didn't have a name, but it had been sent from Orlando. Figuring it had to do with their wedding, she lifted the two silver prongs, peeled back the flap, and pulled out a photograph. Her eyes widened, and her mouth cracked open in surprise.

"Donovan!"

He rushed out of the bedroom. "What? What is it?"

She turned the photo in her hands so he could see it. He snatched it from her. As he studied it, his jaw flexed, and his glare burned with rage. He slapped the photo on the counter and snatched up the cordless phone.

Beth looked down at the image of herself in full hooker costume, with her hand on her hip and her finger crooked in invitation. It was the same come-hither look she gave to the driver of the sedan, thinking it was Ramirez. In the corner of the photo, written in bold black letters, was a message.

We see you, bitch.

"Thorn, you need to come over. Now."

Donovan's demand brought Beth around. He was on the phone, and the look on his face was intense, as if he could murder someone for threatening his fiancée and nearly killing her mere hours ago.

"Beth got something in the mail from them. You

need to see it." A few seconds later, he jammed the phone back on the hook.

How he was acting, and the things he was saying, scared her.

"Donovan, what's going on? Ever since you got back yesterday, you've been acting strange. You know I don't like being kept in the dark."

He braced his hands on the counter and lowered his head. That stance told her what he was about to say was hard for him.

"I saw Buck yesterday."

Beth blinked. She was stunned into silence.

"I wanted to know who was threatening you. He told me to talk to Jackson Storm, so I had Thorn take me to maximum security."

Her eyes widened. Her hand shot out, and she gripped his arm. When he turned, she gaped at him.

"Jackson said the threats you've been getting are from his men, because he put out a kill order on us."

Her knees weakened. She wanted to sit but couldn't make her brain follow any commands. Two words kept replaying in her mind. *Kill* and *order*.

No one survives a kill order.

Chapter Seven

Donovan sat across from Thorn at the dining room table as he had a few days ago. This time, though, Beth sat at the head of the table, and the photo—in a clear evidence bag—lay in the middle like a morbid centerpiece.

"What do we do?" Donovan said, breaking the awkward silence.

"I'll take the photo to the crime lab," Thorn said. "It'll be checked for fingerprints, and the handwriting will be run through our database for any possible matches. As for the sedan, we can have officers patrolling the city keep an eye out for any suspicious sedans with damaged bumpers, but without a full plate number, we won't be able to get information on the owner."

Donovan knew that was the most that could be done, but it didn't feel like enough. "What about the threats?"

Thorn sighed. His shoulders lowered. "I think it's time we take drastic measures with that."

Donovan frowned. "Like what?"

Thorn's gaze shifted toward Beth, and then back to Donovan. "Like the two of you staying under lock and key. At least until you can leave for your honeymoon."

"And when we get back from our honeymoon, and if Jackson's men are still at large, we're back to house arrest?"

Thorn nodded. "Unfortunately."

Donovan mashed his teeth together. *Will we have to hide for the rest of our lives? Screw that!* He was about to shut down the idea when Beth lifted her head.

"You've got to be fucking kidding me." Her voice was a deep growl. He had never heard her sound so enraged. Her glare shot flaming daggers at Thorn. Her chest heaved. "I'm not going to be a prisoner in my own home. I'm not going to let these assholes win."

She shoved to her feet, knocking over her chair. It hit the tile with a loud smack. Her hands were balled into fists. She looked ready to beat the crap out of someone.

Donovan understood why.

"They tried to kill me! They want us dead. Dead! But there's nothing we can do to stop them? There's never anything we can do!" She picked up her empty coffee mug, whirled, and chucked it at the far wall where it shattered into several large chunks.

Her fingers dove into her hair, and she stood facing the wall as she tried to rein in her anger. After a moment, her hands fell to her sides. Her arms were limp as her fight fled, turning her body to gelatin. She turned to them. Her cheeks were a fading fuchsia.

"I'm sorry, I'm just…" She paused as if to consider the right word. "Pissed."

Tears gleamed in her eyes like glass. She padded to the living room on bare feet and plopped onto the couch as if exhausted.

Thorn appeared to be at a loss over how to deal with a distraught woman. His wide eyes, pale face, and sweaty brow briefly amused Donovan.

"You're excused, Thorn."

Thorn's features dissolved with relief as he sprang to his feet. "I'll do everything in my power to find these guys. You have my word." He hurried out and shut the door with a soft click.

Donovan went to Beth. He picked up her feet from the coffee table and placed them in his lap. His fingers rubbed the heels of her feet.

Despite her anger, Beth couldn't suppress a giggle. She tried to free her ticklish feet, but he stole them fast and continued to massage. She scrunched up her toes, hiding the pink polish on her nails.

"Donovan, you know I hate it when you touch my feet."

"Shut up and enjoy it."

He applied pressure to a few points and had the satisfaction of watching her melt at his touch. "We're going to get through this, Beth. Jackson Storm isn't going to win, and his lowlife followers will be caught." He held her gaze. "This will end."

She shook her head. Her face registered an utter lack of hope. "When?"

He shifted. "I don't know, but it will." He kissed her frowning mouth. "A week stuck inside with me won't be so bad. Imagine the things we can do." He winked.

The corners of her lips twitched. "No, it won't be so bad."

****

Beth called her assistant to take over her self-defense classes, and Donovan bolted the door and shut the blinds. For the next five days, they stayed indoors. They played poker and Scrabble, the two games they used to challenge each other, as well as Monopoly and chess. They had movie marathons and had a lot of fun in the bedroom. By the sixth day, however, the day before their wedding, they were suffering from cabin fever.

Donovan woke with the intense urge to escape, to leave the shrinking confines of the apartment and see the vast sky above him. He slipped out of bed, changed into clean clothes, and snuck out of the apartment.

At noon, he would be picking up his mom and grandma. Not having Ryan there was going to be difficult. Ever since Donovan was born, Ryan had always been there. He taught Donovan to ride a bike, gave him pointers to ask out a girl he liked in fifth grade, and slipped him his first beer at the age of sixteen. But now, for the day that trumped all, Ryan would be absent. Donovan wanted Ryan to have his back at the altar and to talk him through his cold feet. More than that, he wished Ryan could've met Beth. Ryan would've approved with a wink and a slap on the back, but knowing that and experiencing it in real life were two different things.

Ryan would be missing from all of Donovan's future happy moments too—the birth of his first child and all of those family milestones. Donovan didn't know how he'd get on without Ryan there to share his joy.

Needing to feel close to his brother, he drove to the cemetery. The sun was warm and the wind cutting through the oak trees cooling as Donovan walked over vibrant grass between rows and rows of neat graves. Arrangements of plastic rainbow-colored flowers poked brightly out of the ground in front of carved stones. He passed an elderly woman kneeling at a gravesite. She pressed a crinkled handkerchief to her chest and held a worn picture in her other hand. Her frail body shook with her grief. Donovan's heart tore for her. He disliked seeing women in tears; from young girls to grandmothers, he always wanted to comfort them. He trudged silently past, not wanting to intrude on her sorrow.

A couple of minutes later, he stood at his brother's grave. The stone inscribed with "Beloved son and brother" made Donovan's throat constrict. He sank to his knees and stared at his brother's engraved name.

"Hey, Ryan."

His voice caught. He cleared his throat.

"I miss you every day. I miss having a beer with you and watching the game. I miss your ridiculous bear hugs. But most of all, I miss you being a phone call away." He took a shuddering breath. "I never told you how much I appreciated everything you did for me. You were my only father figure and the best brother anyone could ask for. I don't know where I would be without you." Tears swelled and pressed against his eyelids in their desperation to get free. "If it weren't for you, I would not be the man I am today."

He dropped his head and let his emotions break free. His chest heaved with each strangled breath he tried to take.

Over the past year, the painful grief he felt had lessened, but moments like this punctuated Ryan's absence. After several minutes, he lifted his head. His gaze landed on the gravestone. "I'm marrying the woman of my dreams tomorrow. Her name is Beth, Beth Kennedy. She's smart, strong, and sexy as hell.

She's one in a trillion...the one for me. You would've liked her." He smiled at the bitterness of the statement. "Although you're not here, you'll be with us tomorrow. That'll have to be enough."

He pushed to his feet and laid his hand on the top of the headstone, as if it were his brother's sturdy shoulder. "I love you, bro, and I'll always miss you." Stuffing his hands into his pockets, he turned from the grave and walked back to his truck feeling as though he were leaving a giant part of himself behind.

Twenty minutes later, he arrived at home. He let himself in to find Beth pacing.

She clutched her cell phone in one hand and held the landline to her ear with the other. Her eyebrows were stitched together, and her mouth was drawn down at the sides. When he walked in, she tensed as if ready to fight. Then her jaw went slack.

"Oh, thank, God! He's here. He's back." She dropped the phones on the couch and sprang toward him. Her eyes were wild with a fierce mix of fear and anger. Her cheeks were as red as five-degree burns. She shoved him, making his back collide into the closed door.

"Where the hell did you go? I was worried sick."

Her anger caught him off guard. "What's the matter with you?"

Her lips parted. "What..." Her voice failed. While shaking her head, she took a step back. "What's the matter with *me*? What's the matter with you? Damn it, Donovan, we're not supposed to leave the apartment. Isn't that what Thorn told us? Isn't that what you've told me? Repeatedly? I woke, and you weren't in bed. Fine. No big deal."

She waved her arms in the air.

He feared she was hysterical.

"But then you were nowhere in the apartment, and I find the chain off the door... For the past five days, that chain has been in place." She pointed at the gold chain. "When I saw it there...dangling...I freaked. I thought something happened to you."

Her arms went lax. Tears gleamed in her eyes.

"I thought you were kidnapped." Her voice was small. "I tried to call you, and there was no answer. Every time, there was no answer. I was so scared I called Thorn. He couldn't get a hold of you, either. Why? Why would you leave the day before our wedding?"

Liquid diamonds streamed down her cheeks, lingered on her jaw line, and plunged to the tile.

Seeing how upset she was over his disappearance tugged Donovan's heartstrings into knots. He hadn't meant to worry her. The fact he had made him feel like a major jackass. His regret and her emotions choked him.

He pulled her to him and tucked her into his body. "I'm so sorry, baby. I really am. I wasn't thinking."

"That's obvious." Her reply was muffled against his chest. She inched back and peered up at him with pink eyes. "Where'd you go?"

He wiped her cheeks dry with his thumbs. "I went to Ryan's grave."

Grief flickered over Beth's eyes before she squeezed them shut. She slowly nodded. "I understand." She peered at him. "But I wish you would've told me...left me a note...something. I would've understood. I would've told you to be careful, ask you to take Thorn along for safety, but I wouldn't have stopped you from going."

Donovan sighed. "When my grief and anger take control, all rational thought goes out the window."

"I'm your fiancée," she reminded him. "I know that, too."

He cupped her chin with his fingers. "I think you know me more than I know myself." He touched her lips with his. While gazing into her red-streaked eyes, his fingers combed through her hair. "Did you really think I'd let someone take me away from you on the eve of our wedding?"

"I didn't think you'd have much say if they did," she mumbled.

His hands moved to frame her face. "Look around, baby. Do you think I would've gone quietly?" Nothing was out of place. No chairs were knocked over, and no lamps were smashed on the ground. A fight hadn't been put up. If someone had tried to take Donovan, he would've fought with everything he had in him. If he had gone quietly, they would've killed him. And then her. They both would've fought for their lives, for each other.

"You're right," she said. "This place would've been a war zone." She gave him a strained smile. The corners of her mouth twitched.

Worry flitted through Donovan like the wings of a raven. Beth had been through so much since they met—a hurricane, an earthquake, and almost being Jackson Storm's hostage. Then pile on everything that had happened recently. How was she holding herself together? Or was she?

After his brother's murder, he went through all

sorts of hell. He didn't doubt he had suffered from post-traumatic stress disorder. Now he feared she could be suffering from the same illness. The one thing he wanted most in the world was to protect Beth, and he felt as though he wasn't doing a good job of that. He wished he could take her away from there. Their honeymoon couldn't come fast enough. He thought they would be safe in Hawaii with the Pacific Ocean between them and Jackson's puppets.

He stroked her arms. "Are you hungry?"

She shrugged.

"How about I make us breakfast?"

"Sounds like a lot of grease." Her smile was less strained. "Sounds good."

He scrambled eggs, fried bacon, and buttered toast. On the side, he managed to make parfait cups with vanilla yogurt and sliced strawberries.

That night, he drew Beth a bath with the lilac bubbles she loved. Mountains of fragrant foam floated atop the warm water. Along the ledge of the tub, he lit a few candles. The flickers from the flames made shadows on the ceiling. Satisfied with his work, he sought out Beth and found her curled in a corner of the couch, looking as delicate as a porcelain doll. He slipped his fingers between hers, coaxed her to her feet, and led her to the bathroom. At the door, he gently pushed on the small of her back.

"You did this?"

He shrugged. "Who else?"

She looped her arms around his middle and pressed her cheek to his chest. "It's lovely."

He kissed the top of her head. "I thought it might help you relax."

Drawing back, she looked up at him. "Thank you."

Shadows darkened the skin around her eyes, making them look bruised, and the whites of her eyes were an exhausted pink. He knew the bath couldn't fix all that, but it was a good start.

She slipped her T-shirt over her head, revealing a black bra. When she started to undo her jeans, he turned to leave.

"You're not joining me?"

He paused at the door. Her tan torso was exposed. A bit of purple silk peeked out from her jeans. She looked sexy, and yet, fragile with the fingerprints of fatigue on her face. He shook his head. "This one is for you. Enjoy it."

While she soaked, he pulled out a piece of paper from his sock drawer—his marriage vows. He read through the words he had been perfecting over the past year and added one more oath—*Protect.*

Chapter Eight

Early the next morning, Leighton whisked Beth to her apartment to get ready. Her stomach was as unsettled as a storm cloud ready to spit lightning bolts. She sat in a chair with her robe fastened around her shivering body. No matter what she did, she couldn't stop herself from shaking like a flag in tornado winds.

"Oh, for goodness sakes! You're getting married, not going to the gallows." Leighton stuck another bobby pin into the masterpiece she was creating atop Beth's head. "The two of you have been living together for over a year, so there won't be any surprises. It's just a short walk and an exchange of vows. After that, everything will go back to normal. You'll just have the title of wife. Besides, you're madly in love, and tonight, you'll be able to have your way with him." She winked her fake lashes at Beth. "You don't have anything to worry about."

Beth hadn't told Leighton about what had been happening lately. She flattened her palms against her thighs and the soft cotton of her robe. "I know," she whispered. But her nerves continued to clang like church bells.

"Would you like something to take the edge off?"

Beth shook her head. "I'm fine." But her heart beat erratically.

Leighton picked up an aerosol can and created a

cloud of hairspray around Beth's head. "All right. Your hair is done. I'll start your makeup now."

Beth sat as still as she could while Leighton painted her face. The whole time, her thoughts circled round in her head. Marriage to Donovan was all she wanted, but the past week weighed heavily on her. If she hadn't been chased. If there was no threat on their lives. If Jackson Storm didn't exist, this moment would be lighter, happier. But because those things had occurred and Jackson Storm was more dangerous than ever, she was bursting with a dozen emotions. At the top of the emotional peak was her deep love for Donovan. Only that could destroy the others. Only that gave her strength.

Leighton presented Beth with a handheld mirror. She gazed upon her reflection. Her hair was arranged in an artistic knot of curls and adorned with a small, silver tiara. Her cheeks were a pretty mauve to match her tan, and her eyes shimmered with a stunning blend of browns.

"I feel beautiful."

"You've always been beautiful," Leighton corrected. "Now you're a bride. Or you will be once you put this on." She picked up the white garment bag from the bed.

Beth slipped on the dress and stood before the mirror. The bodice was a vibrant purple that faded degree by degree into a soft lavender and then white. A smile dawned on her face. She was going to marry Donovan. For better and for worse.

Leighton drove her to the Kraft Azalea Gardens in a red sports car with white streamers and flowers trailing behind it from the chrome bumper. During the drive, they were in the middle of a police car sandwich. Donovan, Thorn, Officer Burnett, and Chief Cormac agreed on one thing for the wedding; Beth's safety took precedence. She didn't mind the presence of the police cars, though.

A peace descended over her as if hundreds of butterflies had landed on her. Their beautiful, calm energy seeped into her pores. Jackson and his murderous minions could not ruin her wedding day. She wouldn't let them.

When they arrived at the Kraft Azalea Gardens, she spotted the cops posted along the perimeter. Their presence comforted her even more. She stepped out of the car and into a spear of sunlight breaking through a fluffy, white cloud. The golden embrace warmed her skin and reminded her of her mom's hugs. She could almost feel her mom's arms around her and her hands stroking the back of her gown. In that moment, her mom wasn't dead but alive in Beth's memory and in her heart. Alive in the sunlight and wind.

Beth heard her mom's soft, sweet voice speaking to her. *Look at you, my baby girl. You're all grown up, and it's your wedding day. I'm so proud of you, sweetie. You're going to live an extraordinary life with Donovan. Now go and grab that life with both hands.*

With a teary nod, Beth took the bouquet of white tea roses from Leighton and stepped toward her destiny.

Donovan stood atop a stone monument. He wore a gray tux and looked delicious. His hair was slicked back, and his gaze reached out to her from across the distance between them.

Thorn stood behind Donovan in a darker gray tux, and Leighton walked ahead of Beth in a violet, A-line dress. Meredith and Lilly, Donovan's mom and grandma; Corissa, Beth's assistant; and a few close friends of theirs were scattered over the lawn. They were all looking toward Beth with smiles on their faces.

Standing on a patch of grass, with the hum of a harp touching her ears, Beth felt her father as if he had taken his place beside her, ready to walk her down the aisle. A small smile stole her lips. She dipped her head to her roses and whispered, "Are you ready, Daddy?"

A tingling sensation cupped her elbow. Her dad was telling her it was time. He was ready to give her away. Her gaze lifted, locked with Donovan's, and she took one step toward him. And then another and another until she stood on the platform beside him, and he held out his hands. She gave Leighton her roses and clasped Donovan's hands. Her heart swelled at the contact. Swelled so big, she marveled it didn't erupt from her chest. Her hands vibrated. Not out of fear, but with the force of sheer happiness. Donovan's grasp tightened, steadying her hands. He lifted them one at a time to his lips and pressed a kiss to them. His smile, serene and loving, warmed her inside and out.

She couldn't hear a thing. Not the hum of nature or the wind rustling through the palm and cypress trees. She could see and feel, though. See Donovan's violet eyes radiating love like solar flares. Feel the pressure of his fingers twined with hers.

Then Donovan opened his mouth. "Beth." His voice cut through the sound-proof bubble around her. "When I first saw you, I thought you were an angel. It could've been because I had just bashed my head against a steering wheel—" Beth laughed. "—but it was because you *are* my angel. Fate tossed us together, but nothing that fate can dish out can tear us apart. No hurricane or earthquake will ever be strong enough. I promise to forever love you, to forever protect you, and to forever be your home."

Tears coated Beth's eyes, making the image of Donovan swim. She blinked them away and cleared her throat when she was told to share her vows with Donovan. She smiled at him. Her heart fluttered in her chest, and her mouth was dry, but she managed to say what she had wanted to tell him for so long.

"I thought I was strong before I met you. I could deliver a mean punch, there's no question about that." She grinned at him, and he winked back. "But I didn't know what true strength meant until you came into my life. You've made me stronger than I could ever imagine. With you by my side, I can handle anything. Your love is like my armor. I wear it proudly. And I vow to return that strength to you. To be your warrior. To fight for us and our love every day of my life. To be *your* forever and always."

Donovan's chest had started to rise more quickly. His gaze had intensified. He took a small step to her, closing the distance between them. She could feel his need to kiss her slam into her body as strong as a tidal wave.

They both looked to the officiant.

"Do you have the rings?" he asked.

Thorn handed Donovan a silver ring. Donovan took it and slipped it onto Beth's ring finger while repeating the words that would bind them together for life.

Leighton passed a matching band to Beth. Heart racing, hand shaking, she eased it onto Donovan's finger. Putting a ring on a man was an odd experience. The strangeness and intimacy behind it made her breath catch in her lungs. She had to take an unsteady breath to finish her oath. "For all the days of my life," she whispered.

"You are now husband and wife. You may seal your vows with a kiss."

A spark flashed in Donovan's eyes. A smile lifted the corners of his mouth. He took her hands and tugged her forward. She fell into his body.

She looked up at him; he looked down at her.

The air around them thickened with the electricity of their passion. Whistles and excited yelps touched Beth's ears, but she didn't tear her gaze from Donovan. His hands lifted and framed her face, causing her heart to stutter. He dipped his head. Their lips grew closer but stopped short. His breath warmed her lips. Her eyelids drifted shut. She gripped him tighter as her breath hitched.

"I love you," she whispered.

With those words, Donovan erased the gap between them and took her mouth. Cheers erupted.

Their tongues twined. Their hearts joined. Their lives linked.

****

Beth sat in the window seat on a plane in First Class. She wore a white track suit for comfort and to state her newly acquired title—wife. Donovan lounged next to her in jeans and a polo. They hadn't had a moment alone to indulge in each other, to celebrate the start of their marriage. After the reception, they had changed into plane-friendly clothing and had rushed to the airport to make their flight.

The plane hadn't even lifted off yet, and Donovan already couldn't stop touching her. He held her hand, and his teeth nibbled on her fingers. The sensation of his teeth scrapping against her skin was driving her mad. She shifted to him, pressing her leg to his. Laying a hand against his cheek, she nipped at his bottom lip, hoping to give him a bit of the insanity he was giving her. He caught her chin and took her mouth with a savage hunger. She inched closer to him. The armrest dug into her side, stopping her from climbing onto his lap.

A throat cleared. "Excuse me?"

Beth pried her mouth free. Her face burned with embarrassment. She covered her mouth with her hand. "We're so sorry," she told the flight attendant.

"No, we're not," Donovan corrected. "We got married two hours ago."

The flight attendant beamed at him, forgiving their public display of affection. "Oh, congratulations! Would the two of you like some champagne once we're in the air?"

"That would be great," Donovan said.

The flight attendant left with a bounce in her step.

After takeoff, they enjoyed their glasses of champagne, stole kisses, and murmured promises and seductions into each other's ears.

The flight took twelve hours with one stop. Too long. When they finally landed, Beth was ready to have their honeymoon night.

They exited the plane and were greeted by gorgeous Hawaiian women with luscious, brown hair down to their hips. They had lovely complexions, deep brown eyes, and wore grass skirts around their voluptuous hips. A woman dropped a fragrant lei of pink, white, and yellow flowers around Beth's neck. She kissed Beth's cheek and said, "Aloha! Welcome to Oahu."

Chapter Nine

Donovan drove a rental car to their hotel. They opted against a hotel on the beach for a less expensive one inland, in the middle of all the places they wanted to visit during their stay. Volcanic mountains rose in the distance; their peaks hiding in the haze of clouds. A riot of flowers grew wild everywhere he looked—the spiked and brightly-colored birds of paradise, the large trumpet-shaped hibiscus, and the showy spears of red ginger. Palm trees loaded with fat coconuts shot out of the ground every few feet, stretching up to the cornflower-blue sky. Other trees bursting with clusters of bananas, ripening papaya, and fragrant mango sprouted here and there. People of all different nationalities from Hawaiians to Japanese and Filipinos clogged the streets and sidewalks. They walked, rode bikes, and hung out in groups chatting in the sunlight.

The hotel was a tall structure with trimmed bushes out front and an L-shaped pool in the back. The lobby smelled strongly of gardenias. At the front desk, Donovan got their keycard and pushed the button for the top floor. He opened the door to the penthouse suite and let Beth in ahead of him. She stepped inside and did a full circle. Taking up one wall in the living room was a widescreen TV. Across from it was a tan sectional. A full kitchen, a dining room with a wood table, a private porch with a hot tub, and a master bedroom completed the suite. For the price he was paying for it for the month, it had everything they could want or need.

Beth faced him. "You got us a suite?"

"Of course, I did." He put his arms around her. "This is all ours. And the best part is we're alone up here."

She smiled. "And how are you going to take advantage of that?"

"Like this." He swept her into his arms and carried her into the bedroom. The bed was enormous with a sea-green comforter and white pillows. As he walked with Beth in his arms, he could feel her body trembling. A frown pulled on his face. Was she scared? She had nothing to be afraid of; she knew him, knew what he was like when they made love. It wasn't as though this were their first time. They knew each other from head to toe, inside and out. He set her on the edge of the bed and lifted her chin with his thumb. Her eyes shone with unshed tears.

"Are you scared?" he asked. "Nervous?"

Beth's fingers curled around his wrist as she shook her head. "No."

He touched her shoulder. "You're trembling."

"I know." She gave a small laugh. "I've been waiting for this moment for a long time. I'm excited and happier than I've ever been. This is the first time I'm going to be with a man who is as much mine as I am his."

Donovan cupped her face. "I've been yours since I first looked into your beautiful, brown eyes."

"But now we're husband and wife."

His heart expanded. That was it. They weren't just linked in love but life. They would forever be a part of each other. Beth wasn't his girlfriend or fiancée. She was his wife, his other half. And from this moment on, they would be sharing a life. All the things he wanted for her, with her, swallowed him whole. He wanted every part of her, as he wanted her to have every part of him. Good and bad. Beautiful and ugly. He would love it all, and he knew Beth was the woman who would love all of him, too.

Dipping his head, he took her lips. He kissed her with every promise inside of him, with every dream he harbored, with every bit of hope that beat within his heart.

He kissed her as if he wanted to taste her soul.

On the bed, she scrambled onto her knees, bringing her face level with his. Her arms looped around his neck, and her fingers dove into his hair. She deepened the kiss. Her intensity burned him.

He matched her power, needing the heat as much as the softness.

Their tongues knotted, and their lips molded. Moans escaped.

His hands slipped down her body. The tracksuit kept his hands from her skin. With a groan, his fingers caught the zipper and whisked it down. The fabric parted, revealing the scar on her chest, the swell of her breasts, and the lace of a pink bra. His hands sought her warm skin. He marveled at how silky she felt beneath his palms, but he wanted more. She pulled her arms free of the sleeves, letting the jacket slip off. His gaze feasted upon her. Her skin glowed. Her body hummed. She was strong and sexy; everything he could ever want and more.

She worked the pants off her legs and slung her

arms around his neck. Her gaze was locked on his. She looked at him with all the passion within her, which was as vast and as deep as the ocean. A small smile tilted her lips, and she whispered one word, "Husband."

His hands caught her hips, and he lifted her knees off the bed. Her legs came around him, and he crawled onto the bed where he settled her in the middle. Hovering over her, he stared into her eyes. He saw so much there. Love. Trust. Joy. Anticipation. She was brimming with all of it, because of him, for him.

"Wife," he whispered back and brought his mouth to hers. He kissed her as if he could sink into her. When she purred, he drew back and reached into his pocket. He pulled out a long piece of black fabric.

"Ah. So that's where the blindfold went."

He winked at Beth as he slipped the blindfold over her eyes. He gently knotted it at the back of her head, not wanting her to be uncomfortable. Then he sat back and studied her. Her lips were pink and swollen. Her chest rose and fell with each excited breath. Her fingers curled into the comforter.

He didn't touch her or say a word, just enjoyed the sight of her as her excitement built.

"Donovan?" Her voice was breathless.

He leaned over her and lay his lips next to her ear. "Ssh."

He traced her lips with the tip of his finger. They quivered apart, wanting, seeking, ready to accept. But his finger trailed down the length of her neck, between her breasts. He skimmed the smooth skin of her thigh with his knuckles. Her fists tightened around the comforter. Her legs twitched. Each touch was brief, and yet, it was enough to have her quivering. He traced a heart over her breast and a line down her panties.

A soft moan floated out of Beth's throat. He looked up to see her biting her bottom lip. Deciding to change the game, to heighten her reaction, he laid his lips on her ankle. He kissed his way up to her knee, skipped her thigh, and planted kisses up her torso.

Straddling her hips, he untangled her fingers from the comforter. He laced his fingers with hers and kissed her knuckles. As he bent over her, he lifted her arms above her head. With her hands caught in his, he hovered over her lips. They were parted as her breath escaped between them. He rubbed his mouth over hers. Her fingers contracted on his.

With a smile, he nipped her bottom lip. Her hips elevated, bumping into him. He licked the inside of her lips. At the lightest contact, her mouth opened for him. He slipped his tongue into her mouth, meeting hers. Their kiss was greedy and roaring with passion. Her fingers unknotted from his and grasped his shirt.

"If you know what's good for you," she panted, "you'll take off this blindfold and let me rip off your clothes."

Laughter rumbled up his throat. He tugged off the blindfold. "Hey."

"Hey." She shuddered beneath him a moment before she yanked the shirt off his body and started to work on his belt. Once their remaining clothes were gone, she pushed his back onto the bed. Seeing her looking down at him, her hair mussed, her eyes gleaming, made him want her even more.

She rose over him and paused to look into his eyes.

His hands molded over her hips, but she didn't move. The way she watched him, without a scrap of fabric on her body, succeeded in making him harder. Her hands flexed on his shoulders, and his hips contracted.

"Beth." His voice was an impatient groan. How could she be so still when he knew her body was yearning for him as much as his body craved hers?

A smile formed on her flushed lips. She sank onto him.

As he moved with her, he realized she had waited for him to say her name, to show he was as undone by her as he had made her.

Mission accomplished.

****

For two days, they did little that didn't involve being locked inside their suite with the "Do Not Disturb" sign on the door. But on the third day, Donovan took Beth to the beach. They rented surfboards and went to Waikiki. Kneeling on the white sand, Donovan rubbed a bar of sex wax onto the surface of his board. Across from him, Beth had her surfboard on her lap. Her ponytail had fallen off her shoulder while she worked her arm in circles. She wore red board shorts and a black, long-sleeved surf top to protect her arms. She never looked sexier.

"If it gets too rough for you out there, come in," he said.

She lifted her head and squinted her eyes against the sun. "I know, Donovan. I've promised you about ten times I won't get crazy out there. I won't take any wave that's too big for me. I'll be careful."

He nodded. He had to trust her to know how to handle herself on the water. For a year, he had been teaching her everything he knew. He turned his head to the waves in the distance. This would be a real test for them, though. Not everyone could surf the waves in Hawaii.

"Watch out for the reef. It hurts like hell."

"That's why I've got these nifty little shoes on. I'll be okay." She smiled at him and rose to her feet with the board under her arm. "Ready?"

They ran together to the shore, jumped onto their boards, and slid over the water.

Side by side, they paddled out. When a wave blocked their path, they dove under it and broke the surface on the other side. Water sprayed Donovan's back. His arms stroked through the water, pushing him and his board farther. On the way through the breakers, they had to dive under two more waves. Each time Donovan came up, he made sure Beth was beside him. Water coursed down her face. She sucked in a breath and surged on. Grinning, he pushed harder.

When they made it past the cresting waves, he sat on his board. Beth pushed herself into a sitting position beside him. Her hands rested on the sides of her board, and her feet made gentle circles in the water. They caught their breath as they waited for the next set of waves to appear on the horizon.

"The past few days have been amazing," Beth said. "I can't believe we're going to be here for a whole month. We could surf every day."

Donovan laughed. He was glad she enjoyed surfing as much as he did. "I do have other activities in mind, but we'll have plenty of surfing time."

She beamed at him. "Good."

He looked out at the water. It was strange to think they were halfway across the world, surfing in a different ocean. Beth had never been to Oahu, and although he had been indulging himself in her, he wanted to show her the island. He wanted their honeymoon to be memorable, in more than one way.

A wave rose out of the water. He watched it as it moved toward them. From where they floated, it didn't look too big. "Do you want to take the first one?"

Beth glanced at him. "Really?"

"Yes, really. Get going."

Without another word, Beth whipped her board around and started to paddle. The wave picked Donovan up and continued to follow Beth. When she charged it, his chest swelled with pride. Her form and speed were perfect. But then he noticed the wave grew taller than he had anticipated. Waves were unpredictable, and Beth had a beast on her tail. It lifted her up and when she stood, Donovan's heart stopped. She could've let it slip beneath her, but she was making the drop.

She vanished from his line of vision. He kept his stare glued to the wave, searching for her surfboard flying into the air, a sure sign she wiped out. As the wave rolled in on itself, he craned his neck. When he caught sight of Beth hunching over her board and gliding along the inside of the wave with her head inches from the cresting water, he threw his hands up. She had successfully made the drop and was riding it like a pro.

Looking toward the end of the wave, he held his breath. If she didn't get there before the barrel closed, she'd crash into it, and a ton of water would slam into her.

His gaze snapped back to Beth. She was cruising

along the length of the wave as if it were nothing. He thought she'd slip out of it unscathed, but white froth churned at the backdoor. He was helpless as the wave closed in on Beth and knocked her off her board. She fell backward, and her board rocketed into the air. The board was yanked down by the cord attached to her ankle. It bobbed up and down as water crushed her, twisted her around, and pounded her.

Donovan held his breath until her head broke the soup, the foam left from the wave. She grabbed onto her board and paddled to safety. When he finally reached her, she was panting for breath.

"Are you okay?"

She nodded and sat up. "Yeah, but damn, those waves can beat the crap out of you. Is that what they call 'eating it'?"

He couldn't stop himself from smirking. "Yeah. That's what it's called."

"Shut up." She splashed him.

"Are you sure you're okay?"

"I'm fine. I just need to catch my breath. Let's go to the lineup. You can have the next wave."

They paddled back to where they had been and waited for the next set to arrive. The lull lasted several minutes before four waves rose up. Donovan stayed put while another man went for the first wave in the set. He was eyeing the third wave when a shout lifted over the roar of the passing wave.

"Hey!"

He peered over his shoulder to see a second surfer drop in on the one who had already claimed it. The two surfers collided so hard they went flying together over the wave.

Donovan winced.

"Isn't that illegal," Beth asked.

"Oh, yeah. Surfers don't take it lightly when you drop in on them. Those two are probably going to end up on the beach to kick each other's asses."

"Really?"

He looked at her. "If someone ever dropped in on you, I'd rip 'em apart." He turned his attention back to the oncoming waves. The second wave was close, and someone was paddling off to claim it. The third wave was behind it, and it was clean.

"I want this next one," he said. "Don't take off on one until I get back."

"I won't."

He turned his board around, waited a heartbeat to make sure he was exactly where he wanted to be, and started to paddle. No one had been charging it when he made a move, but out of the corner of his eye, he saw another surfer a few strokes behind him, trying to catch him. He clenched his jaw as he paddled harder. No way was this snake going to steal this wave out from under him. The surfer inched closer. It was a paddle battle. Whoever could pop up first and make the drop would win the wave.

Donovan threw his arms down faster and pushed the water with his hands harder. His board surged forward, giving him enough headway. He popped to his feet and maneuvered his board to make a clean drop. The face of the wave was beautiful, and the overhead was so high he could stand straight. He easily rode the length of the tube, carving the top every now and then. At the end of the barrel, he kicked out by jumping into the air and turning his back over the wave. When he came back up, Beth cheered.

"I was about to hit that kook with my surfboard when I saw him trying to steal your wave," she said when he rejoined her.

Donovan chuckled. "See, you're getting the surf attitude."

They rode two more waves each, sharing with the other surfers there, before they decided to call it a day. After they passed the breakers, they leisurely paddled back. Once the water became shallow, they stood and walked to the shore with their surfboards under their arms.

"So, how did you like your first surfing experience in Hawaii?"

"I'm stoked. No wonder surfers want to surf every day. There's nothing like it." She glanced at him and smiled. "Well, okay, sex is up there."

He threw back his head and laughed. "Thanks for that."

"You're welcome."

The water on the shore flowed back, making it difficult to walk as the wet sand sucked their feet into holes. Beth tilted into him as she tried to free her feet. He caught her shoulder.

"Got it?"

"Yeah. I hate it when the sand does that," she said while shaking globs of sand off her reef shoes.

A scream made Donovan stop.

Another yell hit the air. This one a warning, "Rogue wave!"

Donovan turned to see a large wave crashing onto the shore behind them. Two things rushed into his mind. The first was a curse. The second was Beth. He was reaching for her when the wave rushed into them. He was shoved backward with the force of a stampede. Something tugged harshly against his foot. His body slammed into the ground, and his hands grabbed fistfuls of sand that dissolved in the water. When he managed to get his head above the water, he saw he had been tossed up the sand dune. The sensation of being pulled back had him flailing as he tried to get to his feet, but he couldn't. It yanked him back down the shore and dragged him over a rock. He latched onto it and held on as water rushed around him. It rose up his neck, tugged on his arms, and pulled on his legs.

When the water lowered and drew back, he peered around. The water would be coming back, and the rock he clung to would be submerged. He shoved to his feet and leapt off the rock. Running up the shore, he yanked his feet out of the sand's greedy hands with each stride. He scanned the shore where several people were scattered around. Beach chairs had been thrown sideways, and coolers were upside down.

His gaze sprang to a spot of red and black. *Beth.* She was sprawled face-down on the sand. Her surfboard was broken in half. The bottom half was clasped in her hands; she had rammed it into the sand to stop the wave from sucking her out to sea.

His own surfboard had been ripped off the rubber string connected to his ankle.

He ran to her as another wave rushed in. When he made it to her, he ripped the Velcro off her ankle and grabbed her arm. "Hurry." She shot to her feet, and they ran up the sand dune. It wasn't as tall as it had been moments ago. Water splashed at their heels, but they kept on climbing. At the top, he saw the shore was flooded again. The people who had been sunbathing dashed after their possessions before they could lose them.

Beth collapsed onto the sand at his feet. "What the hell was that?"

He lowered next to her. "A rogue wave. They're rare, but they can happen. Two or three waves in a set might've fused together."

"Shit, and I thought wiping out was bad."

Back at their suite, they assessed the damage; Donovan's knees and hands had been scraped from the rock, and Beth had sand burn on the side of her left leg. Neither of them had serious injuries. Nothing that would deter their honeymoon.

From the edge of the bed, Beth rubbed ointment over her rash. "I take back my wish to surf every day. Maybe every *other* day."

Donovan squatted in front of her and kissed her thigh. "I'm sorry."

She frowned. "For what? You're not Poseidon. You have no sway over the ocean and the tides."

"No, but I'm your husband and feeling responsible comes with the territory."

She put her hand on his face and pressed her mouth to his. "A rogue wave is out of your control, dear husband. Besides, we're fine." She capped the tube of ointment. "What were you thinking of doing for dinner?"

"How does going to a luau sound?"

"Fun."

****

Flaming torches lined the outdoor restaurant. Several low, long wooden tables overflowed with flowers and food. Beth and Donovan sat on pillows on the ground. Roasting pig scented the air, mingling with the salt of the ocean. Smoke from the firepit drifted in a soft breeze and rose to the night sky.

The platters on the table consisted of beef, chicken, and fish wrapped in taro leaves. Chicken long rice; baked sweet potato; and poi, a starch staple of Hawaii, were also available for feasting, along with many fruits, including pineapple chunks; watermelon; and lychee, the pink and rough rind covered fruit with a delicate, almost translucent meat on the inside.

Beth and Donovan loaded their plates with nearly every food available. Each bite was like a storm of flavor. They ate until they were full, and then watched Samoan fire dancers. The dancers were shirtless with shredded green leaves around their shins and a red piece of fabric wrapped around their waists and legs like swim shorts. They danced and spun their flaming knives, making flashes of art in the darkness. When they did acrobatic stunts to the beat of the drums, Beth and Donovan cheered along with the audience.

Hula dancers in bright bikini tops took the stage next. Their grass skirts were low on their hips. Leaves adorned their ankles and wrists. Beth turned and covered Donovan's eyes. He chuckled, and she laughed along with him. He put his arms around her, and they watched the dancers perform with Uli'Uli rattles made of gourds and red and yellow feathers. The sound of the seeds shaking inside them and the movement of the dancers' hips was hypnotizing. Donovan couldn't deny it. After their dance concluded, they invited audience members to join them on the stage.

Donovan brought his mouth to Beth's ear. "You

should go up there."

She rotated around. Firelight reflected in her wide eyes. "Are you crazy?"

"No. I've seen you move your hips before." He winked at her.

She fought not to smile as she twisted her lips to the side. "Fine, but you better record it on your phone, because I won't do it again." She rose to her feet and slipped out of her flip-flops. She wore a form-fitting, knee-length, blue and white Hawaiian dress.

As she walked away, Donovan ogled her tan legs and shapely butt. A smirk flitted over his face. Her body could mesmerize him more than a room full of hula dancers.

Beth stepped onto the stage with six other brave people, two of which were men. She was given a grass skirt to loop around her hips. Then the dancers taught her and the other participants how to bend their knees, move their feet up and down, and rotate their hips. It was a quick lesson before the music started and they all began to hula dance.

From the table, Donovan only had eyes for Beth. She moved with a grace he'd seen her use on the blue mat in her studio, but this was more seductive. Her hips bobbed up and down with a speed that had his eyes widening in satisfaction. Across the distance, she stared right at him. He couldn't help but feel she was luring him in. His gaze couldn't stay on her face, though. It kept traveling down her body from her breasts to her feet, but zeroed in on her hips each time.

When the song ended, he clapped for Beth, but all his hands really wanted to do was cup her hips and feel her shake against his body.

She came back to their place at the table and slipped on her flip-flops. He looked at her feet and the pink polish on her toes. She lowered next to him. "So, how was I?"

"Breathtaking."

She smiled and kissed him. "I hope you know I did that for you."

"I know," he whispered back.

In their suite, Donovan unbuttoned his black shirt with a Hawaiian pattern down one shoulder. He put it onto a hanger and set it back in the closet. The sound of Hawaiian music drifted into the room. He peered over his shoulder to see Beth standing bare foot on the carpet a few paces away. She was bouncing her hips, like how the dancers taught her, and moving her arms fluidly at her sides.

A smile lifted the corners of his mouth. "I thought you said you wouldn't do it again?"

"I lied."

He went to her as he had wanted to before and put his hands on her hips. Her hips continued to jump. His gaze feasted on them as they moved. His mouth watered. He took a final step so their bodies molded. The tempo of her hips slowed so they rubbed sensuously up and down against him.

"You're good at that." He lowered the zipper at her back.

"Yeah?" She pressed into him. "How good?"

He playfully nipped her bottom lip. "You should *feel* how good."

"Mm." She didn't stop moving her hips. "Yes, I can."

He pushed Beth's dress to the floor. Underneath,

she had on sheer, black panties. He eased the straps of her bra off her shoulders. The flimsy fabric clung to her nipples. He tasted the soft, warm skin of her breast. The whole time, her lower body ground against him, intensifying his needs. Unable to resist any longer, he maneuvered her onto the bed where they shed the rest of their clothes and engaged in their own dance.

Chapter Ten

In the morning light, Beth and Donovan lay next to each other, sated after a night of excitement. Donovan had Beth's right hand caught in his. His fingers were lightly locked with hers, but he kept moving them along the length of her fingers so they rubbed against her skin. The contact was sweet and intimate. They were content enough to lay in bed and just touch fingers.

"We haven't talked about it since I proposed..." Donovan paused, but his fingers continued to slide with hers.

Beth couldn't think of what he meant. "Haven't talked about what?"

"Kids."

She craned her neck to get a look at his face. His stare was so penetrating her heart skipped a beat. "Of course, I want to have kids with you. I haven't forgotten our deal to have three."

Donovan's smile was quick and boyish. "At least one boy. You remember that."

"I'll give my ovaries the memo."

"And I'll have a talk with my boys."

Beth covered her face, smothering her giggle.

"So...when do you want to start trying?"

She watched their fingers glide up and down. They both knew she was on the pill and would have to stop taking it to get pregnant. "I think it would be nice to experience our first year of married life without morning sickness," she said, gauging his reaction. "What do you say to trying for our first baby on our one-year anniversary?"

Donovan lifted her hand to his lips and kissed her palm. "You've got yourself another deal."

Beth threw back her head in laughter. "Is that how we're going to plan our future? By making deals?"

"Why not?"

She smiled. "I guess it'll be our thing."

"That's the spirit."

Beth sat up then. She faced Donovan and crossed her legs on the bed. His gaze trailed down her body, eyeing her sheer black bra. Lower down, she wore a pair of his blue flannel boxer shorts. A slow grin filled his face. That look caused the pit of her stomach to churn and a wet heat to bloom between her legs.

She nudged him. "Hey, eyes up."

His gaze traveled leisurely up her body. That grin was still flirting with his mouth.

She tried to ignore it. "What do you imagine for our first year as husband and wife?"

The tips of Donovan's finger stroked the curve of her knee. "I imagine everything we already have…coming home to each other, waking up to your beautiful face, watching football games together, cooking side by side, surfing, and learning things about you that I still may not know. I also imagine much more, things I can't anticipate, good things."

His words made her heart soar. He might be embarrassed if she said it, but he had a great way with words. She leaned forward and pressed her lips to his. "I like that."

"What do you envision?"

She tilted her head back as she considered the possibilities. "Being partners in everything from home life to work life." She paused. "Laughter, adventure, poker. Lots of poker. Going to your monster truck competitions and losing my voice from cheering so loud."

"In appreciation, I'll fix you hot water with lemon and honey," he offered.

"Thanks. Then there's the little things like smelling your cologne every morning after you first put it on."

He tilted his head. Curiosity shone in his eyes. "You've never said you like my cologne. Is that why you kiss me so passionately after I spray it? I thought it was because you liked goodbye kisses."

Her cheeks warmed, and she bit her bottom lip. "Oh, I definitely like goodbye kisses, but the smell of your cologne combined with how sexy you look…it does it for me every time."

The grin he wore earlier returned. "Nice to know."

She teasingly whacked his arm. "Back to being serious…above everything else, I envision being happy. And I'm looking forward to all of our firsts as a married couple, like the first time I get to sign my new name, our first house, our first baby, and even our first fight, because I know no matter how angry we get, our love is a tougher opponent and can defeat our anger with a TKO."

Donovan nodded. "You've got that right."

He pulled her to him so she leaned into his chest. Their mouths fused. He lay back, and she stretched out on top of him. Their mouths didn't so much as part a fraction. They rode out the long, languid kiss to the crest.

Donovan's hands slipped up the backs of her thighs, snuck beneath the cotton boxers she wore, and massaged her backside. She eased back just far enough to say, "I also envision something else."

"What's that?" His lips moved against hers.

"Sex. Lots of sex."

"More sex than poker?"

"Hm. Let me think about that a moment." She sucked on his bottom lip. Then her lips moved down his neck. She caught the fading scent of his cologne there. Even that could cause her stomach muscles to clench in pleasure. She lifted her head to look into his face. Her finger followed the sharp line of his jaw. She lowered to his lips for another languid kiss. Their tongues stroked silkily, hotly against each other's, drawing out moans.

Before she could sink too far, she pulled back to whisper, "I don't know. I like poker."

****

After a late breakfast, Donovan persuaded Beth to climb aboard a helicopter and fly over an extinct volcano. The land below was lush with green life. Splashes of color dotted the landscape like fireworks in the sky, and turquoise water stretched for miles all around. Diamond Head rose in the distance, a king on his throne overlooking his land.

Beth was awestruck as they flew closer. "So, you're sure this thing is inactive," she shouted into the mike strapped to her head.

The pilot chuckled. "Positive. It's been dead for over one hundred thousand years."

With the reassurance it wouldn't send a lava bomb

into their helicopter, she stared out the window at Diamond Head. It dominated the whole corner of the island. The base had a thick green carpet, and the center was a massive crater of brown rock. What surprised her the most were the roads and buildings built in the middle of the crater. Not to mention the thousands of houses cluttering the foot of the mountain. If the Hawaiians didn't fear it, then she knew she needn't fear it.

"And there are no active volcanoes on Oahu, right?"

"That's right, ma'am."

She nodded at the pilot's words and glanced at Donovan's smirk. "What? I'm just making sure."

After a snack of teriyaki chicken on bamboo sticks and cherry cones of Shave Ice, they ventured to Pearl Harbor. At the USS Arizona Memorial, a strange hush fell over Beth. The presence of the sailors who died on the battleship enveloped her. Sadness filled her heart. Even though the memorial was beautiful, the reason it was created broke her heart. She could feel the terror they experienced on that horrible day. It sank into her bones and made her shiver. The marble shrine with the names of the sailors who lost their lives made a lump form in the back of her throat. So many useless deaths.

Hand in hand, Beth and Donovan moved to a window and peeked over the edge at the water below. Seeing the ship right there, close enough to touch, made her suck in her breath. With the gently rolling waves and the sunlight reflecting off the water, the ship appeared surreal, ghostly.

"Wow." The word came out on a gasp. "This is a grave for many men," she whispered.

"Maybe this wasn't a good idea to come here," Donovan said. "Not exactly a happy expedition to do on a honeymoon."

"No." She squeezed his hand. "This is a once in a lifetime opportunity. I would've been disappointed if we left and I didn't get to see it, but it is heartbreaking." She peered at the ship again, tried to imagine the fright they felt. It overwhelmed her, swamped her, drowned her. Lifting her face, she took a deep breath. The sun warmed her face. Whispers slipped into her ears. It could've been the wind, the waves, but she had a feeling the soft voices were from the lingering spirits.

Please move on, she said to the ghosts. *You don't need to be here anymore. You're courageous, and we thank you. You're safe. We release you.*

The hairs on her arms stood. Warm tears pressed the backs of her eyelids.

"Are you ready to go?" Donovan asked.

She opened her eyes and looked out across the harbor. "Fair winds and following seas and long may your big jib draw." A smile tugged her lips. She lifted her hands off the rail and faced Donovan. "Yeah. I'm ready."

****

That night, they walked along the beach during sunset. Beth held her flip-flops by the straps with her left hand. Her right hand was joined with Donovan's. The surf rolled over her feet, cool and soft. Puffs of foam clung to her toes.

The day had been one of adventure. Now it was ending with notes of relaxation and beauty. So far their honeymoon had been a dream. Her tan had darkened, her surfing skills had improved, and she would have lovely memories of the island to recall for the rest of her life. She had been happy on her wedding day, and she truly had been from scalp to toenail, but she had been wrong when she thought she wouldn't be able to exceed her happiness when she married her soul mate. That happiness didn't compare to what she felt at this moment. They were husband and wife. Forever. They were living new experiences with each other, as they would every single day of their lives together. She wasn't happy. She was elated.

"So far, our honeymoon has been a dream," she said. "If it ended tonight, I would be content for the rest of my life."

Donovan lifted their hands and kissed her knuckles. "But it's not ending tonight or tomorrow. We have weeks to enjoy this."

She tried not to think about why they were staying on their honeymoon for so long, didn't want to think about Jackson Storm. "I don't know how it can possibly get any better than this."

"It will. I have plans."

She slowed. "Plans? That sounds mysterious, Mr. Goldwyn. I'm intrigued."

He shifted in front of her and smiled. "You'll like what I have planned. Trust me."

The wink he gave her sent heat flowing through her body. It collected between her legs. With a single wink that was what he could do to her.

"I've always trusted you," she said and pressed her mouth to his.

When his arms circled around her, she dropped the flip-flops and slung her arms around his shoulders. With her body flush against his, ocean water swirling around her ankles, and her feet sinking into the wet sand, she indulged in the feel of his lips. Kissing him in paradise, half a world away from where they said "I Do" thrilled her. The sound of the crashing waves deafened her, making her believe they were alone on the beach. Alone in the world. She tilted her head and deepened the kiss to claim every part of his mouth. His flavor and heat intoxicated her. Her head spun.

She inched back and leaned her forehead to his. "You're an amazing man, Donovan. An amazing husband." She gazed into his eyes. "Every day is an adventure with you."

He kissed her forehead. "I'm an amazing man and husband because of you."

Heart melted, she lay her head on his shoulder and held onto him. Floating on cloud nine, her gaze lowered to the sand. A piece of seaweed had looped around her ankle. Her toes were buried in the sand. She laughed when she noticed her flip-flops were gone, swept away by the tide.

****

Beth woke to Donovan lavishing kisses over her face, down her neck, and over her chest. "Mm." She stretched. Her toes curled. "That's a good way to wake up."

Donovan smiled and hid his face in the crook of her neck. His lips were soft and suckling.

"Is this one of your many plans?" she asked.

"Oh, I plan on doing this…" He kissed her mouth. "This…" Lowering her lace bodice, his teeth gently closed around her nipple. "And this…" His hand slithered beneath her nightgown. His fingers tweaked the flesh between her legs. "All the time."

She let out a sigh as he fondled her. Her hands curled into the silk of her nightgown. "I could get used to this every morning," she breathed.

"I'm sure, but I have other plans for you today." He continued to touch her as his lips feasted on her body.

"Well, this is a great start," she said and enjoyed the rest of his wake up call.

Breakfast in bed, a shower for two, and a trip to Ala Moana Beach Park were Donovan's surprises for her. The crashing waves and grassy area was a neat contrast. On a park bench overlooking the bluest of waters, Beth rested her head on Donovan's shoulder. "I know we live in a state with over six hundred miles of beaches, but *this* is truly paradise. I can't imagine anything bad happening here. It's so beautiful and peaceful. I'm inclined to think they don't have thunderstorms here."

Donovan chuckled. "They get storms here. There's also bad people."

She lay her finger over his mouth. "Ssh, don't spoil my delusion."

He squeezed her shoulder. "Sorry."

"I want to pretend good things exist here. At least during our honeymoon."

"And you have every right to."

She could almost hear his unspoken words. *Especially after the last year.*

Sighing, she lifted her head and pulled Donovan to his feet. "Let's keep going."

The salty breeze followed them on their stroll. Curved palm trees lined the walkway, and lizards darted in front of their feet. In Donovan's left hand, he lugged a basket of goodies. At a picnic table, she pulled out sparkling water, strawberries, a container of cold pasta salad, pate, and crackers. She divided the food onto paper plates and handed Donovan a plastic fork.

The sun warmed her shoulders. The salt in the air added extra flavor to the food, making everything taste better. Full and content, Beth propped her chin in her hand and gazed at her surroundings—people walking and surfing, children playing tag and rolling in the grass, tall palm trees and rolling waves.

A scream pierced the air, cutting through Beth's serenity. She jumped in her seat, knocking her knee into the picnic table. A splinter poked her thigh. She twisted this way and that while looking for the source of the alarm. At a nearby picnic table, a woman pointed at a tree. Her face was as white as ocean foam.

"Mom, it's just a black snake. It's harmless."

The woman's children stood next to her, laughing.

Beth settled back into place and tried to ignore her racing heart.

After their lunch, they walked back to the car, loaded in the basket, and piled inside. Donovan pulled out of the parking space and glanced at Beth. "Do you want to talk about what happened back there?"

She continued to look straight ahead. If he saw her eyes, he'd be able to read her. "What do you mean?"

"I noticed how you reacted to the woman's scream."

She shrugged. "I'm a self-defense instructor. I react when I hear a scream. It's a knee-jerk reaction." She rubbed her knee where a pink circle was already forming. "Literally."

Donovan drove the car out of the park. "That's all

it was?"

"Yeah." She looked out the window at the buildings and passing cars, not really seeing them. Flashes of the stories domestic abuse survivors told her fluttered through her mind. She saw April's inflated, mutilated face and heard her own scream when she fled from Ramirez's sinister smirk and speeding bullets.

Her gaze drifted to the side mirror. The sight of a black SUV driving too close for comfort made her sit up straighter. Her hand gripped the door. She stared at the SUV. Her breathing was rapid, and her heart pounded.

No, not here! She tried to peer through the tinted windshield but couldn't see faces. The fear she felt when the sedan chased her through the city and off the road returned and coursed through her veins like lava.

She turned from the window. *They're not here.* She thought it as if scolding herself. *You're being ridiculous, Beth. Jackson's men aren't in Oahu, and there's no way they know we're here. We were careful. Weren't we?*

She peeked at the side mirror.

The SUV zoomed up and stopped short of ramming their bumper.

It's them!

Chapter Eleven

"Donovan," Beth spoke stiffly as if she were holding every bone in her body rigid. "There's a black SUV on our asses."

She didn't have to say anything else for Donovan to understand her alarm.

His gaze flicked to the rearview mirror. His hands tightened upon the steering wheel, stretching the skin taut over his knuckles. "I see it."

"Do you think…?"

He glanced at Beth. Her face was pale, and her eyes were wide. He hated seeing fear stamped across her face, hated knowing he couldn't erase it. "I don't know, but we'll find out." He made a sudden right turn.

The SUV swerved with a squeal of tires and roared to catch up to them.

"They found us." Beth's words came out on a panicked rush. "How'd they find us?"

Donovan reached over and squeezed her hand. "It's okay. We'll lose them and call Thorn at the hotel." He maneuvered around a car and pressed the gas pedal to the floor. The light ahead turned yellow. He glared at the intersection. His foot never flinched off the pedal. They breezed through the intersection. As they passed beneath it, the light changed to red.

The SUV didn't stop. It shot forward in the path of oncoming cars. Through the rearview mirror, Donovan watched a car swerve out of the way. Horns blared. He released his captured breath when the cars didn't crash.

The near collision didn't deter the SUV one bit, though.

Beside him, Beth had one hand on the door and the other wrapped around her seatbelt. "Are you okay?"

"I'm fine, but I'll be even better if you lose those fuckers."

Wanting to do just that, Donovan switched to the other lane and made a tight turn. The SUV followed. A quick glance made his heart plummet to his colon. The passenger's window rolled down, and a gun emerged.

"Get down!"

Beth ducked and covered her head with her hands as the gangster opened fire. Bullets punctured the back of their car. The sound of bullets creating craters in the metal echoed in his eardrums. Glass flew at them when the back window shattered.

Donovan scrunched low in his seat. Two bullets punched through the windshield inches from his head. At the next light, he made a fast U-turn that brought them onto a sidewalk. Metal scrapped concrete. The car jostled. He brought the car back onto the road with more grinding metal and rocking that had them bouncing in their seats. The top of Donovan's head rapped against the roof. With a curse, he ignored the pain and focused on getting away from Jackson's men.

Beth bent forward and dug through her purse. She took out her cell phone.

"What are you doing?"

"I'm calling the cops," she shouted. "If we can't lose them, we can lead the cops to them."

"I'm sure a bunch of people have called the cops

already."

She tapped on the screen. "I don't care. They need to hear about the situation from us." She put the phone to her ear. "Busy signal? You've got to be kidding me!"

More gunshots sounded.

A tire blew. The car swerved. Donovan wrestled it back into their lane, catching it before it could clip the car beside them.

"Try again," he urged through clenched teeth.

Beth redialed. "Ugh..." She lowered the phone, made sure the call went through, and brought it back to her ear. "What the hell? There's nothing. Not even a busy signal."

In San Francisco, a down emergency system wasn't a good thing. Donovan hoped it didn't mean the same in Oahu.

With a growl, Beth dropped the phone into her purse. "We're on our own."

Donovan glanced behind them. The SUV weaved from lane to lane, coming close to pedestrians and other vehicles.

"It's okay," he repeated. "I'm going to the Ala Moana Center. We'll ditch the car and go on foot."

"On foot?" Beth's voice was dry, deep.

"We'll be able to hide easier. Trust me."

Thanks to the traffic, the compact size of their car, and breaking the speed limit, he was able to create distance between them and Jackson's men. He turned into the shopping center, sped to the end of the parking lot, and shoved the gearshift into place.

An alert screeched from the radio's speakers at the same time Donovan cut the engine and leapt out of the car. As he rushed around the car to Beth, he glanced at the entrance of the mall. The SUV was trapped behind a line of cars, and they weren't letting the erratic SUV through.

Grasping Beth's hand, Donovan hopped the curb and ran across the street to a chorus of horns. They sprinted from one side street to another, paused behind delivery trucks to check for cover, and peered over their shoulders to make sure the thugs weren't catching up to them.

Staying close to Kapiolani Boulevard and staying hidden in the backstreets was Donovan's one plan of escape. He didn't want to go into a building, caging themselves for Jackson's men to corner and slaughter in creative and brutal ways. He wanted to stay out in the open.

Fear and anger clashed inside him like gladiators fighting to the death. He couldn't believe these men had crashed their honeymoon, and he didn't know if he'd be able to get him and Beth home alive. Would he be able to live up to the promises he swore to Beth on their wedding day? Would he even get the chance? He had to do everything in his power to keep his vow.

The sound of gunfire brought him around. A lone man in jeans and a black T-shirt was at the end of the street, charging toward them.

Donovan led Beth along Kapiolani Boulevard. The cars on the road were at a standstill, horns blaring. As they fled down the sidewalk, the vehicles were a blur of color. Donovan briefly wondered if the lunatics chasing them had caused a car accident, but that thought was fleeting. His main concern was getting them out of there alive.

After a couple of blocks, he directed Beth to a side

street. They ran from one alley to another until Donovan felt they had lost Jackson's men. Keeping close to the building, he slowed to a stop. With her hand on the brick wall, Beth panted next to him.

A couple hurried past. The sound of a woman wailing had Donovan looking after them. Did one of Jackson's men accost them?

He put his arms around Beth's waist and held her close. "We'll stay here a moment to catch our breath. Then we'll go into a shop and call a cab."

She nodded. He hated how she shivered against him. He wanted to give those assholes a hell of a lot of pain for the fear Beth felt, but he had to get them to safety first.

Chapter Twelve

"I think the coast is clear," Donovan said. He stepped out of the alley first, looked both ways, and then waved Beth forward.

She joined him on the sidewalk. Her legs wobbled. "I can't believe those assholes are trying to kill us on our honeymoon."

"It's okay, baby." He stroked her hair.

She shook her head. "No, it's not, Donovan. It's not going to be okay. They'll follow us everywhere we go. They won't stop."

"We've seen at least one of them. We can ID him and help Thorn catch him. Finding him could lead us to the rest. It will be okay."

She nodded again. It's true she had enjoyed, to some extent, the undercover work she did for Thorn, but she didn't want to relive what happened when they helped to take down David Buckland and Jackson Storm.

As she considered this, a flock of birds flew overhead. She looked up to see not one flock but several different species—ducks, geese, tropical birds—flying away from the coast as fast as their wings could carry them. While looking at the birds, a roaring sound grew louder. The rumble was so powerful the windows in the shops shook. At first, she thought it was the wind, but the more aggressive it became, she realized it sounded wet.

"What's that noise?" She frowned at Donovan in confusion. "It sounds like…the surf."

A blast of wind slammed into Beth's back, knocking her forward. Mist swooped around her. The smell of salt tingled her nostrils. She turned to see a wall of water surging toward them. Cars were whisked away as if they were toys, and palm trees were flattened. People were screaming and running past them, but Beth was paralyzed with fright. The wave reached far above the buildings it engulfed. It was massive. Incredible. Terrifying.

Tsunami!

The word blazed through Beth's mind. Even though she knew what it was, it was too impossible to believe. A tsunami couldn't strike on her honeymoon. A tsunami couldn't wash her away. The thought was crazy, something that could happen in dreams or fiction. Too impossible for real life, and yet, it was happening.

Donovan pulled Beth to him.

She grasped his arms. Fear of the wave, of not telling him she loved him, and not having a life with him beyond their wedding rippled through her, tearing her insides to shreds with long, curved talons. Water washed over her feet and flowed up her shins. She sucked in a breath a millisecond before the wave plowed into her, tossing her backward, knocking her down, and yanking her from Donovan's hold. Her body slid along the black pavement. The feel of her skin peeling away made her grit her teeth. Then the water lifted her and sent her rolling. She fought against the sheer power of it as she would fight off an attacker, but this wave was fiercer than any opponent she had ever faced.

Terror had her failing her arms, kicking her legs, using up more of her oxygen. The water twisted her around and around until she couldn't tell which way was up. Debris pelted her body—parts of trees, chunks of buildings, random objects from the street. She couldn't see anything in the murky, churning water, but she could feel it. Her arm got stuck in something with metal strings that cut into her skin. She tried to wrench her arm free. Her other hand grasped a tube of rubber, and she realized it was a bicycle tire. Panic rose high in her. The wires scrapped against her skin. The second she pried it off, she slammed into a vehicle and rolled over the hood.

Branches smacked her. Glass cut her.

Desperate for air, she forced herself to go lax. When bubbles danced along her body and floated upward, she worked her arms and legs until she broke the surface.

Air filled her lungs a precious second before she was dragged back down. Water flowed into her mouth and down her throat. She pushed herself to the top and coughed up water. Each time she made it to the surface, she gasped for breath only to be shoved under again. She paddled hard. When water pooled off her face, she blinked it from her eyes. A log floated in front of her. Holding onto it, she was able to see everything.

Water lapped at the roofs of buildings. She turned to look behind her and found an endless ocean. *How can there be so much water?* Her gaze ticked left and right, searching for Donovan. Debris zoomed past. Large objects banged into her.

"Donovan!"

The roar of water deafened her. If Donovan was calling out to her, she couldn't hear him.

A car floated past. The driver and passenger were pounding on the windows.

Tears flowed down Beth's cheeks. The water was so fast she didn't think it would stop. She screamed for Donovan and searched the torrents for him. Heads bobbed up and down, but she couldn't see any of their faces. She turned her head to see a boat slam into a building. Glass and concrete flew into the air and splashed into the water. Right behind the boat was a second wave piling more water on top of the roaring flood. A gasp flew from her lips.

No!

She latched her legs around the log and linked her fingers. A second before the wave rushed over her, she sucked in a breath. She kept her grip on the log, but the force of the wave sent her and the log rolling as if she were in the middle of a tornado. She had to focus her strength on not releasing the log in panic. When the log bobbed to the surface, she unhooked her legs. The log rotated and brought her to the surface. She greedily inhaled air and swallowed sea water by accident. The taste of it was revolting. She gagged and coughed.

The water was faster than before. Everything was a blur. White torrents surrounded her. She tried to keep her legs tucked beneath her to prevent further injury, but it wasn't easy. Her muscles gave out, and her legs dangled below. Something wrapped around her ankle, nearly pulling her off the log. She hoisted her upper body over the log and tightened her hold. As water sped her past buildings, she kicked her leg. Whatever had hooked around her ankle wasn't letting go. She scraped the sole of her sneaker down her leg and pushed whatever it was off her foot. At the same time, she lost her sneaker. Not having shoes could be a bad thing once the water went down, but there was nothing she could do about that now.

She looked up before she collided into a building. The impact punched a yell loose from her chest. She released the log to put her hands against the wall. The water was so strong it flattened her to the building. Gritting her teeth, she clawed her way to the edge of the building and pushed around it. The moment she cleared the building, water snatched her and carried her away. She kicked her legs to keep her head above the water, but it splashed over her head. Gasping for breath. Spitting out water. Paddling with all her might. She battled her way to the surface when the torrents overpowered her and shoved her down. She came up and blinked water from her eyes.

A tree bumped into her side and pushed her off course. As it zoomed past, she was sucked back under. Stroking with her arms, her hands cutting through water and vegetation, she made it back to the top. Pieces of long grass clung to her head. She ripped them off to see a concrete post with a light fixture at the top sticking out of the water. She aimed her body to it. When she got close, she reached out and grabbed hold of it. Fighting the water, she snaked her arms and legs around the rough concrete and latched on to it for dear life.

Branches, a toy ball, a beach chair, and other random objects sailed by her, some of it hitting her back and limbs. She cried out when something crashed into her legs. Fresh tears coursed down her salt-slicked cheeks.

A high-pitched scream caught her attention. She turned her head to see a young woman battling to keep her head above water. She was desperately flapping her arms and swallowing mouthfuls of water. Her scream gurgled as she was dragged under.

When she came back up, Beth realized she was racing right toward her.

"Hey," she shouted. "Grab my hand!" She tightened her legs around the post, making sure her ankles were locked, and stretched out her right arm.

The girl looked and reached for Beth. Their hands touched. Beth grasped the girl's fingers. She couldn't get a good hold, though, and before the girl could grab on with her other hand, the wave ripped her away.

Beth tried to snatch her hand again but missed by mere inches. "No!"

The girl's eyes widened. She tried to swim to Beth but couldn't beat the tide. "Help me," she cried.

Beth wanted to help her, but there was nothing she could do. If she released the light post, they'd both die. "Grab on to something," she shouted. "Grab on to a tree. Anything!" Feeling helpless, she watched the girl until she couldn't see her anymore.

Minutes drifted by. After a while, the flow slowed to a standstill. Water lapped at her back.

All seemed calm. And would've been if the Pacific Ocean wasn't smothering Oahu. The sky was a crisp, cloudless blue. It was a perfect beach day. Beth's eyes misted when she thought about Donovan. *Is he alive? Will I see him again?* She couldn't stop her thoughts from turning morbid, couldn't stop herself from imagining what her life would be like if he died before they got to taste married life.

Her mind drifted to the happy families, the surfers, and sunbathers at the beach when the tsunami swept over the shore.

She was considering swimming to the nearest building and clambering onto the roof when the tide began to retract. She inched her body around the post so her back was to the rushing water. It started slowly but quickly escalated. The water roared around her, pressing her roughly into the concrete post, pulling on her arms and legs. The pressure was so great she cried out in pain.

Screaming, she felt as though her ribs would crack and her limbs would be yanked from their sockets. The current was so strong, and she was so tired, she wanted to surrender, to let the water whisk her off to the middle of the ocean. The second that thought came, the water's level dropped. It leaked down her body, uncovering her bloody knees.

Her muscles quivered. When the water receded far enough to eliminate the threat of drowning, she scooted down the post. A few feet from the ground, she unlatched her legs and dropped. Her legs shook, and she fell into a foot of water. Her body shivered with exhaustion.

Frightened thoughts whirled in her head. Tears spilled down her cheeks.

She wrapped her arms around the light post and hugged it as she cried. The fear she had when she was underneath the water, caught in the wave's clutches, broke from her body in loud sobs. She had thought she was going to die. Never in her life, not during Hurricane Sabrina or the earthquake that struck San

Francisco, had she been more scared. She couldn't contain her emotions. They broke free from their dam, and she surfed them until she was depleted.

On top of her fear and desperation were questions. Didn't Hawaii have a tsunami warning system? Why hadn't sirens gone off or emergency messages been broadcasted? Everyone could've gone to safety before the tsunami hit.

What happened?

Aches and pain radiated from every part of her body. She peered down at herself to assess the damage. Her right arm was scrapped raw from the bicycle's wires. A large bruise was already forming on her leg. Smaller bruises dotted every inch of her skin along with several lacerations. None of the cuts were fatal, though, thank God. Her hip bone and shoulder felt tender, and she was covered in blood and dirt.

Stomach muscles heaving, she used the concrete post to pull herself to her feet. Her legs wobbled uncertainly. She kept her hand against the post as she took a careful step to test her strength. Her legs held.

She looked left and right. The people who had been there were gone. *What if I'm the last person on the island?* She shook her head. That was a silly thought, but she couldn't help wondering where everyone was. She didn't want to be alone. Not now. *Not ever again*! Where were the locals? Where was Donovan?

What she saw while searching for people shattered her heart. Rooftops sat in piles of wood and shingles on the ground. Buildings were reduced to heaps. Trees, with their tangled roots, lay in the road. Brush and other debris created huge knots. Everything was filthy and coated in grim. Seeing what Oahu, a once bright and happy island, had been transformed into lodged a cork of grief in the center of her chest. She rubbed her chest as more tears clouded her vision.

Not knowing if Donovan was ahead of her or behind her, she decided to walk in the same direction the wave had been taking her, in case he had been carried farther. She called out Donovan's name. The other part of her knew that if she kept going straight, she'd find a part of the island the wave hadn't touched. And people. She'd find people.

She longed to hear Donovan's voice shouting back to her, but silence only answered. *He could be dead. I'm on my honeymoon, and I might already be a widow.* She tried to banish that thought but couldn't dislodge it. It clung to her mind like sap on a tree.

She came up to a door ripped off its hinges. White flowers decorated the pink paint. It was a little girl's door. She pressed her palm to a flower.

Had the girl been in her room when the tsunami hit? Did the wave tear apart her home? Was she alive?

Beth snatched her hand away as if the door had burned her skin. Her watery gaze rose to the sky. The brilliance of the blue horizon and the golden sunlight angered her. She had seen a sky like it before, after Hurricane Sabrina slunk away from the Sunshine State. She'd rather the sky mimic the hurt and destruction left behind by the disasters with rolling black clouds. Seeing the sky looking so pristine, when the world was in ruins, was cruel.

She walked past the pink door—her steps awkward with one sneaker—and felt as though she was leaving behind the corpse of a sweet girl in a pink, flowered dress.

Blades of grass created a blanket atop the standing water. Pieces of it stuck to her bare legs. An eerie quiet had swallowed the land. The roar of the water and the horrified cries were gone, replaced with a death-like silence. Sunlight reflected off the water, blinding her. She tore her gaze off the water to look ahead. Buildings were husks of what they used to be. Windows blown out. Walls crumbling.

Concrete skeletons.

Bones of a community.

A graveyard of twisted metal and broken concrete.

Everything looked like a war zone, as if the tsunami had grenades in it. She never knew water—something so serene and beautiful—could be so explosive.

Her gaze lowered, and she froze. A body lay in the muddy water a few feet from where she stood. It appeared dead until it shuddered and gasped for breath. Her feet launched into action. She fell to her knees next to the body.

A shard of glass was embedded in a woman's chest. Blood soaked her shirt and seeped from the corners of her mouth.

Beth looked into the woman's face, and a pang of dread stabbed her heart. It was the young woman she had tried to save.

"Oh, God." She gripped the girl's trembling hand.

The girl was crying and gagging on blood. Her eyes gleamed with the knowledge she was dying. Seeing that realization in the eyes of someone so young stole the breath from Beth's lungs, stole it like a thief.

The glass protruded from the girl's chest and vibrated with her beating heart. A sick rolling sensation dominated Beth's intestines. She forced down the urge to vomit and tightened her grasp on the girl's hand.

"You're not alone," Beth said. "You're not alone."

The girl's shaking increased. Squeaks escaped from her mouth. Drops of blood splattered onto her chin.

Tears blurred Beth's vision, distorting the girl's features. All she saw was her blonde hair, pale skin, and blood. Beth's own shaking was magnified by the girl's spasms. Her heart thudded frantically, and her chest constricted. She wanted to be strong for the girl, but her emotions were haywire. Instead of holding it in, she sobbed.

Staring at the girl's face, Beth saw the life leaving her eyes as if they were doors, but it was leaving slowly, reluctantly. The girl convulsed as she fought to breathe through the blood filling her throat.

Beth held her still and looked up at the sky. "God, take her. Take her now. Please, please, please." The girl's suffering was too much. She wanted the young woman's pain and misery to end. "Take her, take her, take her," she whispered. Grief had its hands around her throat, choking her. Her chant continued until the girl's shaking ceased. She closed her eyes as her heart sank like an anchor. When she peeled her eyes open again, she looked at the girl's immobile face and wished she knew her name so she could give her a proper goodbye.

Her hand trembled as she lifted it. The feel of the girl's warm and lifeless eyelids gave her chills as she lowered them. "I'm so sorry."

This girl would be alive if Beth had held on tighter, reached farther.

Her gaze lowered to the slick, pink glass. The urge

to remove it was combatted with having to pry it free from dead flesh. She couldn't do it.

Drawing herself to her feet, her muscles quivered and her body swayed. She searched for something she could use to cover the girl's body—a blanket, tarp, or jacket—but found nothing. She hated leaving her there, exposed. Except there wasn't anything she could do about that, as much as it hurt.

"I'm so sorry," she repeated. "Please forgive me." She took one faltering, sloshing step then another. Although she was moving away, her mind stayed with the girl.

****

She continued to walk. Her soggy sock slid down her foot. Her gaze roved over the water, looking for bodies and debris that could hurt her. Caught in a nest of wood and grass was a chunk of black rubber. She stared at it, unbelieving. A lone black sneaker. She hurried to it and plucked it out of the water. The brand and size were the same; it was her shoe. Laughing, she hugged it to her chest. What were the odds of finding her shoe when she couldn't even find her husband? Tears leaked from her eyes as she wedged her foot and the wet sock back into her sneaker.

Several minutes later, she came across a woman trying to carry two young children. She staggered and the boy and girl slid down her hips. They whimpered as they clutched her.

"H…" Beth's voice was a weak croak. She cleared her throat and tried again. "Hello?"

The woman paused. When she turned, the children slipped down to her knees. Their little arms wound like ropes around her legs.

Beth trudged toward them. "Are you okay?"

The woman nodded, although tears coursed down her face. Beth saw the same relief at finding another person alive mirrored in the woman's eyes. Blood streamed down her face from a gash close to her hairline. The little boy had a nasty bump in the middle of his forehead, and the little girl had a scratch down her neck. She didn't have any shoes on her tiny feet.

"I can help," Beth offered. "Please, let me carry one of them. We can look for shelter and medical aid together."

The woman nodded again. "Okay." Her voice was rough with unshed tears. She sniffed loudly. "You can hold Ali."

Beth smiled at the little girl. "Hi, Ali. I'm Beth. I like your polish." She pointed at the little girl's shriveled toes. "My toenails are pink, too." She gave her a smile and held out her hands. "Is it okay if I give you a lift, so your mom doesn't have to carry you?" She waited for the girl to open her arms, to accept her.

Ali scrutinized her with big, brown eyes. When she recognized a tsunami survivor, she reached out.

Beth lifted her from the woman's arm and settled her onto her good hip. Ali looked as light as a feather pillow, but her twenty pounds weighed Beth down.

"There." She tapped the little girl's nose. "That's not so bad, is it?"

The little girl shook her head and shoved her thumb into her mouth.

Beth smiled and looked to the mother.

"Thank you," the woman said. "I'm Nikki, and this is Evan." She hefted the boy higher on her hip.

"Hello there, Evan. You look like a strong, little

boy. You are, aren't you?"

He raised his arm and gave her a salute. If she had the strength and a free hand, she would've saluted back.

She searched the ruins and buildings for a street sign or name, but everything had been stripped away. She didn't recognize a thing. The fact she was lost in yet another city she was unacquainted with didn't escape her notice, but she couldn't dwell on that. If she survived this, she'd remind herself to get a map of any city she visited in case of a natural disaster.

She looked to the woman who appeared to be a local. "Do you know where a hospital is?"

"There's a few specialty hospitals farther inland. I think Kapiolani Medical Center would be our best bet, but it's a ways from here."

"That's okay. We need to go farther inland and get to higher ground, if possible. Another wave could be coming. We'll make it."

They had to.

With Ali in her arms and Evan in Nikki's, they shuffled on. For the longest time, the only sounds Beth heard were the sloshing of their steps. No chirping of native birds, no laughter or Pidgin talk met her ears.

All color had also been erased, too. The exotic wild flowers and stands featuring rainbows of ripe fruit were missing. Mud painted everything, turning the once beautiful island ugly and depressing.

After a while, Beth felt the heaviness of Ali's head on her shoulder. Ali's arms were limp at her sides, and her lips were pursed into a pout as if her thumb were still in her mouth. Beth smoothed the damp, brown curls from her forehead. The scent of a child's sweat teased her nostrils. It was a comforting smell.

"We were getting Shave Ice," Nikki said, bringing an end to the quiet.

Beth looked over Ali's head at her. Evan was asleep, too. His hands were in fists in Nikki's shirt.

"Evan wanted root beer, and Ali wanted strawberry. I had just handed the cups to them when I heard screams and turned to see the wave coming at us. I grabbed Ali first. Her cup tipped, and the ice fell down my shirt."

Beth's gaze lowered. The front of Nikki's shirt was pink.

"Then I grabbed Evan's hand, and I ran with them. The wave hit us, and I lost them. When I finally made it to the surface, I saw them several feet in front of me. They were holding onto a pink inner tube. It must've come from a hotel. Wherever it came from, it saved my babies' lives." Her voice cracked. "I swam to them, and we held onto the inner tube. It spun us around and around, but I kept a hold of their hands. I was determined to never let go of them again.

"When the current stopped, we paddled to the roof of a building. It was level with us, and I pushed them over the ledge. I was pulling myself over when the water started to pull back. We stayed up there as the water went down. The door to the roof was unlocked. Praise, God! And we made it down to ground level, but my babies didn't want to step a foot into the water. I was picking up Evan when I noticed he still held the cup of Shave Ice in his hand. His little fingers had poked through the Styrofoam. The ice was all gone. I had to tear it apart to get it off his fingers." She dropped a kiss onto Evan's sweat-dotted forehead. "They'll probably never want Shave Ice again."

Beth swallowed. She couldn't image going through something as devastating as that at such a young age. Seeing a vendor selling Shave Ice would no doubt cause the terrible memory of the tsunami to flood back to them every time.

"I can't say this won't haunt them. It'll haunt all of us," she said. "But the fear will eventually dissipate. Be there for them. Wipe their tears. Hold them. Kiss them. Tell them you'll keep them safe. And they will grow. They will move on from this horror."

"The problem is…I'm afraid I won't be able to."

Beth glanced at Nikki. She was crying and stroking Evan's back.

Beth didn't have children. She couldn't imagine the terror Nikki felt when her babies were ripped from her arms. It must've been one hundred times worse than losing Donovan. Just thinking about him made her heart palpitate and her eyes fill. She took a slow breath to get her emotions under check.

"Are they twins?" Beth said, indicating Ali and Evan.

"Yes."

"They're beautiful."

Nikki smiled.

They continued to walk side by side. Oahu's sweltering heat was back in full force. The sun beamed down on them, depleting their body of water, and zapping their energy. Beth's T-shirt stuck to her back. Beads of perspiration snaked along her spine. Where Ali was curled against her, she was soaked with sweat. Her mouth was dry. Her tongue stuck to the roof of her mouth. She licked her lips, desperately wanting something to drink. The longer they walked, the stiffer, weaker, thirstier she became.

Ali was growing heavier with each step. She shifted her onto her other hip and winced when her bones protested against the weight. Gritting her teeth, she pushed on. Even when she wanted to collapse, she kept her arms locked around Ali and her legs moving. Mechanically. Robotically. Mindlessly. It wasn't long before she was panting with exertion. Her arms burned from holding Ali. Her leg muscles vibrated. Sitting and resting was an appealing thought, but if they caved into their exhaustion, it could take hours for someone to find them. Hours they couldn't afford. Not without water. Not in that heat. And not banged up from head to toe.

Her gaze shifted to a cage in the water. She stared at it, wondering if an animal was trapped inside. A few steps closer and she saw it was empty. And it wasn't a cage.

"A shopping cart." Her hopes soared as she hurried to it. Her feet kicked up water. One handed, she managed to upright it. Water leaked from the holes. "All right, sweetie, you're going to go inside this cart." She set Ali on the bottom, and Nikki added Evan.

"Let's push it together," Beth said. She wrapped her hands around the handle.

Nikki stepped up beside her.

Beth's arms felt like doughy pasta. Her leg muscles were on fire. She tightened her grip and used every part of her body to push the cart through the water. Salt drops drizzled down her face. Her mouth felt drier than ever.

"Where were you?" Nikki's voice brought Beth away from her pain. "When the wave came. Where were you?"

"I was…" Memories of what happened before the tsunami rushed through her mind. It all seemed so long ago. "I was with my husband. We were…"

Running.

Guns firing.

Jackson's men.

"We were going for a walk and enjoying island life." She didn't want to tell Nikki about the men who had been after them. "We came here for our honeymoon. We were married four days ago. Birds flew overhead, and wind blasted me. I turned to see the wave. We didn't even try to run. We held on to each other, but when the wave hit, I lost him." She paused as emotions filled her and almost came loose. "I don't know where he is. I don't know if he's dead or alive. I don't know…"

"I'm sorry…that is truly horrible. I hope you find him."

Beth nodded. Her voice was thick with unshed tears when she said, "Me, too."

They fell silent. Their grief for each other gave them the strength they needed to push the cart harder, faster. The water level gradually shrank the farther they went. Although the wave could've stretched for blocks yet, Beth knew they would soon reach an area untouched by its wet, vengeful hands.

"Wait. Did you hear that?" Beth forced the cart to a stop and laid a hand on Nikki's arm. She strained to hear a male's voice calling out for someone; Donovan calling out for her.

"I don't hear anything," Nikki whispered.

"Hold on." Beth's heart thundered. Wind whistled past her ears. Tilting her head left and right, she listened with all her might. Surely, she hadn't imagined it, hadn't hoped for Donovan so fiercely her mind conjured his voice. How could her brain be so cruel to torture her in that way? She started to shake her head. "I thought I heard—"

"Hello? Is anyone out there?" The voice, clearly masculine, echoed around them.

The women looked at each other with wide eyes.

"Stay here," Beth said. "I'll be right back." She took off at a run; her energy restored with the hope of being reunited with Donovan.

"Donovan! Where are you?"

"Over here!"

She splashed past an intersection. "Keep shouting. I don't know where you are." She followed the shouts to the next intersection and turned. A man was rushing toward her. The closer she got to him, her feet slowed. It wasn't Donovan. She dropped her hands to her knees and lowered her head as she cried. Her heart plunged to her bowels. Her strength dissolved. She was about to sink to her knees when a hand caught her arm and pulled her to a stand.

"Are you okay?"

She looked into the man's face. He had blonde hair that dripped over his forehead and blue eyes as clear as the sky. "I'm fine. I thought you were my husband."

The man shifted from side to side, unsure of what to say to being mistaken for a woman's husband. "You're the first person I've found," he finally said.

"I'm not alone. I found a woman and two children a while ago. We could use your help." She led him back to Nikki.

"Is he your—"

"No." Beth cut off Nikki. "No, he's still out there. Somewhere." She had to believe Donovan was alive. If she believed the opposite, she would curl up on the ground, in the dirty water, and wait for death to take her. There was no reason for her to live if Donovan was gone, so she had to believe he was safe. Not hurt. Not dying. Not already dead.

"I'll find him," she whispered.

Nikki gave her a reassuring smile.

Beth looked away when she noticed doubt creep into Nikki's eyes. She couldn't afford to let doubt seep into her. She inched away as if it were contagious.

"I can push the cart," the man volunteered.

Beth and Nikki walked on either side of the cart as the man pushed it. They were moving through the next intersection when Ali's tiny fingers curled around Beth's pinkie. Beth looked at her. Ali took her thumb out of her mouth with a loud smack and pointed toward the water. Beth's head whipped up.

At first, she couldn't see anything. No one was there. But Ali tugged her pinkie and jabbed her finger in the air more urgently. Squinting her eyes, Beth searched the ground. Did the child see a snake? Her gaze roamed over the brown water. Sticks and leaves littered the top. Then she saw it. A bottle of water. She hurried to it, snatched it up, and held it like a trophy. Smiling, she walked back to Ali.

"Good job," she said. With a crack, she unsealed the cap. She gave it to Ali and Evan. They each took several gulps. Evan passed the bottle of water to Nikki. She took a deep swallow and gave it to Beth.

Cool water soothed her parched throat. Pulling the bottle from her lips, she coughed. Her throat wasn't prepared for the wet. She handed the bottle to the man and realized then that she didn't know his name. They passed the bottle around once more. When she held it out to the man again, he shook his head.

"You guys need it more than me," he said.

An inch of water was left in the bottle. She took a sip, gave it to Nikki for a last taste, and then they let the children drink the rest.

With a bit of water in her system, Beth felt marginally better. She studied the man beside her as he pushed the cart. "What's your name?"

"Kevin."

"I'm Beth. This is Nikki and her kids are Evan and Ali."

He nodded at each of them. "Saying it's nice to meet you doesn't sound right considering the circumstances."

"But it is nice to meet you," Beth insisted. "I thought I was alone. When I saw you, Nikki, I was thankful I wasn't alone and that two kids could survive this. Then when I saw you, Kevin, I was glad because we needed help. We wouldn't have been able to go much farther by ourselves."

Kevin looked into her eyes. "You were glad although I wasn't who you were hoping for?"

"Yes." And it was the truth.

"What's your husband's name?"

"Donovan Goldwyn."

She met his eyes when he looked back at her.

"You'll find him," he said.

She lifted her face to the sky and briefly closed her eyes as she took a deep breath. "I know." She'd find him because she'd never stop searching.

They walked two blocks, and then found an older man and woman huddled together on a tree trunk. Kevin stopped and approached the couple. "Hello? Are either of you injured?"

"My shoulder is dislocated, and my wife has a nasty gash in her thigh. She can't walk."

Beth joined Kevin. "We're looking for shelter and medical aid. Please come with us. We can put your wife in the cart."

The man faced his wife. "Verna, honey, it'd be better if we went with them."

"I know that, dummy," Verna said. "But I'll need this strapping young man with the bulging biceps to lift me off this dead tree."

Beth glanced at Kevin and stifled a laugh. Together, they were able to get Verna into the cart. Evan and Ali took their mom's hands, and Melvin walked beside the cart, holding his wife's hand.

"Everybody ready?" Kevin asked. "Beth's Convoy is en route. Next stop, Kapiolani Medical Center."

Beth smiled. The seven of them walked together. The fact she had found so many survivors already gave her a sense of relief. She hoped someone was helping Donovan at this same moment.

Watching Melvin and Verna, her heart swelled and wept. Swelled because their love was pure and undying. Wept because she longed for Donovan to be by her side. Melvin held Verna's hand in his wrinkled grasp. Their banter made Beth smile. They were utterly cute, and Beth wished to experience marriage with Donovan well through their golden years. She wanted to be in his embrace even when he was frail. She wanted to fight with him and make him laugh even in the retirement home. She wanted to kiss their great grandbabies and lay in bed, at the end of their days, knowing they lived a long and happy life. But would she?

"How did the two of you stay together when the wave hit?" It was a question that had nagged at Beth since she saw them together on the tree.

"I never let go of her hand," Melvin said.

An arrow dove through Beth's heart, shredding it and leaving a gaping hole. "H-how?"

Melvin frowned. "I don't know. I just…didn't."

Seeing their hands clasped now, knowing their love was mighty enough to keep them joined, even when a great force of nature plowed into them, made her lose her breath. Especially knowing how the water had thrown her and Donovan apart as if they were twigs in a raging sea. She turned her attention to her feet and tried to silence her thoughts.

When her sneakers lifted out of the last centimeters of water and touched dry land, it felt strange. Not having water sloshing with each step she took made walking easier, but her feet squished uncomfortably inside her wet socks and sneakers. She wanted to dry her feet, drink a gallon of water, curl up in bed, and sleep for a week. But she had to keep walking, searching, and praying.

Sometime later, with dusk hanging heavily above their heads, they came upon a group of locals crowded around a red pickup truck. The sight of them was a huge weight off Beth's shoulders.

In the blink of an eye, unfamiliar faces surrounded her.

"I'm fine, I'm fine, I'm fine," she repeated as tears fell down her cheeks. She kept Nikki and Kevin in her line of sight. For some reason, she felt protective of them. "They need help, though. Verna has a leg wound, Melvin's shoulder is dislocated, and the kids need to be looked at. Can you take them to the hospital?"

"We sure can," a man said. "Hop in. We'll get ya'll there as soon as possible."

"Mahalo." Beth extracted herself from the locals and went to her group. "They're going to take you to the hospital."

The locals laid Verna in the back of the truck. Nikki huddled in a corner with one arm hooked around each of her children. Melvin sat next to Verna with his hand in hers.

Keven climbed up and held his hand out to Beth.

She shook her head and took a step back. "I can't."

Kevin's hand lowered. "What are you talking about?"

"I can't go with you. I need to look for Donovan."

"He could be at the hospital."

"But he might not be. He could be out here somewhere."

"Beth, it's going to be dangerous out here when the sun goes down."

"I'll be fine. I'll look for him tonight. The military should be here soon to help. I'll get a ride to the hospital by nightfall tomorrow. But I'm not going to quit. I can't give up on him, because he wouldn't give up on me."

Kevin stared at her for a long moment before shouting to the other men. "Does anyone have a flashlight Beth can have? And water?"

"Here."

A bottle of water and flashlight were passed to

him. He bent forward and held them out to her. She tucked the bottle under her arm and reached up for the flashlight. Her fingers wrapped around the tube. She tried to take it from him, but his grip remained firm. She peered into his eyes.

"Be careful," he said, then released the flashlight.

"I will."

The truck roared to life and lurched forward, taking what Kevin had joking called "Beth's Convoy" to their final destination. Beth's own destination wasn't where they were going, though. Her destination wasn't a place at all but a person.

She began her search. Every thirty seconds, she called out Donovan's name. She went back the way she came where the water resided, waded in it until it covered her shoes, and then cut over a few blocks to a different area.

The sun was sinking below the horizon, the sky transforming with oranges and pinks, when she paused to release a yawn that cracked her sunburned lips. Before she could bribe her limbs into moving with the false hope of a bed around the next corner, a hand stamped over her mouth and an arm crushed her shoulders.

"You gave yourself away with that ridiculous yelling, you stupid bitch."

Beth retaliated.

"Grab her legs!"

She yanked her feet loose and kicked furiously, blindly hitting whatever body part she could reach.

"Grab her fucking legs!"

Someone wrestled with her legs while the man behind her restrained her upper body.

"Hold her still," another voice growled.

A hard object cracked into the side of her head. Sparks burst over her vision. Thoughts and sensations fled as darkness descended.

Chapter Thirteen

When the wave plowed into Donovan, something other than water hit him. A metal trashcan bounced against the ground, propelled by the water. He couldn't do anything to escape it, so he braced for the impact. The blow knocked him back, prying loose the breath he held hostage in his lungs. A kaleidoscope of falling stars burst over his vision. Rolling water sent him flipping head over feet. By the time he realized his hand was empty, Beth was long gone.

Part of a fence curled around his body, digging into his skin, smashing his nose, poking his eyelid, and pushing him to the bottom. His fingers twined around the links. He pushed against it, but it wouldn't budge. With his arms and legs constricted, he couldn't move or swim. The water had full sway over him. It tossed him around as if he didn't weigh more than a basketball. He slammed into the ground and was yanked along the grainy, rough surface. The feel of the metal scraping on the asphalt vibrated through him.

His chest was heavy without oxygen. While widening his shoulders and flexing his arms, he pushed his feet into the fence. He wrangled with it as if it were a boa constrictor. After a moment of shoving and kicking, the fence opened wide. He pressed the soles of his shoes onto the ground and launched himself up. His arms and legs paddled furiously against the vicious, churning water. Never before in his life had he experienced a force as powerful. The current didn't stop for a second but continuously flowed with the strength of a raging river. He felt as if he were in the middle of Niagara Falls.

Water cascaded down his face when he broke the surface and was thrown into the side of a truck. Pain radiated up and down his spine. Twisting, he managed to grab hold of the back wheel. Using his remaining strength, he hauled his body up and climbed into the truck's bed. He fell onto the bottom, panting. The rocking of the truck sent him rolling back and forth, his hips and shoulders smacking into the sides. He got onto his hands and knees.

His eyes scanned the rushing water. "Beth! Beth, where are you? Beth!"

He had promised to protect her and already failed. If Beth was dead, he would never forgive himself.

The truck collided into a building, and he tumbled toward the water. His hand lashed out and caught hold of the tailgate. The lower half of his body trailed behind the truck like a lure on a fishing line. His muscles strained as he pulled himself up. With much effort, he managed to get onto the bumper.

He rode the tsunami in the back of the truck as if he were on a surfboard. The whole time he kept an eye out for a brunette's head in the water, but one never appeared. When the flow stopped, the truck was parked alongside a building near a window. Being knowledgeable about waves, he knew the water would reverse, and he didn't want to be on the truck when it did. Nothing would be safe from the power of the wave going back out to sea. Not vehicles, houses, and certainly not people. He clambered onto the roof of the truck. The metal dented under his weight. When he stood, the truck wobbled.

The window was at the height of his waist. He braced his hands on the ledge and heaved his body into the small space. Back pressed against the glass, he hunkered down. He didn't have to wait long for the water to change direction. The truck bumped into the surrounding buildings, chipping away chunks of concrete before being swept away. From the ledge, he watched trees, a lawn mower, and a table fly by. The building shook around him, and he prayed it wouldn't crumble beneath him.

As fast as the wave came, it went.

Once everything calmed, he peered at the ground two stories below. Having no desire to jump that far, he shifted toward the window. Across from a large armoire was a four-poster bed. Light streamed through the open bathroom door.

Keeping one hand on the frame, he knocked on the glass. He waited a few seconds before rapping again. No one stepped into the bathroom light or came searching for the source of the knocking. So, he didn't think twice when he swung his elbow back and smashed the window. Glass dribbled on the carpet. He maneuvered his tired, hurt body through the opening. Standing on sturdy ground with no water around him felt strange. His limbs didn't quite know how to react, and he stumbled when he took his first step.

He went to the bathroom first. The mirror revealed a man with scratches leaking blood down his face. Lifting his torn T-shirt, he craned his neck to see his back. The skin along his spine was red. Already his back felt bruised. Every movement he made caused a bone-deep ache to spread like cobwebs from his neck to the base of his spine. He checked the medicine cabinet, found cheap pain reliever, and swallowed three with a mouthful of water from the faucet. With more water, he cleaned away the blood on his face and neck. Then he stashed the pill container in his pocket, figuring he'd need more later.

He stiffly moved through the hotel room. The TV was still on. Black and white static consumed the screen. He grabbed a bottle of water from the mini fridge. Two plates of half-eaten food sat on either end of a wood table. He picked up a roll and ate it in three bites; he didn't know when he'd have food again.

When he opened the door, he was bombarded by weeping, screaming, and loud talking. People stood in small groups in the hallway. Women were hugging and comforting children. Men were arguing over what they should do next.

"I think we should stay here," one man said. "We're in a standing building. We have shelter."

"This place might not be safe for long," another said.

"Do you think it'll be safer out there?"

Donovan slipped past them, not offering his own opinion. All he cared about was finding Beth. He couldn't think about the possibility she had been carried out to sea with the water or was dead somewhere for critters to feast on. If he thought about that, he wouldn't be able to go on.

A voice called out to him. "Hey, where you going?"

He stopped and turned.

Everyone looked at him.

"I'm going downstairs," he said.

"We don't know the condition of the lower levels," the skeptical man said, who thought it would be safer to stay in the hotel.

"I don't care what the conditions are. I'm going down there."

The man studied him. "Wait a second. Were you outside?"

Donovan didn't have to look to know the man saw his dripping clothes. "Yes. I was able to climb into a window. My wife was with me when the wave hit. We came here on our honeymoon." He glared at the men staring at him. "I have to find her, and no one is going to stop me from going. If anyone wants to come, you're welcome to join me. If not, stay."

He was rounding the corner when footsteps pounded after him, and a man appeared in his peripheral vision. Donovan glanced at a black man with a beard and determination set on his face. "My wife and daughter went shopping two hours ago. They never came back."

Donovan nodded. "I'll help you find them."

"I appreciate that, man. I'm Tray."

"Donovan."

They clambered down the first flight of stairs and were met by a pool of water clogging the stairwell. Donovan cursed. The two men looked at each other.

"There's no other way down," Tray said.

"I figured." Donovan peered at the water. "I'll go. I'm already wet, and I can hold my breath for a while. I can do it."

Tray looked at him skeptically. "Are you sure?"

"Yeah."

Beth counted on him. That alone pushed him to do whatever he had to, even dive into a flooded stairwell to open the door blocking his way out.

He slowly breathed in and out twice. On the third breath, he trapped oxygen in his lungs and plunged into the water. Keeping his hand on the railing, he swam down the stairwell and around the curve. At the bottom, he encountered the metal door. His hand wrapped around the knob. It twisted but the door didn't budge. He planted his feet into the last step and thrust his shoulder into the door. Baring his teeth, with his lungs burning, he strained against the pressure of the water and pushed as hard as he could. The door cracked open an inch. Shoving with his knees, he pressed his shoulder more roughly into the metal. Suddenly, it flew open, and he was propelled out of the stairwell.

White torrents clouded his vision. His body rolled over the ground and crashed into a wall. Water piled on top of him, keeping his head below the surface.

When he got to his feet, water forced his back against the wall. He examined his surroundings. The windows in the lobby were broken. Water flowed out of them, seeking freedom. Chairs bobbed like buoys. The paintings that had decorated the walls with elegant splashes of color floated atop the surface. His gaze lifted. Droplets clung to the ceiling and streamed down the walls; the first floor had completely flooded.

Something bumped into Donovan's chest. He looked down to see a man's body face-down in the water. Images of his brother's waterlogged body flashed in his memory. Turning his head, he pushed the corpse away. When he took a few steps, he found another.

Tray came running down the steps and hopped into the three feet of water drowning the lobby. "Hey, are you okay?"

Donovan nodded. "Sure." He looked left and right. Bodies floated all around, bumping into each other. Few people usually occupied hotel lobbies, but many of them had probably run in for shelter. They ended up dying in a place they thought would keep them safe. But nothing could protect you when Mother Nature was your opponent and she wielded water as her weapon.

Donovan and Tray made their way through the water and bodies to the front door. Seeing the destruction at eye level took Donovan's breath away. A couple of buildings had been shredded. All that was left were a few pillars and their concrete bases. Trees lay in the road like pick-up-sticks. A car door drifted in the foot of remaining water. Donovan didn't even know where to begin. Should he backtrack or go forward?

"Where would they set up a place for survivors to go?" Tray asked.

Having been in other natural disasters, Donovan knew exactly where. "The hospital."

They walked together. Silently, at first, until the silence weighed too heavily on Donovan. "Your wife and daughter…what are their names?"

"Meg is my wife. Katie is my daughter. She's eight. They were wearing matching white sundresses." He paused. "Meg's hair is curly, and Katie's hair was in pigtails with those little pink plastic ball things tied around them. She's been wearing them for years and I still don't know what they're called." His smile wobbled as tears gleamed in his eyes. "And your wife?"

Donovan's heart strings tangled at the thought of Beth. "Her name is Beth. She has brown hair and eyes. She was wearing a purple tank top, jean shorts, and black sneakers."

"I heard you say you're here on your honeymoon. When was the wedding?"

"Four days ago."

"Shitty thing to happen four days into married life."

"No kidding."

They walked side by side, searching for their loved ones. Wood and rubble stood in mountains. They had to climb over piles of trash—branches, cardboard, lumber, chunks of plaster, and concrete. Donovan took tentative steps so the pile wouldn't crumble under him. A nail stuck out of a piece of wood. The sharp end pointed up. He set his feet on either side of it and warned Tray to avoid it. On the other side, more debris was spread out before them.

Donovan's gaze scanned the ground. Paper, money, and books splayed open, their pages matted into clumps, covered the asphalt like wallpaper. He almost didn't notice the black sneaker sticking out from beneath layers of garbage. It was the tan ankle that caught his attention.

His heart plummeted to his gut. "Beth!"

Fear spiked in his veins. His worst nightmare was laid out in front of him. He ran and fell onto his hands and knees beside the leg. The ankle was thin and smooth, like Beth's. A lump formed in his throat. He began throwing pieces of wood and palm tree branches. With each new piece of debris he tossed aside, the lump in his throat grew larger. He unearthed two legs and one arm. As Donovan shifted to remove the objects burying the upper body, Tray felt the inside of the exposed wrist.

"There's no pulse," Tray said. His voice was solemn.

Donovan lifted a branch, revealing a brunette. The face was bloodied. He couldn't tell if it was Beth or not. Desperation settled over him. He grabbed rocks and wood and flung them aside. The black demon of fear with its cold, damp flesh and oily intestines possessed him. His heart raced with the speed of a jackhammer attacking granite. He pulled away a sheet of torn Styrofoam and froze. The woman wore a yellow T-shirt.

"It's not her," he whispered.

"Are you sure?"

Tray's question had Donovan reflecting back on that morning. Purple was Beth's favorite color, and she looked great in it with her golden skin and rich, brown hair. He had watched her slip a leather belt through the loops around her slender hips. The buckle was silver and had peeked out from beneath her tank top.

This woman wasn't Beth, but that didn't stop him from checking her left hand. The ring finger was bare. Not even a tan line was visible.

"I'm positive," he said. "She's not Beth."

Those words brought him short-lived relief followed by throat-clenching panic. Beth was still out there somewhere—hurt, lost, scared…dying.

"Let's move her."

The woman was limp in Donovan's arms. Her head fell backward as if she didn't have any bones in her neck. Her arms dangled by her sides like ropes of gelatin. He set her on the sidewalk and positioned her hands over her stomach.

"Here." Tray handed him one end of a beach towel.

"Where'd you find this?"

"I pulled it out while we were digging her out."

The towel had a giant peace sign on it. Although it was soaking wet and filthy, it helped to hide most of the woman. Donovan tucked the edges under her body to keep her concealed if the wind picked up strength. He looked down at the peace sign resting over her joined hands and the shape of her head beneath the black cotton. His throat tightened with tears. If Beth were dead somewhere, he hoped someone would cover her as he had covered this woman.

Chapter Fourteen

Beth's eyelids cracked open. The brilliant, blue sky greeted her. She felt as though she were floating, heading toward the few fluffy clouds above her. She closed her eyes. The back of her head throbbed. A net of electrified pain sparked from temple to temple. She tried to move a hand to the back of her head, to probe the pulsating knot with her fingers, but her arm was trapped behind her back. Something ensnarled her wrists. It was hard and tight, sending an ache through her bones that made her eyes sting.

"The bitch is waking up."

Those words, said with a nasty bite, penetrated the hazy sphere cocooning her. She wasn't floating; she was being carried. Her eyelids flipped open, and she thrashed her body.

"Fuck! She's a wild one."

She yanked a foot free and aimed it at one of the men restraining her legs. The bottom of her sneaker rammed into his face. The crunch of bone was a satisfying sound.

"She broke my nose!"

Cocking her foot back again, she tried to kick the other man and succeeded in hitting his shoulder with her heel. He stumbled, but as he fell back a few steps, he caught her foot.

"Put her down!"

Her feet smacked the asphalt as half of her body was released. She wrestled back and forth, trying to free her arms. The men in front of her were shoved aside by another. This man lifted a gun and jabbed a silencer into her forehead.

"I will fucking shoot you and leave your body here for vultures to feast on," he said. "Try me, bitch."

She didn't move. She barely breathed. These men were capable of anything. She envisioned a bullet blasting through the back of her skull, leaving a gaping hole, and taking out half her brain with it. She imagined Donovan stumbling upon her body and the gore around her. Her heart palpitated. She couldn't let that happen.

"I'll cooperate," she whispered.

"Of course, you will." The man lowered the gun to his side. "If you don't, I'll kill you."

Her mouth went dry. Her heart banged against her ribcage. Each throb muted the pain at the back of her head.

"If you wanted down, all you had to do was say so," he taunted. "You can walk." He turned, and the two men restraining her arms yanked her forward. She purposefully let her legs go slack. Her feet dragged behind her, and she dug the toes of her shoes into the mud. They made two long streaks. The men cursed and hefted her up, setting her back onto her feet.

The man with the gun spun around. "What the fuck's wrong now?"

"She's not walking."

Beth looked at the man as his black eyes pinned her in place. "My legs are asleep."

He pointed the silencer at her left knee. "A bullet will bring back the feeling."

"Stop," she shouted. "I'll walk."

"Good choice."

When the men started to move again, she took halting footsteps. Her gaze eagerly sought for signs of their location. She couldn't tell where they were, but the ground was becoming less muddy, which meant they were going deeper into the city, away from the places devastated by the tsunami. There was a lesser chance of this area being searched for survivors. Not good for her.

Her gaze jumped from left to right as she sought landmarks. Her eyes widened at the sight of a street sign—South King Street. She had no idea where that was, but it was nice to know a street name.

When the mud disappeared, her heart dropped. If it didn't rain, someone could track the footsteps they left behind, but without mud, there wouldn't be any evidence. She looked down at her feet as she lifted her sneakers. Lines of mud clung to the asphalt in the shape of her shoe. But with each step she took, those lines became thinner until the mud was gone.

Several minutes later, they came upon an intersection. She was forced to make a right turn that took her away from the path their footprints had made. Panic swam through her veins. She needed to do something, leave a mark in some way. She wouldn't be able to tear off a piece of clothing without them hearing it. Not to mention her hands were cuffed behind her back. Her thoughts roamed from her sneakers to her hair tie. She couldn't step out of a sneaker. That would be too obvious. She couldn't reach her hair tie, but that wouldn't be a good clue anyway. A black hair tie could belong to anyone. Her thoughts jumped to her charm bracelet. No one else wore a bracelet with a hurricane charm on it.

She moved her arms. Not enough to tip off her captives, but enough to make it seem as though she was readjusting their position. She let out a groan and rolled her shoulders. When her hands were at her wrists, she stretched her fingers and prayed she'd feel the thin chain.

Had it fallen off?

She couldn't feel it against her skin. Her breathing stopped as she searched for the bracelet. Even her heart seemed to stop beating. She wiggled her fingers. Where was it? A sob was about to burst from her lips when something tapped her finger. Her eyes widened, and her mouth fell open. It was the hurricane charm.

She caught it between her fingers and tugged. But the bracelet didn't budge. Her fingers slithered up, following the bit of chain to the cuff around her wrist. The bracelet was stuck under the handcuffs. She carefully worked it free until she could grip the chain with her other hand. Mashing her teeth together, she pulled on it. The thin links cut into her skin.

She yanked harder.

Her wrist cried out in pain, but she didn't stop. Even when it felt as though the chain were on fire, as though her skin would start to bleed. Before a whimper could break free from her lips, the chain snapped. She curled her fingers around it and closed her eyes in a silent prayer. After a quick thank you, she lifted her foot and purposefully tripped herself.

The men holding her stumbled. She released the bracelet from her fingers; it fell as they righted themselves.

"Sorry," she muttered. "My legs are weak."

The men mumbled under their breaths, and she smiled to herself.

The charm bracelet was in the middle of the road, waiting to be found.

****

The longer they walked, the darker it became. The moon was a giant disk in the sky, glowing upon Beth like a reassuring figure, a higher power reminding her she wasn't alone. She couldn't see anything except the three men in front of her. One with a gun, one who kept putting his hand to his smashed nose, and the other with shoulders like a two-by-four. She had to give it to them. They didn't let a tsunami stop them. Somehow, they had managed to stay together and beat the wave. Beth and Donovan couldn't even do that. And the fact they went back on the hunt for her the moment the water went down showed their determination.

When the sky was pitch black, they pulled her to a stop outside a one-story building. She looked up to see the business's name but was yanked through the doors before she could read the sign.

"No one will be coming here for weeks. By then, you'll be dead," the man with the gun said.

They tugged her inside, past cubicles and offices, to the back of the building. A flashlight shone their way. She wondered if it was the one Kevin gave her.

"Let's lock her in this closet."

She was forced to stand in the hallway, with the gun at her head, while the other men cleared everything out of the janitor's closet. Not a single bucket or mop was left inside.

The man with the gun yanked her around so she

was face to face with him. "Home-sweet-home," he snarled and shoved her inside.

She pitched backward but caught herself before she could fall to the ground. When the door slammed shut and locked, she didn't throw her body against it and scream for them to let her out, because she knew they'd do no such thing. Instead, she waited until her eyes adjusted to the darkness. The space was bare. No window. No carpet. A tiny vent near the ceiling was the one source of decoration.

Her only way out would be through that locked door.

In the corner of the closet, she sank onto the floor. Her shoulders burned. Her muscles shook. She was exhausted and in pain from scalp to pinky toe. She wished for a bed, for a blanket and pillow...for Donovan.

What she had was a cold, hard floor and a wall.

The buzz of silence lulled her to sleep.

****

She was awakened when the door swung open. She jerked awake, not knowing what to expect.

The man with wide shoulders slammed a metal chair in the middle of the floor.

Next to him stood the man with the gun. "Get up."

Using the wall for support, she pushed herself up.

"Sit." He pointed the gun at the chair.

She lowered herself onto the edge of the chair and looked up at him. Her body was braced for a punch. When his hand vised around her upper arm and he whirled her around on the chair, a gasp flew from her mouth. Then the cuffs opened their jaws and released her wrists. She quickly pulled her hands into her lap and massaged the bruised skin around her wrists. They were tender, and her shoulders were stiff.

When she looked up, the gun was in her face.

"Call Donovan and tell him we have you."

She blinked. They wanted her to call Donovan? She shook her head. "Even if he has his cell phone, it'll be useless because of the water." She paused, not wanting to say the next sentence, but it came out anyway. "He might be dead."

The man laughed. "He's not dead. Donovan is a hard man to kill. A bit of water can't kill that motherfucker. Leave him a message. If he's smart, he'll check it."

"Why?"

"Because we want him to come running. We want him to fall into our trap, so we can kill the two of you with one bullet."

"And how is he supposed to find me?"

"He's not going to find you. He's going where we want him to go. And we'll be there waiting." He turned to the open door. "Bring it in here."

The man with a bloody T-shirt and crooked nose came in with a satellite phone.

Mr. Gun took the phone in his other hand and held it out to Beth. "Call him." He raised the gun. "Tell him you're in a building across from the Hawaii Ocean Church."

Beth took the phone. Her hand shook. Her palm was cold and sweaty. She pushed the first three buttons for the area code with a numb finger. Heart racing, lungs paralyzed, she quickly dialed the one number that came to mind. Pressing the phone to her ear, she prayed for him to answer it.

"This is Thorn."

Hearing Thorn's voice was like hearing a choir of angels.

She took a slow breath before speaking. "Donovan, it's Beth."

Thorn sighed. "Thank God you're okay. Wait…" There was a pause. "Did you call me Donovan?"

Beth continued. "I don't know when you'll get this message, but I'm okay. For now…Jackson's men have me."

"Fuck."

Thorn's hiss was a pang to her heart.

"They want me to tell you I'm in a building across from the Hawaii Ocean Church." She struggled to keep the emotion from her voice, because it was a weakness the men crowding around her would exploit for their sick humor, but her words wobbled. "They want you to come here."

"Are you really there?" Thorn whispered.

"No." Beth swallowed. She kept her gaze from the men towering over her. "That I love you. Know…that I am waiting for you."

"I'm coming, Beth."

His words made the tears she had been holding back slip down her cheeks. "Goodbye." Her farewell was barely audible even to her own ears. She ended the connection and thrust the phone at Mr. Gun.

"Convincing," he said. "When Donovan hears that, he'll surely come running."

One by one, the men left.

While staring at the door, the wall of tears over her eyes thickened. Anger inside her metastasized until her body shook with rage. She imploded with a scream.

Launching to her feet, she grabbed the metal chair and beat it against the door. Again and again. The metal chair collided with the solid door and sent vibrations up her arms. She threw the chair across the room with another yell and crumpled on the floor. She bent forward, her arms over her head, her forehead touching the floor. Screams and sobs blended into something inhuman. She let her anger and terror take full control until she was empty. With her emotions gutted from her body, she fell onto the floor with her cheek against the dusty tile.

Sometime later, the door opened. She didn't stir or lift her head. After a moment, the door closed, and she was alone again. This happened two more times. Each time, she drifted back to sleep. By the third time this happened, she was curious. She pushed herself into a sitting position and pressed her back against the wall. While eyeing the door, she thought about what she could do to get free.

The door opened. One of the men poked his head in through the gap. She glared at him. He was startled to see her sitting there, staring at him with malice. He took a step back and shut the door with a snap.

Her gaze strayed from the door to the vent at the top of the wall. She rose to her feet, picked up the chair, and positioned it below the vent. Standing on the chair, her face was right in front of the vent. Cold air didn't blast her cheeks. The air conditioning was off with the rest of the power. That was evident by the amount of sweat slithering down her spine.

The vent was too small for her climb through, but the metal covering could aid her in retaliation. She worked off her belt and pinched the metal prong with her fingers. Aiming for the screw's head, she stuck the tip of the prong into the X. Grasping it tightly, she turned the prong. The screw twisted. A glorious burst of optimism filled her. Readjusting the prong with every turn, she managed to get the screw to lift high enough to grasp it. Pricks of pain stabbed the tips of her fingers, but she didn't give up until the screw slipped out of the hole.

One side of the cover slipped down the wall.

She stuck the screw into her pocket and began working on the next screw. When it was loose enough to pull out, she grabbed the vent to keep it from clattering to the floor. With the second screw in her pocket, she climbed down with the cover in one hand and her belt in the other. Both would help her escape.

She moved the chair to the wall directly in front of the door. Then she hunkered in the corner. As she waited, she wondered why they checked on her. Did they think she would make a miraculous escape? Or kill herself? She had no plan to do the latter. But the former was definitely part of her plan.

Smirking, she wound the belt around her hand so the buckle was over her knuckles. In her other hand, she grasped the metal grate.

She waited.

Her eyes didn't grow tired. Her energy didn't wane. Her mind didn't change.

When the key entered the doorknob, she tightened her fist.

"What the hell?" The man stepped into the room with his gaze on the empty chair.

Beth rose and shouldered the door shut. When he faced her, she cracked the metal grate into the side of his face. His body slammed onto the ground, and she pounced on him. She pounded his face with the belt buckle, punching him until her arm weakened. He wasn't moving when she got to her feet. If he was breathing, she couldn't tell and didn't give a damn.

She picked up the grate and fastened it to her back with her belt. The buckle was bloody. With a glance at the man, she saw his face was drenched with blood. Not a drop of remorse touched her.

She made sure the belt was tight around her ribs before she made a run for it. As she ran down the hall, she thought of Donovan. Although she didn't have to fear him getting caught in their trap, if he was out there, alive and looking for her, they could hunt him down as they had hunted her. They could kill him.

She flew around a corner. Laid out before her were the cubicles. Beyond them was her way out. She launched forward, pushing her leg muscles to take her farther and her feet to be quicker. This was her chance.

"She's getting away!"

Teeth clenched, hands curled into fists, she rushed through the aisle between cubicles. With each stride, she was closer to freedom.

"Shoot her!"

That order made Beth's heart come to a screeching halt, but her feet didn't get the same memo. The final stretch of ground was before her. If she could get outside, she could find somewhere to hide until the coast was clear.

Her hand reached for the door handle. Her fingers curled around it. She yanked it open and leapt over the threshold. Then something tore through her shoulder with flaming teeth. Pain snaked through her body from shoulder blade to shoulder blade, fingertip to fingertip. It was a pain she had never felt before, so powerful her legs went slack and her body punched the ground. Her breath expelled from her lungs.

She couldn't move or breathe. Her eyes stung, but she couldn't blink.

Shouts came from behind her. The angry voices were like a shock to her heart. She gasped for breath. A burning, throbbing pain enveloped her shoulder.

She lifted her head to see she had made it outside, but the bullet had tackled her to the ground before she could disappear into the shadows.

Stomping shoes came toward her.

She tugged her right arm out from under her and grabbed her left arm. A moan escaped her lips. Shoving the pain aside, she wiggled off the infinity knot ring from her finger and tossed it into the road. It rolled to a stop a few feet away.

Hugging her shoulder, she squeezed her eyes shut and let out a wail.

Hands grasped her ankles like shackles and dragged her all the way to the back of the building. She tried to sit up, to keep her upper body off the ground, but a tearing sensation caused her to drop back each time. Every bump, every turn caused her to cry out. Blood slicked her fingers and drenched her tank top.

She couldn't fight back. She was at their mercy as they towed her back into the closet. Eyesight blurring, she could barely make out the outline of the man unhooking the belt from her middle. He whipped it away then slapped it across her cheek.

A scream ripped from her lungs. Her skin seared.

Hands rolled her over and removed the metal grate.

She shut her eyes, expecting it to smash into the back of her skull. It didn't.

They left her on the floor, bleeding and in agony.

The door shut, locking her into the darkness of captivity.

Chapter Fifteen

Donovan and Tray searched all night as helicopters flew overhead. Their lights were giant beams that shone down from the sky. The darkness was brilliant. Without a single light from a building or car, the night sky and its flickering stars bore down on them. Trucks carrying loads of injured people and volunteers passed them. They flagged down those trucks to see if their loved ones were onboard. The survivors vowed to keep an eye out for Beth and Tray's family, as did the volunteers, but Donovan didn't have any faith in them remembering. They even checked the dead bodies piled three or four deep in the backs of trucks. The smell was sickening. Donovan pulled his shirt over his nose, but a tear near the collar admitted the rotting smell.

They shifted bodies aside, rolled them around to see the faces of the people on the bottom. None of them were Beth, Meg, or Katie. So they went on. They didn't stop searching even when they yawned.

One of the volunteers had given them a pair of flashlights. Donovan's flashlight illuminated a small path. It couldn't show him what lurked in the standing water, behind piles of debris or behind him. It showed him the tips of his ripped shoes and the gleam of an animal's eyes when he roved the light left and right. Whenever he'd seek the critter with the neon eyes, it would vanish into the night. Chills rolled up and down his body. Minutes extended into hours.

Helicopters blazed through the night, shaking the air with their blades and offering a splash of light. Every time one flew by, Donovan took the opportunity to scour the ground for any sign of people—limbs, clothing, hair. But the light always came and went too quickly.

His stomach growled with hunger. He didn't dare think about food. Not while Beth could be out there starving. They traveled up and down the blocks, picking up debris, and calling out names. Every once in a while they came across a body. Donovan removed his shirt and ripped off strips of fabric to tie to sticks that they stuck in the ground next to the bodies. Posting flags was the least they could do to let Search and Rescue know a body was there. By dusk, Donovan had a patch of cotton left; it limply hung in his hand.

The sky lightened degree by degree from smoke-gray to a translucent blue with streaks of yellow and orange. The sun was a bright orb peeking above the buildings when they reached the hospital. Seeing the hundreds of people crammed in the parking lot stunned Donovan. He stood next to Tray and looked out at the expanse of people in utter bewilderment. So many. Their bodies were caked in mud. Their clothes dirty. Several tents and makeshift shelters with tarps for ceilings were set up in the parking lot for treatment. People with minor injuries were being treated. Those who needed surgery were rushed into the building on gurneys.

Two HI-EMA trucks—there should've been a lot more—were parked in the middle of the throng. A few workers passed out water and Meals-Ready-to-Eat as fast as they could to the needy hands reaching out to them. Random volunteers handed out blankets, clothing, and shoes to people who could use it. There were far too many people, though, and not everyone would be able to get what they needed. In no time, the food and water would run out, leaving these survivors hungry and thirsty. With the sun beating down on them, unforgiving, many would drop from dehydration. The hospital could give some of them intravenous fluids, but they probably didn't have the equipment to hook everyone up to IVs.

Donovan moved along the rows of people alongside Tray. A woman with bloody arms wrapped gauze around a man's head. A young boy, who must've been no more than ten, held a bottle of water to a younger child's lips. Were they alone in this chaos? Everywhere he looked, he saw suffering being battled by the beauty of strangers helping strangers. They were comforting and nursing one another.

For hours, Donovan searched. When hunger deteriorated his strength, making his muscles burn and twitch, he suggested getting something to eat. They got in line and waited as person after person retrieved a meal. Donovan's tongue was dry in his mouth. His head spun with fatigue. He was handed a brown plastic container by a female HI-EMA worker. As he stepped aside, he peered behind the workers to see one box of MREs. The worker caught his eye and gave a shake of her head. Her silence told him everything. When they hand out the last MRE, they'd be left to starve. Even her. Donovan knew he'd have to ration out his food and single bottle of water until more help arrived.

He ripped open a package consisting of two thin

pieces of multigrain snack bread and ate them with the cheese spread he squirted from another package. It actually wasn't bad. He put the remainders of his meal—a plastic bag that would heat up his main meal with a bit of water, a package of grilled chicken breast, a lemon poppy seed cake, and cinnamon candy—in the pockets of his shorts. Throughout the day, he popped Red Hots into his mouth to trick his stomach into believing it was full; it didn't work.

An hour later, he stood in front of boards posted near the hospital's front doors. These boards were covered in spreadsheets full of names of the people at the hospital. More were filling up as survivors added their own names in case loved ones came looking. Donovan's finger trailed down every list from top to bottom, from the front of the three boards to the back. Beth's name wasn't there. He found a couple of Katie's but not Tray's little girl.

Donovan picked up a pen and added his name to the bottom of a list. Before he handed the pen to Tray, he drew an infinity symbol beside his name, hoping it would catch Beth's eye. Would she see his name listed there? He imagined her falling to the ground with joy if she did. As he would've done if he had seen her name.

What if she were dead?

The thought sickened him, but he had to know regardless. With heavy feet, he walked through the crowded doors of the hospital and found a nurse.

"Excuse me?"

"Sir, I can't help you right now."

"I just have a question to ask." He put a hand on her shoulder to keep her from turning away. Stress and exhaustion mirrored on her face. She had dealt with many distraught individuals and wasn't looking forward to dealing with another. "I'm trying to find someone—"

She cut him off. "Then check the lists outside. We have no other way to document such a large quantity of people coming in and out of these doors." She tried to leave again, but Donovan stopped her.

"I have," he said. "I want to know where the dead are being taken."

The woman froze. Sympathy washed away her lines of impatience. "The dead in this area are being taken to Cartwright Field." She pointed in the general direction. "Past Shriner's Children's Hospital. Keep cutting through the parking lots and you'll find it."

Donovan told Tray this bit of information. They agreed to go and then return to the Medical Center where they felt they'd have a better chance of finding their loved ones. After checking the lists tacked to the boards at Shriner's Children's Hospital and adding their names with Kapiolani Medical Center in parenthesis, they continued on to Cartwright Field, a large baseball field. The green grass was full of black body bags. Bodies were also wrapped in tarps and other plastic covers. White writing was scrawled on many of the body bags with names. Most documented genders. Some just said "child." Tray checked those. Donovan couldn't imagine Tray's fear over seeing his little girl's face every time he unzipped one of the bags. He was petrified of seeing Beth's face, but Tray was looking for his wife *and* his daughter.

A few of the body bags had plastic baggies of jewelry on top of them for identification purposes. Donovan kept his eye out for Beth's charm bracelet and rings, as well as her name and "female." He peeked into the bags and partially lifted tarps to see the faces of the women. Row after row, he went. After a while, the women's faces began to blur. Every time he blinked, he saw their glossy eyes staring up at him.

They finished their morbid task and headed back to the Medical Center. Donovan went to the boards and found his own name. From there, he looked over the additions. None of them were the right ones.

He sat on the outskirts of the parking lot and nibbled on the lemon poppy seed cake. Tray sat next to him. Neither of them said anything. The day had been a long, hard one, and it wasn't over yet.

Every hour or so, Donovan returned to the boards. Sheets of paper were starting to overlap each other and still Beth's name wasn't there. On his way back to Tray, a woman stopped him.

"Here." She held out a T-shirt to him.

"No, thanks," he said. "Give it to someone else."

"I'm giving it to you," she said and extended her hand. "You'll have a terrible burn if you don't take this shirt. I can see you've been in the sun for too long without protection."

Her words rang true. His skin was burning in the sunlight. A look at his chest revealed red skin. Already the skin on his shoulders was peeling. He gratefully accepted the old T-shirt. Slipping it on, it rubbed against his burned skin.

At dusk, when his stomach growled for food, he poured a bit of water into the bag from the MRE package, slipped the grilled chicken breast inside, and propped it up on a small rock. Steam seeped from the bag as it heated his meal. He stared up at the sky, at the pink and orange clouds. With the chemical smell tingling his nostrils from the MRE and the cool breeze touching his skin, he wished Beth were with him. For all he knew, Beth was a corpse. She could have died when the first wave hit them or been swept out to sea. Her soul could be long gone. He may never see her again, may never hold her.

"Meg! Katie!" Tray shot to his feet.

Donovan looked up to see Tray lifting a little girl into the air. He crushed the girl to his body and opened his arms to a weeping woman in a tattered dress. The small family embraced, crying and kissing.

Reunited with his family, Tray walked away with his daughter on his hip and his arm around his wife's waist. Donovan was forgotten. He ate his meal alone as tears clogged his eyes.

Chapter Sixteen

Beth used the soles of her sneakers to push herself to the wall. Seething, she inched into a sitting position. She touched her shoulder. Her index finger dipped into a hole. She bit her bottom lip. The bullet had passed straight through the meat of her shoulder, which was a good thing, because the bullet didn't have to be dug out, but not so good considering she had two holes for blood to escape through. Her arm was streaked with blood, and her shirt was soaked with it. She pressed her palm to the hole in the front of her shoulder. If she lost any more blood, she'd lose consciousness, and death would soon follow.

"Hey!"

Her voice cracked.

"Hello, somebody? Come on! Hello." She lay the back of her head against the wall. "Somebody, please. Hello."

Her energy was depleting when the door opened. Mr. Gun crossed his arms in the doorway. "What?"

She took a shuddering breath. "I'm going to bleed to death. If I die, you won't be able to use me for bait."

"And what do you want me to do about that? I'm not a fucking medic."

She didn't like the option that came to her mind, but she didn't have any other choice. "I can cauterize it," she said. "I need something thin and long and metal." She considered office supplies and kitchen utensils usually found in the workplace. A ruler wouldn't work. Neither would a spoon. "A metal ballpoint pen might work. And a lighter. You might be able to find one in a desk."

Smokers always had spares, right? Surely someone who worked there sucked down a cigarette during his or her lunchbreak.

"I'll see what I can find."

She almost thanked him, but realized he was the bastard who shot her. Why would he care if he wanted to kill her in the end? He could be sitting with his buddies, laughing about his lie to help her. But if she died before their plan came to fruition, he wouldn't be able to use her as leverage. How would he make sure Donovan was on his way if she was a corpse?

Grasping her shoulder, she asked God to help her through this ordeal. *Please don't let me die. If Donovan is alive, I can't leave him. I can't put him through more misery and heartache. And you shouldn't want to put him through that, either. So, please, help me to survive this. Help me, help me, help me…*

Her bottom lip trembled. Her mind repeated "help me" like a broken record. She was slowly sinking into unconsciousness when the door finally opened.

Her eyelids fluttered.

"Here."

Her gaze lowered to the hand stretched out to her.

"This is what I found."

In the middle of his palm sat an expensive silver pen and a yellow lighter.

She peeled her hand away from her wound and took the items with blood-stained fingers. "Thank you," she whispered and meant it.

She set the pen in her left hand. Her fingers barely had enough life in them to hold it. With her other hand, she flicked the lighter to summon a tiny flame. Slowly, she rotated the pen, letting the flame lick every inch of the metal cap. She did this until the metal was hot enough to burn. Then she felt for the hole at the back of her shoulder. Taking the pen in her hand, she reached around and penetrated her wound. The instant the red-hot cap touched her flesh, her shoulder ignited with flames. She threw back her head as a scream ripped from her.

Fire coursed through her arm. Her brain shouted, *STOP!*

But she couldn't.

She held the pen in place until the searing sensation ended. Pulling the pen back out sent pain rippling through her. She dropped her head as tears flowed down her cheeks. Even as she cried, she wiped the blood off the pen with her T-shirt. Body shaking, she spun the wheel on the lighter and reheated the cap. Her hand quivered when she brought the pen to the hole at the front of her shoulder.

She hesitated.

The pain radiating from her wound would quadruple the moment she stabbed herself with the pen. But she had to do it. She took three fast breaths before jabbing the fiery pen into the hole. A wail soared out of her throat. She bent forward as she sobbed. The smell of burning flesh touched her nostrils. Nausea flirted with her stomach. She would've thrown up, but the pain was too great.

Blackness pinched the corners of her vision. Her

head wobbled. She wedged the pen back out. No more did she feel pain. No more did she feel sick.

A weakness drew her away from herself. She collapsed into the wall. Her eyelids sealed, and her body slid to the ground. A second before she fell into unconsciousness, the pen and lighter were snatched out of her feeble grasp.

****

Beth seesawed in and out of consciousness. Every time she cracked open her eyelids, colors burst like fireworks—blinding white, blood-red, and scorching yellow. Seconds later, she'd dizzily sink under the influence of anguish only to have it vomit her back up into the waking world. The ground felt unsteady beneath her body, as if a whirlpool had opened up and was swallowing her in its great, watery mouth.

When the dark released her for the umpteenth time, she was able to withstand the temptation of its pull. She moved her fingers over the ground and felt the grit of sand and the silky powder of dust.

Sweat beaded on her face. Her shirt clung to her back. Whimpering and panting, she maneuvered herself into a sitting position. Her head spun like a toy top. She tapped her fingers over her wound. Crusted blood flaked off her skin. There was no fresh blood, which meant she had successfully cauterized it. The skin around the bullet hole was burned. Every inch of her shoulder throbbed. She moved her fingers to the pulse point in her neck. Her heart beat was slower than normal.

Leaning her head back, she focused on her breathing. Her logic was that if she brought her organs oxygen, she could hold out until help arrived. To keep her mind off the prospect of death, and to ward off the drunken feeling of blood loss, she sang songs in her head from "Baby One More Time" to "God Bless the USA." She was on her encore of "Bittersweet Symphony" when the door opened. Mr. Gun stepped in. He dropped a paper plate with two slices of white bread next to her. She eyed the bottle of water he put next to it. Hunger gnawed at her stomach with shark's teeth. Saliva pooled in her mouth. Plain white bread was tasteless and far from what she'd want if she could have anything, but it was something to fill the cavity in her stomach. Except, it wouldn't give her the nutrients her body needed. Protein, vitamins, calcium. That was what her body needed to produce more blood.

"Can you look for a packet of sugar and salt?" she asked. Her voice was faint.

"What for?"

"A bomb." She sighed. "My body needs the nutrients. I'll add it to the water. It won't be as effective as an IV, but it may help."

Mr. Gun stared at her. His inner dialogue played out across his face. Should he help her? His job was to kill her, but not before he killed Donovan.

"Fine," he hissed.

The door released a groan when he flung it open and stalked out. Beth counted to one hundred and thirty-three before he returned. He tossed a tiny white packet of salt and a pink packet of sugar at her. They hit her in the chest, tumbled down her stomach, and fell onto her lap.

She muttered her thanks and reached for the bottle of water. In order to unscrew the cap, she had to hold the bottle with her left hand and wrench off the cap with her right. Her muscles strained. Taking off the cap was almost too much work for her. With a trembling hand, she lifted the bottle to her lips and took a sip. Then she set it between her legs and used her teeth to tear open the packets. She poured the salt and sugar into the water, twisted the cap back on, and gave the bottle a couple of half-hearted shakes. Her arm fell. She set the bottle on the ground as if it weighed five pounds.

Her gaze lifted to Mr. Gun. She plucked the empty packets from her lap and held it out to him. "Do you want these back? I could give someone a paper cut with them."

He sneered at her. "Fucking eat them for all I care," he spat and slammed the door shut.

She picked up the paper plate and tore off a piece of bread. Chewing was even too much for her, but she worked her jaw until she consumed all the bits from the first piece of bread. Throat dry, tongue plastered to the roof of her mouth, she took a swallow of water. The salt and sugar gave it an unpleasant taste, but she forced herself to take another drink. Saving the second piece of bread and the rest of the water for later, she hugged her arm and settled into the corner of the wall.

She drifted off to sleep. In her dreams, she relived the tsunami, the churning water, and the lack of oxygen. She tried to paddle to the surface, but something had her ankles. She looked and screamed. Bubbles rose from her mouth. Jackson Storm held onto her ankles and was pulling her into the pitch-blackness.

A bang jerked her awake. Her heart thudded. Her mind twirled. She stared at the group of men in the closet.

So they're going to kill me now.

Broken Nose, the man she had kicked, and the man with the big shoulders stepped forward. She winced when their hands came toward her. The blows she expected to come didn't. Their hands seized her arms. She cried out when her shoulder was jostled. They half carried, half dragged her to the chair in the middle of the floor. She dropped onto it with a thud and protectively grabbed her shoulder. Tears crowded her eyes.

"Call Donovan again." Mr. Gun thrust the phone in her face. She flinched back. "If you die, we lose our advantage. Donovan is the main objective. We need him, so you better make your plea convincing."

She took the phone.

The numbers danced.

She blinked, jabbed one button, and had to wait for her eyesight to stop blurring to dial the rest. The phone was heavy. She thought it would break her wrist.

The ringing ended, and Thorn's voice came on, "Beth, is it you?"

She met Mr. Gun's watchful glare. "It's his voicemail again."

"Then leave another fucking message."

"He may never get my messages. I'm going to die because you're too stupid to realize he doesn't have access to his cell phone."

Mr. Gun jabbed the silencer between her eyes. "Hearing his wife get her brains blown out in a voicemail will make him come after us. I don't need to keep you alive."

He was right. If she really was leaving Donovan messages, hearing a gunshot would sicken him with rage. He'd seek them out to kill them.

She took a slow breath. "Donovan, I don't know if you heard that or not, but they're going to kill me if you don't come soon."

"Tell him we'll offer a trade," Mr. Gun said. "If he comes, we'll let you go."

She relayed the information though it made her sick.

"I'm at the Bay Area American Red Cross," Thorn told her in hushed tones. "They're trying to figure out how to deploy volunteers. They've agreed to let me come along."

Knowing Thorn was in California, a plane ride away, gave her fuel. She spoke quickly. "Go to Honolulu, past South King Street, away from the mud. Look for the spiral and infinity. Look for—" She was going to repeat those instructions when a hand lashed out and backhanded her across the face. The phone clattered to the floor.

"What does that mean? Look for the spiral and infinity?"

She didn't answer.

"What does it mean?"

She kept her head bowed.

"She probably doesn't even know what it means," another voice mocked. "Look at her. She's lost a lot of blood. Her brain isn't functioning right."

Silence buzzed in her ears as the men watched her. After a moment, she heard muttered curses and the sound of them retreating.

The door locked.

She lifted her head toward the ceiling. "Look for my bracelet and ring," she whispered, hoping God would carry her plea to Thorn.

Chapter Seventeen

A ruckus pulled Donovan out of his sleep. He opened his eyes to dawn. It took some effort to sit up. His body was weak, battered, and aching. Even his toes and heels hurt from walking. He scanned the parking lot for the source of commotion. A delivery truck was creeping through the crush of bodies to the center of the parking lot. It came to a stop, and the back door was lifted. Crates were stacked inside, taking up about half the space. Cheers erupted as small silver objects were tossed to the waiting crowd.

He slowly got to his feet and went to the boards while everyone pushed to get closer to the truck. In the pale light, he ran his finger down the lists. He spotted a Bethany, but no Beth Kennedy. He trudged back to his spot, pulled out the small patch of cotton left from his other T-shirt, and draped it over his eyes so he could sleep a couple more hours.

When he woke again, the sun was blazing down on him, trying to burn him through his clothes. He shifted into a sitting position, and his knee bumped into something. Metal hit rock. He looked down to see a tin can lying on its side with a plastic spoon. He picked them up and turned the can over in his hand. Minestrone soup. His gaze flitted over the people closest to him, but no one looked at him. Someone had left him this soup. Whomever it had been, he sent them a silent thank you.

The smell of herbs and savory broth made his mouth water. He had been sure there wasn't any water left in his body, but the saliva pooling in his mouth proved him wrong. He meant to only eat half the can of soup, but it was so good he gobbled down every last kidney bean and shell noodle and scrapped the sides for good measure. His stomach was still impossibly empty, but the soup gave him enough strength to get to his feet.

He moved along the gathered people, looking at faces, but not finding the one person he yearned for. At the delivery truck, he paused. Empty crates were stacked beside it. Inside a single row of crates remained.

"Where did this come from?" he asked the man organizing crates.

"Walmart was destroyed. We spent all day yesterday searching what was left of it for canned goods." He hopped out of the truck and spoke with a hushed tone. "This is all we found. One can for each person here, and we are dangerously low. We won't have enough for everyone a second time."

The MREs were gone, and soon, so would the canned goods. What would they do next?

He walked along the stretch of black top with the heat bearing down on him. He was beginning to think Beth would never find her way there.

As the hours went by and the sun grew hotter, he went to the side of the building for some relief. He found a shaded spot. All alone, his sorrow and fear began to build inside him until it burst free. He buried his face in his hands and wept for the faces of the dead women he saw yesterday, for the people who died in the tsunami, for the families who wouldn't ever find each other, and for his soulmate who he may never get to hold or kiss again.

At noon, a car's horn beeped.

He peeked around the corner. A few vehicles with red plus signs on the doors were driving into the hospital. The American Red Cross. He hoped they brought provisions. Not interested in getting up, not even to see if they had food, he turned his head and let his eyelids drift shut.

A voice broke through his peace from the hospital's crackling PA system.

"Donovan Goldwyn."

His eyelids snapped open. He leapt to his feet.

"Donovan Goldwyn, come to the nurse's desk ASAP. I repeat, Donovan Goldwyn, Donovan Goldwyn, come to the nurse's desk ASAP."

Static erupted from the speakers.

The message ended.

Donovan shoved through the crowd with his heart pounding. Hearing his name elated him. He had one thought as he fought through the hospital's front doors.

Beth.

He went to the front desk. "Excuse me? My name was called over the intercom."

"Donovan!"

He turned at the shout. Confusion pounded his head. It took him a moment to place the face in front of him because there was no way he could be there.

"Thorn?"

"God damn, you're an indestructible son-of-a-bitch!" Thorn threw his arms around him and clapped him on the back.

Donovan stood stiffly, not returning the hug.

Thorn stepped back and surveyed him. "Take these. I don't want you falling down dead."

Falling down dead was what a lot of people had been doing since the tsunami hit.

Donovan looked at the water and protein bar Thorn shoved into his hands. They looked foreign, but not as foreign as Thorn standing before him, looking clean in jeans and a T-shirt.

"What are you doing here?"

"I came because…" Thorn looked around. "We need to find somewhere to talk."

Donovan took him to where he had been napping.

"Donovan, Beth called me."

Those three words almost brought Donovan to his knees. He sagged against the wall. A grin split his face. "She's alive?" A mixture of relief, that conjured tears and stole his breath, and happiness that made his heart light, overtook him.

"Yes, she's alive. Or at least, she was." He paused. "Donovan, what I'm going to tell you isn't going to be easy to hear."

Donovan didn't understand. If she was alive, why'd Thorn make it sound as though it could be temporary? "Why? What happened to her?"

Thorn took a deep breath before saying, "Jackson's men have her."

The sweet emotions he had felt were robbed by this new information. The weight of Thorn's statement sent him sliding down the wall to the ground.

Thorn crouched in front of him. His words echoed inside Donovan's head. What he said didn't make sense. How could Beth be locked up somewhere with her life in the hands of Jackson's gang?

"She called me pretending to call you," Thorn explained. "She gave me instructions before our last call was disconnected. She said to go past South King Street, out of the mud. Then she said something strange. 'Look for the spiral and infinity.'"

Donovan's gaze flicked up. "She said that? Spiral and infinity?"

Thorn nodded. "You know what that means?"

The jewelry he had been looking for when he inspected the field of body bags flashed in his mind. "Her charm bracelet with the hurricane symbol and her infinity engagement ring. She left them as clues."

Thorn nodded. "That's good. We have a way to find her then. And, Donovan, we have to do it fast. She didn't sound good when I last spoke to her."

Donovan sprang to his feet. "I know where South King Street is. Let's go."

He ate the protein bar and drank some of the water. His stomach felt hollow, but he ignored it. They walked without a single word passing between them. Both lost in their thoughts, in their determination.

Beth meant a great deal to the two men. For one, she was a sister. For the other, she was his true love, his everything.

Thorn suddenly stopped and crouched on the ground. Donovan stood next to him. There in the drying mud were two marks, as if something had been dragged. Thorn's fingers traced a shoe print in front of the lines. "It's about a size eight." He stood and looked up and down the road. "The tracks for these shoes begin here."

Donovan peered up and down the road.

"I think they had been carrying her and set her down here," Thorn said as he inspected the other footprints. "She never said how many of them there were, but I can make out at least three clean prints." He faced Donovan. "Where's South King Street from here?"

"Up ahead."

Thorn nodded. "That's okay. We found where she was at one point, and we know they headed away from here, so we have to go back the way we came. Keep your eyes peeled."

Heading back the way they came, Donovan eyed the footprints, keeping his gaze locked on the tread of Beth's sneakers. When the mud disappeared, a few muddy tracks were left on the road, but soon, not a single line of mud was visible.

"Wait."

Donovan took his gaze off the road and stood in the middle of the intersection. He saw Thorn staring at the road that broke off to the right. "What is it?"

"I think I saw something."

"Like what?"

Thorn met his eye. "Silver. Something silver in the road."

With that, they took off at a jog. They scanned the asphalt.

"There." Thorn ran ahead of Donovan, bent down, and picked up something that flashed in the sunlight. A chain dangled from his fingers.

Donovan snatched it from him. The metal was blistering hot from the sun's rays, but it looked as it did the last time he saw it hooked around Beth's wrist—her bracelet.

Chapter Eighteen

Beth shivered on the floor. The second piece of bread was gone, and a few swallows of water remained. After she begged to be taken to the bathroom, they brought in a small trashcan. She had set it in the corner behind the door and had hovered over it to relieve herself. At least they were nice enough to keep the bag in it so when she was done, she could close the bag to keep the smell of urine from escaping.

Hours had gone by since she had spoken to Thorn. With no light coming into the closet, she couldn't tell if it was day or night, but she figured she was well into the first forty-eight hours of her captivity. The urge to escape welled inside her. She didn't have the energy to run to the door, though, nor did she have a weapon. The chair was still in the room, but she wouldn't be able to wield it. Whoever came into the room next, she had to be able to overpower him, and that would be highly unlikely in her given state.

Weapon. What could she use for a weapon?

Her vision trailed down her body. Shoelaces. Hair tie. That's all she had. She could twist together her shoelaces and choke one of the men, but he'd have to be within arm's reach and she'd have to jump him from behind. No way was she capable of jumping, nor were her arms strong enough to be able to hold the shoelaces long enough to render him unconscious. At this point, she wouldn't even be able to hop. The hair tie? All she imagined doing was flicking it into a man's eye. But her aim, with something so small, wouldn't be so good. More likely, the hair tie would sail past his head and out the door.

She needed something that could cut, stab, or draw blood. Her thoughts went to the underwire in her bra. If she could manage to get out of her shirt and bra, she might be able to rub her bra against the concrete wall until the threads broke enough for her to fish out the underwire. With that wire, she could pick the lock and slip out undetected, unless someone was posted outside the door. She looked to the zipper of her jean shorts. If she didn't mind being in her underwear around four men, she could try to rip out the zipper and wrap it around her knuckles like she did with the belt. The thing was, she knew she wouldn't be able to attack someone like that again. Not with so much of her blood gone and her left arm out of commission.

She stared down at her shorts. If only cotton and jean could make a weapon. She was beginning to abandon the idea of escaping when she noticed a sliver of silver poking out of her pocket. Dipping her fingers into her pocket, she felt sharp metal. She pulled out the two screws she had removed from the air vent. They were two inches long. A smile tugged her lips. She slipped the screws between her fingers and made a fist. The screws jutted between her knuckles like Wolverine's claws.

She didn't have to wait long for the next man to check in on her. Her head swayed as she peered up at him. Garbled words fluttered from her lips.

"What?"

She repeated herself, the words nothing more than a sigh.

"Huh?" He closed the door and crossed to her.

She fumbled with her words.

He knelt in front of her, bringing his ear closer to her mouth.

"You're dead," she said.

The man jerked back, and she swung her arm. Her fist slammed into his face. He let out a roar. Through his opened mouth, she saw the screws protruding from his cheek. She drew her fist away, sliding the screws out of the holes, and jabbed her fist at him again. The screws slipped into the meat of his shoulder.

He screamed. Blood coated his teeth and streamed down his face.

She was aiming for his neck, wanting to give him a fatal wound, when he fell backward on the ground. Now was her chance to flee. She pushed herself to a standing position and took a step toward the door.

She froze as it opened.

Three men stood there flabbergasted to see her standing with two screws caught in her bloody fist.

The largest of them, the man Beth referred to as Two-by-Four, tackled her into the wall. The hit sent pain shooting up and down her arm. She yelled and jabbed her fist at him, puncturing the screws repeatedly into his chest and abdomen.

He brought her to the floor.

Her breath punched from her lungs. Pulsing electricity swaddled her shoulder.

The other men joined in on the fight. Someone gripped her forearm as another uncurled her fist and stole the screws. Then a boot stomped onto her fingers.

She screamed.

The heel tramped down on her fingers again.

A crunching sound was followed by her wails. Hot tears plunged down her cheeks.

Mr. Gun's face hovered over her. "I think we underestimated you, but not anymore. Let's see you try something now." His smirk was wolfish.

She shrank from him.

As the two other men, Broken Nose and Screw Face, supported Two-By-Four, Mr. Gun picked up her bottle and poured out the last of the water onto the floor. On his way out, he picked up the chair.

Alone, Beth sobbed on the ground. Her left arm was draped over her stomach, and her right hand lay mangled on her chest.

Sometime later, her crying stopped. She felt distanced from her pain, hunger, thirst. The silence was deafening. Darkness was her companion.

Her blood loss teamed up with her growing dehydration and hunger, bending the real world. Whenever her eyelids cracked open, strange images assaulted her. A giant blowup snowman, like those grotesque Christmas decorations people put on their lawns, towered in one of the corners. It took her a moment to realize it was falling. She lifted her right arm to stop it from trapping her. Her crippled hand propped it up.

After a moment, she realized the snowman wasn't even touching her hand. She lowered her arm. The snowman's carrot nose was aimed at her face, but it didn't come any closer. She blinked.

The snowman vanished.

Her hand floated back to her chest. She continued

to stare at the spot where the snowman had been in confusion. While eyeing the darkness, her eyelids drifted close.

Sleep was fleeting. Every few minutes, she'd wake and see something new, something terrifying. At one point, a man shrouded in shadows rushed at her with a knife. She grabbed the empty water bottle with her crushed fingers and chucked it at him. It sailed through his torso and bounced off the wall. The man had seemed so real.

Her fear had been palpable.

Darkness accepted her into its arms, and she dreamed frightening things.

Crushing water surged toward her. Instead of crashing into her, it swooped around her like a cocoon. Trapped in the swirling water were hundreds of bodies. Their blank faces pressed up against the wall of water, and their dead eyes stared at her. Screams echoed around her. A part of her realized the screams were coming from her own mouth.

She rotated around and around, desperate for a way out. The whirling water rose to the sky. If she had wings, she could fly out of there, but she was grounded. Her gaze dropped and landed on a face she recognized. Donovan. He was trapped in the water. His eyes gleamed with death.

Her cries magnified.

Suddenly, the wall of water burst, and she was swallowed by it. She woke gasping for air and failing her arms. Pain exploded through her body. Heart thundering, she tucked her arms back to her body. She fought to stay awake, but the lure of sleep was too strong for her to defeat. Her nightmares from then on were swirls of colors and explosive sounds. She couldn't make out a thing. Objects and faces bled into each other.

She teetered out of her dreams and opened her eyes.

Donovan knelt beside her.

"You're alive," she whispered.

"Of course, I am."

His voice. Oh, it sounded so good.

"I've missed you."

"I never left you, Beth. I've been here the whole time." He pointed to her chest, indicating her heart.

She shook her head. "Sometimes that's not enough."

"But it is, Beth." He took her battered hand in his and kissed her bruised knuckles. "Our love is so strong we can live in each other's hearts. Even in death. As long as we are alive, neither of us can truly die."

"I know what you're saying, but will you stay with me until help comes?"

"I'm not going anywhere." He stretched out beside her and embraced her.

In his arms, her pain disappeared.

She closed her eyes.

Chapter Nineteen

With Beth's bracelet in his fist, Donovan marched on. His hunger and thirst were forgotten. All that mattered was Beth and getting to her before Jackson's men could execute her. He didn't believe for a second they wouldn't kill her if they had a chance. The one thing stopping them was their desire to take them down at once.

Well, nothing could stop Donovan from getting to Beth. *Nothing.* Not even a bullet.

The sun began its descent from its perch high in the sky. He judged it to be around four o'clock. The sun's rays were brighter and hotter than ever. The clean shirt he got that morning clung to his back. Sweat poured down his face and slithered into his eyes. The salt burned, causing him to rub his eyes and squint for some relief. He would've stepped right over the tiny, silver circle if he hadn't blinked his blurry vision clear. The silver flashed at him like a warning. When he recognized what it was, he sank to the ground. He held the sun-warmed ring by the tips of his fingers and stared at the infinity knot. The memory of his proposal came alive in his mind, as if he was kneeling on the cold tile in the San Francisco Police Department. He tilted the ring this way and that with his thoughts focused on Beth. That was how he saw the bit of dried blood.

He rose and scanned the area. He took a couple of steps into the road and stared up at the building. It made sense for her to leave a clue where Jackson's men were keeping her. Dropping something as small as a ring wouldn't have been hard to do as they dragged her inside, and it was the last item they could look for.

Spiral and infinity. That was her tip to Thorn.

"Do you think she's in there?"

Thorn met his eyes. "Possibly."

Donovan launched forward. His hand wrapped around the door handle. He was about to fling it open and rush inside with no thought for himself when Thorn tackled him. Donovan fought against him. He swung his fist out, the one grasping Beth's jewelry. Thorn leaned back so Donovan's knuckles grazed his chin. Then Thorn's fist caught Donovan square in the jaw, sending him into the wall. Thorn wrenched Donovan's arm behind his back and shoved the side of his face into the stone.

"Stop it," Thorn hissed in his ear. "If you go in there half-cocked, you'll get yourself and Beth killed. Probably me, too. So cool the fuck down."

"She's all I have."

"Which is why you shouldn't do something as stupid as storming that building with no weapons and no backup."

Donovan knew Thorn was right. They'd all die because of his brashness. "All right. I won't. Now get off me."

Thorn released him and took a step back. "We have to get out of here in case they heard us." He peered around. "Let's go to the roof of that building." He pointed at the building across the street. "We'll have eyes on this building. If we see anything suspicious, we can take the next step."

Donovan hoped that next step involved him getting his hands on the bastards who had been hurting Beth.

They ran across the street, snuck into the building through the unlocked front door, and made their way to the roof where they hunkered behind the wall. Time ticked by with no activity in the building across the way.

The sun sank lower. Clouds drifted overhead and blocked the rays, leaching sweat from Donovan's pores.

Sitting still brought his hunger back in full force. He tried to keep thoughts of fat hamburgers dripping with special sauce and pizzas loaded with sausage and onions at bay, but his mind kept circling back to the foods he wanted to gorge upon. It disgusted him. Had Beth had food since their picnic? Were Jackson's men starving her?

He glanced at Thorn who was scrutinizing the building as if it were an enemy that needed to be taken down. Donovan didn't doubt Thorn was considering ways to get in and out alive.

"Thank you," Donovan said.

Thorn tore his gaze from the building. "Why are you thanking me now? We don't have Beth yet."

"Because I never would've known about her situation if you hadn't come. I wouldn't be this close to her with the hope of rescuing her."

He imagined returning home a widower and Thorn telling him the awful news too late to do anything about it, because by the time he would've arrived home, she would've surely been dead. Killed days before by the men whose patience would've run out while waiting for him. He would've been waiting for a ghost in the hospital's parking lot.

"You and Beth would've done the same for me," Thorn said and turned to the building.

Thorn was right again. He had become a part of their family. They would've risked everything to save him or the woman he loved. Even if Donovan would've been hesitant, Beth would've kicked his ass into taking action. She was a fighter for others, for him when they were strangers, for the students in her classes, and for a battered woman who sold her body for money. No one was unworthy of her help.

Donovan turned his attention back to the building in time to see the door open. He ducked his head.

A man stepped into the dying sunlight. His greasy, brown hair hung over his forehead. A gun was in his hand. He moved to the side of the building, set the gun on a window's ledge, and unzipped his pants to take a leak. A stream of pee flowed between his feet. When he was done, he picked up the gun again. His head swiveled left and right before he slipped back into the building.

Donovan didn't look away from the door. "She's in there."

Thorn went inside the building to call the Honolulu Police Department with his cell phone. He was put on hold until they could verify his position at the Orlando PD, then again to patch him through. For the past several minutes, Donovan listened to him argue with the chief of police.

As Donovan paced back and forth, Thorn's voice grew with aggravation.

"I know about the conditions out there, sir. I came

here with the American Red Cross, and I've walked the streets. I'm asking for your help." A brief pause. "I know your men are out there looking for survivors, but we both know they won't find many, if any at all. Saving a woman who is alive right now, but could die at any moment, should be a top priority. If you do nothing, you're condemning her to death." Thorn whirled around and sank his fist into the wall. "You're going to let these men get away with murder!"

Donovan's own anger swelled as he listened to Thorn's heated words. Thorn's face was a dark red. His chest rapidly rose and fell.

"Sir, if you don't rally your men and send them here, I will tell every news source in America about how you could've saved a woman, who survived the tsunami, only to be kidnapped by ruthless criminals, but you did nothing, which resulted in unspeakable torture and her death. You and your department will be disgraced." He breathed heavily. "Yes, sir, that is a threat. But if you come to her aid, people will praise you for giving this devastated island something positive to hold on to in the wake of this disaster. Which will it be?"

Donovan studied Thorn's face for a reaction to the chief's words, but the anger never left his eyes. Was the chief denying him help? Denying Beth?

Thorn nodded once. "Thanks, sir." He ended the call and slumped onto a chair with his head in his hands.

"Tell me they're coming."

Thorn raised his head and looked Donovan in the eye. "Thirty minutes."

Donovan released his breath. His shoulders

dropped.

Those thirty minutes took forever. The sun sank, and the sky turned granite. Donovan's nerves hummed like a wasps' nest. With five minutes remaining, they snuck out of the building to meet up with the officers down the road, away from spying eyes.

The chief didn't send just any officers, though. When the rumble of an approaching vehicle touched Donovan's ears, he turned and was stunned to see a SWAT truck coming toward them. It stopped beside a building for cover and uniformed SWAT members climbed out two by two. A total of six. The men and one woman wore helmets, body armor, boots, and weapons. In their hands, they held semi-automatic weapons with scopes.

"Are you Detective Thorn?"

"I am." Thorn briefed them on the situation. "I've seen at least one armed man. Based on the footprints, there could be three or more. No activity at the front of the building or near any of the windows. They might be holed up in the back. I don't know where the hostage is, so keep an eye out for a white female, 5'8", brown hair, and brown eyes. These men are highly dangerous. We don't want any of them getting free to do any more of Jackson Storm's dirty work. If they don't surrender, shoot to kill."

They nodded confirmation.

"Do you have a plan of action?" the SWAT captain asked.

"I think we'd be able to take them by surprise if we split up. One group could go through the front and the other through the back. Take out these men, clear the building, and find Beth. Unless you have a better plan.

I'm open to anything as long as the end result is the same."

"I agree, but we wait for nightfall. The dark will be our advantage." He held out night vision goggles and a gun, like their own, to Thorn.

Then he held out goggles and a gun to Donovan.

He took them with a raised brow. He had been prepared to argue all the reasons he should storm the building with them and had been ready to get a firm refusal.

The leader must've noticed his frown because he said, "Thorn said you're training to be a cop."

Donovan's gaze swayed toward Thorn, who gave a discreet wink.

"But since you're not licensed yet, you get this." He pointed to the gun in Donovan's hands. "This gun has rubber pellets in it. It's not lethal, but it can still hurt like hell and leave a nasty bruise. You'll stay behind us at all times, out of the line of fire until the criminals are taken down."

"I can do that," Donovan confirmed. "Thank you."

"We have vests and helmets for both of you, too."

Donovan and Thorn put on the body armor and waited with the SWAT team for nightfall to settle over the island. To occupy the hours, they watched the building from multiple vantage points. No light. No movement. No life. Jackson's men were being careful about keeping their presence unnoticed. Other than the man who came outside to take a piss.

Something in that action told Donovan he was arrogant. Smug. Surely, there were bathrooms inside. Even without electricity to keep the water pumping, he could've peed in a toilet. Why come out in the open?

Because he thought he was safe, smart.

The moment darkness fell they went into action. Thorn slunk off with three of the SWAT members to the back of the building. Donovan took up the rear of the three who would break down the front door. Captain Foster held up his fist, and they pressed their backs to the building. Williams, the other man, went to the other side of the door. The captain counted down with his fingers from three. When he pointed, Williams stepped in front of the door and sent his boot into it. The force of his kick caused it to bang open. Foster rushed in and turned left. Kano, the woman, was a step behind. She swung right. Williams went in after them, and Donovan followed.

With the night vision goggles, he saw perfectly. Everything was cast in a neon green glow. He could make out the desks in neat rows as well as Foster, Kano, and Williams. Seeing them move with such uniformity and precision was a sight. He felt safe trailing behind them, but that didn't stop his heart from beating erratically, thanks to the adrenaline pumping through his veins.

Shouts came from the rear of the building. Gun shots sounded. Donovan gripped his gun tighter but kept it pointed down. Foster, Kano, and Williams picked up their speed but continued to sweep the area, calling out clear whenever they searched a room and found it empty.

At the end of a hall, they came across a body stretched out on the floor. Even with the night vision goggles, he saw the bullet hole in the middle of a man's forehead. Dark stains spread across his wide chest.

He stepped over the body. More shooting echoed

through the hall. He followed Williams around a corner to see another SWAT member standing over a man with a bullet hole in his forehead. As he passed, he noticed the man had a patch covering the left side of his face.

They rounded another corner into a new hallway. Captain Foster and Kano ducked into a room and stepped out.

"Clear. Smells like this one has been dead for a while."

Donovan looked into the room. The smell of a body left to decompose in a room with no air conditioning punched him in the face. He took a step back. The man's face was unrecognizable. His features had been smashed into a bloody pulp.

As they made their way down, systematically checking every room, Donovan's thoughts went out to Beth. *Where are you, baby? Where are you?*

He was following Williams when a dark object blurred the corner of his vision. A breeze swept behind him, tickling the sun-roasted skin on his neck. He whirled around with his gun at the ready. In the green glow, his gaze landed on a man trying to make an escape down the hall. He squeezed the trigger. The man tripped on his feet and slammed into the ground face-first. Gun pointed at the back of the man's head, Donovan advanced on him to make sure he wouldn't rise. There were no holes or spreading darkness on his back. He wasn't dead, just unconscious, and Donovan wished his bullets had been real.

Captain Foster stepped beside him and tightened a zip tie around the man's wrists. Williams stayed behind to keep an eye on him while the three of them joined

Thorn's team.

"How many did you count?" Foster asked the other men.

"We took down two, sir."

"We found one dead in a room, and Donovan took down another."

The other teams' heads swiveled to Donovan. He couldn't make out their expressions with the night vision goggles occupying half their faces; were they shocked or impressed? By the grin Thorn wore, it was easy to see he was amused.

"That makes four. You were right, Detective Thorn."

Thorn shrugged. "I'll feel right when we find Beth."

They split up to check all the rooms. With every "clear" that sounded, Donovan became more and more anxious. Had they taken her somewhere else? Did they kill her and dump her body where Search and Rescue would find her and think she was a victim of the tsunami?

His gaze scanned offices. He even checked under desks to see if she was huddled there in fright. He was starting to believe she wasn't in the building when someone said, "She's in here."

Donovan made it to the closet ahead of Thorn. The faint smell of urine touched his nostrils, making his heart muscles clench. Beth lay on the ground next to a black stain. He fell next to her. The green light from the goggles made her look sickly. Bruises darkened her skin like storm clouds. Cuts resembled tattoos as if someone tried playing tic-tac-toe on her arms. Blood smeared her skin, giving her the look of someone with the plague. Her arms lay on her chest. The fingers of her right hand were bent at odd angles. A spot near her left shoulder made Donovan think of a black hole.

Hole?

Donovan's hands touched her shoulder. His heart shattered as if someone hit it with a sledgehammer. He gently felt the back of her shoulder, and his fingers found another hole. He looked up at Thorn, who was frozen a few feet away.

"They shot her," Donovan roared. "Those assholes fucking shot her!"

He ripped off the goggles. Blackness consumed his vision. He couldn't even see Beth as he lifted her onto his lap. "Beth." He felt for a pulse at her throat. It was faint. Too faint. "Beth." His fingers stroked her face. "Can you hear me? It's Donovan."

She didn't move. She didn't make a sound. Her breaths were too shallow to hear in the silence around him.

He bent down and set his lips next to her ear. "Don't you leave me," he whispered. "Don't you dare. I love you too damn much to say goodbye now. It's too soon for that. Hold on. Please hold on…"

Chapter Twenty

Beth's eyelids fluttered open. Light blinded her. Groaning, she squeezed her eyes shut. *Am I dead*?

She commanded her eyelids to open again. Alien objects surrounded her. Where was the trashcan holding her pee? What were the blurry things that circled her?

A face floated in front of her. The features were distorted. Demonic. Fear shot her into fight mode. She thrust her elbow toward the face and felt something crunch.

A cry pierced the air. Hands pushed down on her chest.

"Help! Help!"

The shouts were garbled. Robotic.

Where the hell am I?

She kicked her legs. Growls rumbled from her throat. This was the sound humans made when they resorted to their animal instincts to survive. And that was all Beth had left. If she could, she would rip off an ear with her teeth. Bite off a finger. Tear out a throat.

During her rampage, she saw a snake feeding on her arm. Her fear of snakes brought a startled sound from her throat. She reached for the snake's transparent body to yank its fangs out of her flesh.

"No!" A hand grabbed her wrist. "No, don't pull out your IV."

Another hand shoved her down, pinning her

injured shoulder.

"Watch her shoulder. Careful!" The order was issued as Beth let out a pained cry.

Something jabbed her in the neck.

Her fight dissolved. Her limbs went limp. And her eyelids sealed with one thought, *where's Donovan?*

****

Sounds came to her first—the beeps of machines and voices she didn't recognize. Then she felt the warmth of a blanket, the softness of a pillow under her head, the cushion beneath her spine. None of it made sense. She was locked in a closet, sleeping on a dirty, hard floor. Her blood loss must be messing with her brain. Not only had she seen a giant, inflatable snowman, but now she was imagining a bed.

Eyes still shut, she went to roll over onto her right shoulder, to relieve the ache in her back, but she couldn't move her legs. Something had her ankles.

The nightmare of Jackson Storm hanging onto her ankles, dragging her to the bottom of the ocean, resurfaced. Hysteria bubbled up inside her. Her eyelids snapped open. Padded belts were strapped around her ankles. Sitting up, she was brought short. She looked down at the strap around her right wrist.

"Get them off," she shouted and tried to pick at the contraption with her fingernails. Every movement of her fingers sent darts of pain up her arm to her shoulder.

She jerked her legs, wanting to break the leather. The bed beneath her vibrated with her rampage. "Get them off!"

People rushed into the room. She looked at them as a cornered animal would, as though she would kill them before they could kill her. Except none of them had the faces of the men who had been tormenting her for days. That didn't make her feel any safer when they surrounded her and pressed her flat against the bed.

"Let me go!" She tried to fight them off, but her left arm was in a sling and her other limbs were tied down. "Let go, let go, let me go!" They weren't letting her go. Their hands applied more pressure to stifle her rocking. All she could do was shake her head from side to side.

"Stop!"

The command halted her heart. She would recognize that voice anywhere. Blinking the haze from her vision, she looked to where it came from. A gap formed in the crowd, and Donovan appeared like an apparition. He shoved the people out of his way to get to her.

His hands tenderly cupped her face. "Ssh. It's okay, Beth. You're at the hospital."

Hospital? Frowning, she reexamined her surroundings. The swirling colors settled, and she made out the objects that were so strange before—the beeping came from the machines monitoring her vitals, the snake biting her arm was an IV, and the monsters were doctors and nurses. Her gaze drifted back to Donovan. A growth of beard darkened his cheeks and jawline. His face was tanner, but his eyes were as bright as ever.

"You're…you're real?"

Donovan's smile melted her heart. "Yes, I'm real." He kissed her forehead. The contact brought tears to her eyes. She hadn't felt love or compassion in days.

"Can you undo the straps? I don't want to be tied down." The tears leaked from her cheeks, leaving wet paths.

He turned to the doctors and nurses. "Take them off her."

"We put them on her so she wouldn't harm anyone, or herself," someone in a white coat said.

"Do you realize the nightmare she was in before we brought her here? She was scared. I'm here. She's not going to hurt anyone." When they didn't move, he advanced toward them. "Remove the straps. Now." His voice was a low growl.

The doctor nodded, and the nurses set to work freeing her. Once her ankles were released, she curled up her legs. An odd burning and pulling sensation between her legs made her shift. The strap was removed from her right wrist, and she lifted her hand to see it bandaged. Her middle and ring fingers were splinted. "Broken?"

Donovan's gaze softened. "Yeah." His answer was a breath. He gently took her wrist with his fingers and held her bandaged hand between his. She could barely feel his touch; he was trying so hard not to hurt her.

Her attention shifted to the foot of the bed. She was relieved to see they were alone. The doctors and nurses had quietly excused themselves.

"How long have I been here?"

"Three days. They patched up your..." his voice cracked. "They patched up your gunshot wound and gave you a ton of medicine to battle the infection you were developing. They gave you a blood transfusion and bag after bag of fluids. You have a catheter and, for a while, you were hooked up to oxygen."

Well, that explained the weird sensation between her legs—a catheter.

Donovan lowered his head. "I was terrified."

"I'm sorry," she croaked.

He shook his head, leaned forward, and kissed her lips, which she doubted felt good against her dry, cracked lips.

"How'd you find me?"

"Thorn…and these." He dipped his hand into a pair of shorts she didn't recognize and showed her what lay in his palm. Her charm bracelet and infinity engagement ring.

She gasped. "You found them." More tears developed. "I hated leaving them like that. I felt as though I was leaving parts of myself behind. The most important parts."

"I know, but I'm glad you did." He wiped her cheeks with his thumbs.

"What about the men who grabbed me?"

"We got them. It's okay now. Rest."

Rest sounded like a great idea, but she was still afraid of what she'd see if she closed her eyes. "You'll be here while I sleep?"

"I'm not going anywhere."

Her mouth tilted up in a smile. "That's what you said before."

His eyebrows lowered.

He didn't understand, so she elaborated, "You were with me in that hellhole during my darkest time. You were with me. It might've been a hallucination, I realize that, but it comforted me."

"I'm glad I could be there for you."

His smile revealed he wished he had really been there, and been there sooner.

For the rest of the day, she slept on and off. In the morning, she woke feeling less groggy than the day before, but in more pain. The drugs they had pumped into her after her operation had worn off, and it was time for another dose. A kind nurse gave her some pain killers. Another brought her some lunch consisting of pureed soup, orange Jell-O, apple sauce, and a bottle of ice-blue Gatorade. Donovan tended to her when she was incapable and fed her the soup one spoonful at a time. She appreciated his patience and affection, but she hated being so injured she couldn't even feed herself. Beth, the self-defense instructor who took on a hurricane and an earthquake, wouldn't even be able to recognize the Beth in that hospital bed.

Later, a nurse removed her catheter. The tug of the small object leaving her body made her wince. She felt better with it gone, though. A couple of naps and another meal of soup and custard replenished her strength.

That night, Thorn visited. He stepped into the room, barely moving beyond the threshold, and stood there with his hands in his pocket as if unsure what to do next.

"How are you doing?"

She smiled. "Better."

"I'm glad." He rocked back and forth on his heels. His eyes resembled the eyes of a puppy staring up at her from the floor while she lay in an empty bed. How could she resist those eyes?

She sat forward. "Thorn, come here and give me a hug."

He crossed to her in two strides. His arms wrapped around her waist, and his cheek pressed to hers. He held on for a moment before kissing her on the temple and pulling away. "I'm so happy to see you." His fingers trailed along the strap of her sling. "Even with this."

She nodded. "I'm happy to see you, too. I could've died from happiness when you answered my first phone call."

His smile wobbled. She never thought about what he went through after she called him. And how in the world did he link up with Donovan?

She asked just that.

"That's a long story."

"Thorn, have a seat and tell her," Donovan said. "She needs to hear it."

Thorn sat in a chair on the other side of her bed. "Right after you hung up the first time, I drove straight to the airport and got on the first flight to San Fran. During the whole flight, I went through dozens of strategies for how I was going to get to Oahu and find you. When I got to the coast, I went to a Navy Yard. I figured if any military force in the United States would came to Hawaii's aid, it would be the Navy base stationed in California. When I got there, I ran into a few problems. Let's just say, there was a fight. I was detained until Chief Cormac vouched for me. I was released and told to never come back or I'd be arrested and charged with some bullshit. Anyway, I went to the docks next and tried to bribe fishing vessels to take me across the ocean. They were tempted but too scared to make the journey because of the tsunami. I tried to tell them a tsunami in the open ocean is about a foot tall, but they wouldn't budge. Not even when I raised my offer."

"To what?"

"Fifty thousand."

Beth's mouth opened in shock. "You...you were

going to pay that much just for me?"

"Just for you?" Thorn glanced in Donovan's direction. "Beth, you're a good person. The best. The lives of so many would be destroyed if you died. You're worth forty times that amount."

She dropped her head. Tears fell onto her lap, creating dark spots on the cotton blanket spread over her lap. She shook her head, not wanting to believe she was worth that much. Or worth the trouble he went through.

"When the fishermen wouldn't help, I was roaming around like a chicken with its head caught off for a while. Then I heard on the radio that the Hawaii Emergency Management Agency in Honolulu sustained damaged and was having a hard time bringing aid to the island, so I went to the Bay Area American Red Cross. They were loading up supplies when I got there. I was able to get the person in charge to agree to let me come along. It took a lot of persuading, but when I said they'd be responsible for another death, one they could have prevented, I was allowed onboard. We landed at the Kalaeloa Airport and drove to Honolulu. Some went to the Shriner's Children's Hospital and another group went to the Kapiolani Medical Center. I went with the latter because I remembered you said you were heading to the same one when they grabbed you, so I went inside and asked if I could use their PA. system. At first, I was told no. But I showed my badge and told the nurse a message wouldn't hurt anyone. She said Donovan's name a few times and told him if he was there to come to the front desk. And he did."

Thorn grinned. "The son-of-a-bitch was alive, and he was there. We went off together. I saw your bracelet, and Donovan found your ring. I convinced the police chief to send help. In fact, he sent a SWAT team. We stormed the building, took down Jackson's men, and found you in the closet." His gaze lowered a moment before he continued. "We brought you here in the SWAT truck. Donovan carried you in with an escort of a heavily armed team. There was no way you weren't getting admitted. They took you straight to surgery."

His eyes said what his voice didn't; seeing her nearly lifeless on the floor would forever stay with him.

The terror she endured in that building, in that closet, came back to her as strong as the tsunami, as strong as a bomb. Combined with the things Thorn did to find her and the unspoken events Donovan went through, she couldn't stop her onslaught of emotions. She broke down. She couldn't bury her face in her hands, though, and felt naked to the world as she wept.

"Beth, I didn't mean to upset you. I'm sorry."

She shook her head from side to side. She wanted to tell him it wasn't his fault, but sobs came forth from her mouth. A hand touched her knee. Through the wet shield over her eyes, she recognized Thorn's hand with the small scar and the plain platinum band he wore. She knew he wasn't married, had never been, but she didn't know the significance behind the ring or why he wore it daily.

"I'm gonna go. I'll check back in tomorrow."

Beth could've laughed. Every time she cried, Thorn wanted to flee. What would he do if he had a woman and she cried for whatever reason? The thought of him panicking wasn't strong enough to make her laugh, though. She continued to sob. Her body rocked with the violence of it.

Donovan sat on the edge of the bed and put an arm behind her. "It's okay, baby. You survived. You're safe."

She cuddled into his side and cried into his chest, needing to feel as safe as he said she was, but unable to believe it.

Chapter Twenty One

The doctors kept Beth in the hospital for two weeks. Balancing a spoon on her splinted fingers, with her hand shaking, she was able to feed herself small amounts. She couldn't eat much, though. Those fourteen days in the hospital, including the three days she was unconscious, plus the three days she was locked up in the closet, resulted in her losing fifteen pounds.

The doctor said losing weight was normal in her circumstance and reassured him she was above the line where they'd be concerned about her weight. Even so, her collar bones and hip bones stuck out of her body. Black hollows swallowed her eyes. Her skin was too pale. The veins in her arms looked like blue snakes. Dark, straight hair grew from her unshaved legs.

She was a fragile creature with a small resemblance to the woman he married. Her voice was even different. Scratchy as if her vocal cords had been burned with acid. Whenever she spoke, she sounded miles away; her words empty. She was like a shell of who she used to be. Seeing her like that broke Donovan's heart. All he could do was be there for her, although he wanted to do more.

During the two weeks the doctors closely monitored her vitals and blood count, making sure infection didn't return. She was extremely lucky the bullet had made a clear path through the meat of her shoulder and didn't shatter bone. Her physical therapy went well, too. Tears would stream down her cheeks as she rotated her shoulder and lifted her arm, but she never uttered a complaint or let loose a sob.

At first, a nurse had to support her frail body whenever she got out of bed, helping her to take baby steps to the bathroom. After a couple of days, she was able to walk under her own power. Then she was able to take short walks with him around the hospital's wing. He'd push her IV pole, and she'd shuffle along beside him.

Once during their walks, she stopped in front of a window. He didn't know until there was a tug on the IV pole. When he turned, he found her immobile. Her right arm, with the IV taped to the crease in her elbow, was stretched out toward him. He had pulled on the IV. "Shit, sorry." He backed up. "What are you doing?"

"I wanted to see the ocean." Her voice was toneless. "I wanted to see if it was different."

He peered out the glass windowpane. The sky overhead was a soft blue. No clouds in sight. The crowds of homeless, helpless people were gone, transported to other hospitals throughout the islands of Hawaii or to shelters. A crew had cleaned up the debris they had left behind. Donovan was glad. He didn't want Beth to see any remnants from the tsunami. Not even a piece of trash. It would be too much for her delicate mind.

In the distance, he could make out a strip of blue.

"Let's go back to your room."

She didn't resist as he took her elbow and steered her away from the window.

Her doctors said she was excelling in her recovery, but Donovan knew psychologically her health was a different matter. He didn't know what happened during her sessions, but he knew what she was like with him. And if she wouldn't talk to him, then he knew there was no way she would talk to a stranger. Unless, of course, it was easier for her to talk to someone she didn't know, didn't care for. That was a thought he didn't like.

The day before she was released, her doctors removed the bandages from her shoulder to inspect the gunshot wound. Beth kept her eyes straight ahead and her chin lifted. She didn't want to see it, so Donovan looked for her. Black stitches closed the holes on both sides. The skin was pink, as if raw. It didn't look as horrific as it did before the doctors rushed her into surgery, but it looked foreign. His jaw clenched.

While staring at the bruises blanketing her skin from shoulder to collar bone, he recalled another nasty bruise he had seen there. When Hurricane Sabrina visited Florida, Beth had risked her life to retrieve him from his crushed car. The gale force winds sweeping down the road pitched a rock the size of his fist into her shoulder. Many weeks went by before that bruise dissolved into the natural color of her skin.

The doctor cut away the stitches. Without them, the scaring became more visible. She'd forever bare a mark of the tsunami, of the pain inflicted by Jackson Storm's men. A small, ragged circle that would remind her of her fear in that God forsaken closet. And she had two of them—one to haunt her from the front, and the other to taunt her from the back. If he could erase them with kisses, he would. He'd kiss them night and day, but his lips held no magic, only love.

The next day, Beth was allowed to go home. Home was half a world away, though, and she wasn't well enough to travel. A cab drove them to their honeymoon suite. Donovan's foresight to get a hotel farther inland to save money had been a smart move, because the surge waters hadn't reached their hotel. With the room paid for a whole month, they were able to settle back into their room with no difficulty.

Beth lowered onto the edge of the bed and onto her right shoulder, with her arm extended to keep her fingers safe. Donovan gently stretched out behind her. He was trying to figure out how to hold her when her arm, trapped in a sling, lifted a few inches. He slipped his arm underneath hers and rested his hand on her right wrist. It was the best he could do until she healed.

They slept together for hours. Having Beth in his arms helped Donovan to sleep more peacefully than he did in the chair next to her hospital bed. Every half hour, he'd wake up, check on her, and try to reposition his cramped limbs and crooked neck. He dropped into a sound sleep, knowing with great certainty Beth was okay. She was next to him, not hooked up to machines or tubes.

When he eased awake, he opened his eyes to a different ceiling than he was used to seeing. For a moment, confusion cocooned him. He had to recall the moments before his nap to remember where he was and to realize Beth wasn't asleep next to him. He sat up with her name on his lips.

Flashing colorful lights and the hum of noise drew his attention to the TV. The words "Devastation in Honolulu" dominated the screen. Then footage from the tsunami and the aftermath flashed by, fading into each other to reveal increasingly more heartbreaking still-shots. A child wailing atop a pile of debris. Strangers carrying a woman through floodwaters; her clothes clinging to her by a few fibers. A man cradling a baby in a bloated diaper to his chest; his bare feet were bloodied. Planes tossed belly-up at the Honolulu Airport, boats stranded inland, houses reduced to nothing, the hotels on the coast stripped away.

Donovan scanned the room. The curtains were tightly drawn. Beth's side of the bed and the two plush chairs were empty. He stiffly rolled out of bed, walked around the footboard, and nearly tripped over her. She was huddled on the floor with her face lifted toward the TV. In the gloom, shadows and light played upon her features, turning the dark circles around her eyes into caves.

"Beth?" He knelt in front of her. On her cheeks, tears gleamed with the reds and blues that projected the sad images. She couldn't turn from them. He cupped her face in his hands and lowered her head, forcing her gaze off the TV. The pain from the people in the news coverage reflected in her eyes. He wanted to shield her sight, but he couldn't make her forget the things now imprinted on her memory.

"Why are you watching this?"

"I had to know," she said. Her voice was little more than a breath.

He could understand that need. While he waited for her to regain consciousness, he had watched the chilling reports. He glanced over his shoulder to see a wide helicopter-view of the parts of the island heavily impacted by the tsunami.

"It's not good," he said. If she wanted to know, it

would be better coming from him. "An underwater quake, far out in the ocean, triggered a tsunami. The Tsunami Warning Center experienced glitches of some kind. They weren't able to detect the quake, and when the tsunami became visible, it was too late. They were hit before they could sound the siren. What happened is unthinkable."

"But obviously not impossible."

He studied her a moment before adding, "The tsunami was thirty, maybe forty-five feet tall and went about one mile inland. Oahu took the brunt of it. The death toll is estimated to be two thousand, but it's rising."

Beth made a strangled sound from deep in her throat as if she couldn't breathe. "Why…why am I alive while so many are dead?"

Donovan shook his head. He wished he had the divine answer to her question. "I don't know why we're alive, and they aren't. Maybe it's because we're stronger, smarter, luckier. Or maybe it's a higher power's doing. I don't know why, Beth, but we are. And we can't take that for granted. We have to keep living for those two thousand and the people they left behind."

Beth's nod was marginal. "For those two thousand people."

Her promise to stay alive relieved him. Although she was out of the hospital, she was so damaged from what happened that he had been afraid she was slipping away. From herself. From him. From life.

"I'm going to order food, and then we can go back to bed. Is there anything you feel like you might be up for eating?"

"Grilled cheese."

The simple request made him smile. "One grilled cheese sandwich coming up."

She ate one triangle of her sandwich before her stomach refused anymore. He gave her a dose of medication, and she drifted off to sleep.

****

Her screams jarred him awake. She was thrashing so wildly he was afraid she'd reopen the delicate skin over her gunshot wound.

"Beth?" He carefully straddled her and caught her shoulders.

Her fight doubled. She thought he was trying to hurt her, kill her. She thought he was one of *them.* That realization was like a knife to his abdomen.

"Shit." He lifted her off the bed, wrapped his arms around her, and held her head to his chest. "Beth, you're dreaming. Can you hear me?" His lips were next to her ear. "Wake up, baby. Please, wake up. Wake up, wake up." He repeated his two-worded plea like a chant.

Her jerks continued.

He squeezed his eyes shut. *Please, come back to me. Please, bring her back.*

He stroked her hair. "Listen to my voice. It's me. It's Donovan."

It's not them. I'm NOT them!

Her movements lessened until her body went slack in his hold. It felt less like surrender and more like her body gave out, that she had given up.

"Beth?" He laid her back on the bed.

Sweat coated her skin. Her face had lost the grimace of fear and now wore a blank mask. She looked at him with glistening eyes.

"You," she croaked.

He sighed. "Me." Bending forward, he pressed his lips to her sweaty brow.

"Always you," she whispered.

He smoothed away the damp strands of hair from her face. "Always." He wasn't merely confirming her words, but promising her he'd always be there for her. Would always come to her rescue if she needed it. Would always wake her up from her nightmares.

"Was your nightmare about the tsunami?"

Her head twitched in his hands. "Everything."

That one word, spoken on a gasp, told him her nightmare incorporated the terror from the tsunami and Jackson's men.

"Will you tell me about it? Any of it?"

She was quiet for a long time.

He settled beside her. *She won't tell me a thing. Not now or ever.* That realization about tore him in half.

Then her voice came out of the darkness. "It always starts when the wave hits us, and I lose your hand. I used to see you among the dead, but you're not dead." She laid her hand on his chest as if needing to make sure it was true. "I'm trying to get to the surface, but something has my ankle. It's Jackson Storm, and he's pulling me into the depths of the ocean. When I get swallowed by the black nothingness, I'm suddenly in that closet. In that closet…"

She told him about her attempts to get free, about getting shot and her hand stomped on. But she said it all in a detached sort of way. There was no emotion behind any of it. Her words sounded rehearsed. Repeated. And it sank in that what she told him was the bare bones of what happened. She told him what he wanted to know, but she was merely listing the highlights of her captivity while keeping herself, her mind, her entire being away from it.

At least she told him something, though. He had to take stock in that.

****

As the days went on, Donovan could clearly see the effect her kidnapping had on her. He'd often catch her sitting in bed, on the couch, even in a corner staring off into space. And every little thing made her jump. If room service knocked on the door, if he came into the bedroom while she was curled up on the floor, if the microwave beeped, she'd jerk. Her eyes would go wide and wild. Seeing her like that pained him. He didn't know what to do to make her feel safe.

On the third day after her release, he found her sitting in a chair in front of the window. Her legs were pulled up to her chest, and her right hand rested on her left shoulder.

His glanced down at the floor. The gray sling lay there like a snake's discarded skin. While approaching her, he saw the index finger on her injured hand circling round and round the jagged circle in her flesh.

"What are you doing?"

She flinched at his voice. Her gaze ticked to him and then back to the window. "It helps me to know what's real and what's not."

He squatted next to her. "What do you mean?"

She kept staring straight ahead. "When I touch this scar, I know I got out. I know it because, in that closet, I had a hole here." Her finger continued to caress the new skin. "There are times when I wake up and think

I'm back in that place."

His gaze snapped to her face when he heard the wetness in her voice.

"Sometimes I blink, and I'm there. I see the trashcan in the corner, the air vent with no cover, my blood on the concrete. I have to blink to make it go away. I tried not blinking at all, but that didn't work. I've found I can combat it if I touch this scar. I tell myself, 'You're out, you're out.'" Tears streamed to her jaw. Her voice trembled. "I was making coffee when the kitchen vanished, and I was there. It's getting better, though." She looked at him and nodded. "It's getting better."

Donovan swallowed. He took her hand, pulling her finger from the scar, and kissed it.

"Is there anything I can do?"

She shook her head and then said, "You're doing it."

Chapter Twenty Two

Beth stood, leaned down, and planted a kiss on Donovan's forehead. She appreciated his presence more than she could voice. Especially in her darkest moments. Whenever she thought she was locked in the dank janitor's closet, and if her scar trick wasn't working fast enough, she'd seek Donovan with her eyes. Seeing him would banish any strands of the hallucinations that were still intact. She wanted to tell him that, but the words got stuck in her throat. The kiss was all she could manage.

The next day, Thorn visited. When Beth saw him, an involuntary smile manifested. It was such a rare thing that it surprised her. Not once during the last few weeks had she cracked a smile. Feeling her facial muscles lift like that felt strange.

"Beth, you're looking ravishing."

She made a soft sound that could've been called a laugh. "I can eat a whole cheeseburger now."

"That must be it." He winked at her.

With a shake of her head, she excused herself to the bedroom. While closing the door, she heard Donovan say, "That was the first time I've seen her smile, and it was for you."

"Jealous?" Thorn said. Even from the other side of the door, she could recognize that Thorn was horsing around with Donovan.

"Shut up, jackass. But seriously, it was nice seeing her happy for once." There was a pause before he said, "She's different. She's jumpy all the time, she stares at nothing for hours, and hardly talks to me."

"Beth..." Thorn sighed.

In just saying her name, Beth felt all his sorrow. It grasped her throat like a hand. Tears pressed against her eyes. Her chest was heavy as if a rope was around her middle and someone was squeezing it tighter and tighter.

"She isn't just a survivor of a kidnapping or a tsunami," Thorn said. "She's both. And not separately, either, but at the same fucking time. That's more than anyone could handle at once. Considering, I think she's handling this well."

"I miss her." Donovan's words jabbed her in the heart.

"Look around, Donovan. She's here. That's more than many people can say."

"I know." Donovan's voice was barely audible through the door.

"And, Donovan, she is going to be different. She may forever be changed by this, but even if that's so, will you still love her?"

"Always."

Always...it was what he had said after he had lured her out of her first nightmare. Since then, she'd had an average of two nightmares a night, and he had been there to comfort her after each one.

She backed away from the door and retreated into the bathroom where she cried into a towel. Her hot breath suffocated her, but she didn't pull the towel from her face. Her weeping rocked her shoulders. The terry cloth dampened from her tears and warmed against her cheeks.

How could she not see she was hurting Donovan? She didn't mean to, of course. Everyone had their own way of coping after experiencing trauma. Withdrawing into herself was a defense mechanism.

Donovan said he missed her, and she missed the woman she used to be, too. Days ago, she had resigned herself to the fact she'd never be that kickass woman again, the one who rescued Donovan from his wrecked car and ventured into a house armed with a shovel to help him. Now, while sitting on the bathtub's ledge, she felt her returning. She had on her purple boxing gloves. The scar across her chest was visible. Determination burned in her eyes.

Beth smiled at her. *Long time, no see.* Except, that wasn't true. Fighter Beth had been there when she made her escape attempts and was slowly dying from blood loss. In fact, she was never far beneath the surface of Beth's skin. Now, Fighter Beth had come back to help Victim Beth get strong—mentally and physically. She couldn't stay scared and weak forever. If she did, she could lose the man she loved.

She wet a face towel to mop the stickiness from her cheeks. Then she met her reflection in the mirror and looked into her eyes, past the dark shadows and red lightning bolts. "You went through something horrible," she told herself. "And then you went through something even more horrible. You have every right to be changed and scarred, but you do not have the right to be a bad wife. Enough is enough! If you sink into depression, if you let PTSD take over, Jackson will win. Pull it together! Heal and fight back! If not for you, then for Donovan."

She knew she wouldn't be able to end her nightmares or stop herself from jumping at random noises, but she could be more open. Didn't all the shrinks say it was best to talk about the bad, the gruesome? If she kept it bottled up inside, she'd eventually explode, and that explosion could take out Donovan.

"You are Beth Kennedy Goldwyn, a self-defense instructor. You have survived quite a few disasters and have been face to face with criminals. You may not be such a bad-ass right now, but you'll get there. Over time. Starting today."

The determination reflecting back at her from her eyes was new. All she used to see before was heavy despair. A fire—albeit a small one that would need daily kindling—now filled the emptiness inside her.

She took out her makeup bag and applied some cover-up to the circles under her eyes. When she was done, she looked less like the walking dead. Not wanting to overdo it, she skipped the blush. If she came out with rosy cheeks, neither of them would be fooled. Makeup wasn't the best tool to bring herself back swinging, she knew that, except it made her look healthier and that counted for something.

Feeling a fraction stronger, despite her injuries, she joined Donovan and Thorn in the living room. The first thing she did was give Donovan a smile. By the way he smiled back, she knew it meant the world to him.

"I thought you would've gone home already," she said to Thorn.

"No. I've been..." He glanced at Donovan before continuing. "Helping with search and rescue and cleanup."

Flashes of the destruction blinded her—the pink door with white flowers and the young woman with the glass protruding from her chest.

Beneath the table, she pinched the skin on her thigh until the images faded.

"That's good," she managed.

She struggled to join the conversation. Every once in a while, she inserted a comment, but all she wanted to do was take another nap. When Thorn mentioned one of Jackson's man who was apprehended, her ears perked up.

"He's not saying a word about why he was in that building or why Beth was there. He's not even bothering to lie to say he went there for shelter."

"Jackson trained him," Beth said.

Donovan and Thorn looked at her with wide eyes. They were startled by her voice, her words.

She met their stares. "He won't say a word. Not even if you torture him."

"Well, he doesn't need to," Thorn told her. "We have enough evidence against him. Plus, with your testimony and mine, he'll get a maximum sentence."

She hadn't thought about testifying. She had mistakenly thought it was over, but it was far from over. Years from now, he'd be on trial, and she'd have to relive every horrible moment while recounting them to the judge and jury. The pain would resurface. The nightmares, if they diminished, would return in full force.

For the next few years, she'd be dreading the day she'd have to appear in court, sit in front of dozens of eyes, and swear an oath to say the truth and nothing but the truth. But the truth was too hard. The worst part? He'd be sitting a few yards away. Watching her. Grinning at her. Knowing what he did, what they all did. And he would still cling to his "not guilty" defense because it'd be all he had left.

What about her? What did she have left? The hope he'd rot in prison? Face electrocution? She didn't want any of that. She just wanted it to be over.

"It would've been better if he had been killed," she said, without a drop of mercy.

Donovan and Thorn peered at each other. "That's what we said," Donovan admitted. "But at least he's the last of the four we have to worry about."

Beth's eyes widened. Her breath caught in her chest. The world turned to black. One word repeated over and over in her mind.

Four.

The men involved in her kidnapping blurred through her mind one by one.

Not four.

"Five," she said.

"What?"

She tore her gaze from the black world consuming her. "There weren't four. There were five."

The looks on their faces confirmed her panic. They were shocked. Worse than that were the flickers of fear flashing across their faces.

"Are you sure?" Thorn's hands clenched into fists atop the table. His jaw ticked.

"I had names for them," she said. "Broken Nose was the man I kicked in the face. DB was the man I beat to death with my belt buckle. Screw Face was the man I stabbed in the face with a screw. Two-by-Four was the man with wide shoulders."

"And we got them," Thorn reassured her.

She shook her head. "You missed Mr. Gun. I called him that because he always had a gun in his hand. He was the one calling the shots. He was the one who shot me, who stomped on my hand. He was the worst one of them all."

She looked from Donovan to Thorn. They appeared as defeated as she felt.

"Five," she repeated. "Not four."

Chapter Twenty Three

One got away. That infuriated Donovan. And it wasn't even a weak link but the mastermind behind Beth's kidnapping and torture. How could that have happened? He had seen Mr. Gun with his own eyes. The man took a piss in front of him for God sakes! How could they have missed him? His vanishing trick boggled Donovan's mind. Maybe Mr. Gun knew Donovan and Thorn were on the adjacent roof and snuck out the back, leaving his pathetic team to take the fall. The better question was how they were going to find him?

"And you think there's a chance he could still be here?" he asked Thorn.

Beth was the one who answered. "I told you. Jackson trained these men. Mr. Gun isn't going to give up. I mean, did Jackson? When we were in San Francisco, he hunted us down to our hotel room and waited until we returned. Mr. Gun will wait for the perfect opportunity. He doesn't want me alone. He wants *us*. And when he can get us together, he'll strike. You can count on that."

Donovan wasn't sure what brought about Beth's change, but her old self was returning, and he was thankful for that.

"If that's true, then why hasn't he come for the two of you here?"

Beth smiled at Thorn's question. "Because he doesn't want to make his boss's mistake. He has another plan."

"If only we knew what that was," Donovan interjected.

Although anyone could've questioned Beth's sanity over the past few weeks, she was sane and her logic was sound. While in the claustrophobic closet, she had been able to get into her kidnapper's head and learn his ways. Neither he nor Thorn doubted her instincts in this matter.

That still left Donovan with one unanswered question. "If we don't know where the bastard is, and he's not coming here, how do we draw him out?"

All three of them were silent.

Donovan thought of returning to the building where they found Beth and doing a thorough search of it and the surrounding buildings. But that would take a lot of manpower and time. There was no way of knowing how far Mr. Gun could've gone to find a safe place to hide and plot his next move. For all they knew, Mr. Gun could be in the hotel across the street watching them through the window with a sniper's scope.

Donovan peered over his shoulder and made a mental note to draw the blinds.

Putting out an APB would be pointless. They didn't know his real name, and he could've disguised himself by now. Besides, he wouldn't be showing his face anywhere.

With one look at Thorn's scowl, he could tell Thorn wasn't having any more luck coming up with a plan.

"There's only one obvious answer," Beth's gaze

locked on to Donovan. "We set ourselves up as bait."

Donovan looked at her aghast. "You already were bait!"

Beth peered at him as calm as ever. "But now we can be bait together."

"This isn't a game, Beth," Donovan shouted.

"To him it is."

Donovan faced Thorn, hoping the cop would take his side, but Thorn shook his head. "I hate to say it, but it's the only option."

Obscenities flew from Donovan's mouth. He stalked away from the table. In the kitchen, he clutched the edge of the sink. His hands tightened. If he could break the counter and bend the metal with his rage, he would.

Beth's words carried to him. "Thorn, can you—"

"No need to ask," he said. "I'll get some food and come back in thirty."

The door closed.

Though she moved silently, he could sense Beth behind him. Her right arm looped around his waist. Her palm flattened against his abdomen, and the splints on her fingers scratched him through the thin fabric of his T-shirt. Against his back, he felt her other arm trapped in the sling as she pressed herself as closely as she could to him with her cheek between his shoulder blades.

After a moment, he turned and wrapped her in his arms, being careful not to disturb her shoulder. They stayed like that for a minute before Beth spoke in a hushed voice.

"I know you don't want to risk me. I don't want to risk you, either, but we have to do whatever we can to get this guy. If we don't, we're always going to look over our shoulders. What kind of life will that be?" She leaned back.

He lowered his head to look into her eyes. They were clear, not clouded with drugs or fear.

"What if we have a baby?" she asked. "How would we keep him or her safe if we can't keep ourselves safe?"

The mention of a baby knotted his gut. "We can't have a baby if you're dead," he whispered.

"But if we get him, we'll be able to live long, happy lives." She lifted her right hand and lay her palm against his cheek. "We're not the only ones who face uncertain futures if Mr. Gun is free to continue Jackson's work. Think of all the other people he can kill. We have to stop him. Not just for us, but for his future targets. I can't sit back and let him hurt other women as he hurt me."

He knew she couldn't. And neither could he.

"Okay," he said. His voice was hoarse. "I'm in."

Those two words felt like a death sentence, but for whom he didn't know.

****

Thorn helped Beth into a bulletproof vest while Donovan strapped on his own. "So, these things can stop bullets?" Beth asked.

"We wouldn't wear them if they didn't," Thorn said as he put the last strap into place.

"What if he shoots at our heads?"

Her words caused Thorn to glance at Donovan, but neither of them said a word.

"Never mind," she said. "I think I know."

Donovan pulled a T-shirt over his head and picked

up the purple flannel shirt Beth would wear. He eased the sleeves up her arms then worked the buttons into place. Each one hid more and more of the vest. His gaze flicked to her face. She was watching him with wide eyes.

His heart clenched.

"I'll be right beside you the whole time," he said.

"I know."

"No one is going to let anything happen to you."

"I know."

"We're going to be okay."

Her lips pulled into a small smile. She nodded, but he felt her doubt.

He captured her lips and kissed her deeply. His heart hammered into his chest. Could Beth feel it through the vest? When he pulled away, he slipped her arm into the sling.

She looked as vulnerable as ever.

With his arm around Beth, his hand on her hip, he faced Thorn, who wore his own bulletproof vest over a black T-shirt. In his hand, he clutched a radio.

"When you go outside, linger a moment, so if he's watching, he'll see you. Drive to the beach. Go the speed limit. If you drive too slow or too fast, he'll know something is up. When you get to Waikiki Beach, head toward Diamond Head. We've drawn an infinity symbol in the sand for you. If you see it, we're close. You won't see them, but undercover police officers will be there. They are getting into position as we speak. Don't do anything suspicious. Don't look over your shoulder. Act like you're alone. We're doing this at sunrise to eliminate the possibility of innocent people getting caught in the mix. If Mr. Gun shows up, play his game. I'll give the order to shoot him when the opportunity arises." He looked at them. "Are you ready?"

"As I'll ever be," Beth said.

"Let's get this over with," Donovan agreed.

"All right." Thorn lifted his radio. "Beth and Donovan are on the move. Everyone into position." He nodded at them.

Hand in hand, Donovan led Beth out of the hotel room, into the elevator, and onto the sidewalk. At the curb, they paused. It took all of Donovan's self-restraint not to look up and down the street, not to search the windows. The sky above was a pale gray. The streets were quiet. Even so, he couldn't shake the feeling someone watched them.

He faced Beth.

She turned to him. A sweet smile was on her face. It tugged his heartstrings. How could she give him such a lovely smile knowing how dangerous of a situation they were in? Knowing their lives could come to an end at any minute?

She put her right hand on his neck and rose up on tiptoe to whisper in his ear. "Kiss me and make it good. Because nothing will piss him off more than seeing us together, in love and kissing."

She dropped back onto her heels. Her smile was wide, showing her teeth.

Donovan grinned down at her. Dipping his head, he nipped at her bottom lip. His arm snaked around her, pulling her body snuggly to his. With his other hand, he caught her chin and held her head in place as his tongue entered her mouth. A soft caress, a gentle bite, a light suck. He drew a moan from her, a sound he hadn't heard in a long time. It ignited a fire within him. He cradled her head in his hands as he eagerly explored her mouth. Her flavors, textures, and scent; he could drown in them. Her warmth, even in this moment, was strong enough to seep into his pores and set him ablaze.

A groan rumbled in the back of his throat. He had to pull away before his needs became too powerful. Beth wanted to give Mr. Gun a show of their romance, not a theatrical. But, by God, he couldn't wait until this was over and she healed so he could make love to her again and reacquaint himself with her body.

Panting, he pressed his forehead to hers. Feeling her lips, her tongue, hearing her moans and breathy sighs invigorated him. He wanted more but couldn't have it. Not on the sidewalk with Mr. Gun watching.

"Damn," Beth gasped. "That was…" Words failed her.

He inched back, but his hands were still tangled in her hair. Her cheeks were flushed. How nice it was to see that versus the pallor her nightmares brought.

"I miss that," she managed.

He smiled. Kissing her, caressing her, holding her to his humming body…he had missed that, too. The kisses he had given her before today were soft and quick. The caresses he had given her were soothing rubs on the back, and the embraces had been to ward off pain, not to heighten passion.

He kissed her on the tip of her nose before leading her to their rental car.

After they crossed South King Street, signs of the tsunami became visible. The roads were clear, but filth and debris were piled along the road. Crews made their way up and down Oahu, cleaning up what they could while machines used their metal jaws to pick apart demolished buildings. It would take Oahu months, years even, to return to its former self. If it ever did.

Donovan glanced at Beth. She sat stiffly in the passenger's seat with her head bowed and her hair curtaining her face.

"Are you okay?"

"Yeah." Her voice was muffled. "It's just better if I don't look."

Heart breaking for her, he put his hand on her knee. He drove like that all the way to the beach. When the coast came into view, his jaw clenched. Many of the hotels dotting the coast were gone. He knew Beth had seen some of these images on the news, but he didn't want her to see them in person. He drove to the end of the beach and parked next to the last hotel that was luckily still intact, except all the windows were busted.

He squeezed Beth's knee. "We're here."

Beth slowly lifted her head. She looked toward Diamond Head and then back at the rest of Waikiki Beach. Her body jerked as if an electric current shocked her muscles. She took a deep breath before turning her head to Donovan.

He was relieved not to see her eyes swimming with tears, but there was pain between her lashes. The same pain he felt while looking at the demolished beachline and thinking about the people who had been there when the tsunami struck.

"Let's get this over with," she said.

They walked toward Diamond Head where Thorn and his undercover team hid. Their footsteps were leisurely as if they had no reason to think danger was near.

A couple of surfers were in the water, undeterred by the ruins as long as they could catch a wave. One person jogged along the shore, and another snapped pictures of the water. Other than that, the beach was stranded.

They were drawing closer to the massive mountain that was Diamond Head when the infinity symbol appeared in the sand. Beth's hand twitched in his. He kicked away the infinity as they passed it.

"How about this spot?" he asked.

Beth peered at the scenery. "I like it. We're alone." She smiled at him and sank onto the sand facing Diamond Head. He lowered next to her and put an arm around her waist.

Gentle waves rolled forward and stretched over the soft sand beside them, reflecting the colors of the sunset—soft oranges and bright yellows. The sky's brilliance wasn't matched in the rolling waves, though. The colors staining the clouds behind Diamond Head struck Donovan with awe. He couldn't remember the last time he admired a sunrise or sunset. If ever.

"So, this is where it's going to end," Beth whispered. "In this pretty place?"

He knew what she meant. Sting operations should be done in sketchy places, not a place as beautiful as this.

"You know I don't think I've ever watched the sunrise before. I like to sleep in."

Donovan chuckled. "I was thinking the same thing." He drew her closer to his side. "Do you know how magical a sunrise or sunset is? Although it looks like the sun travels across the sky, the Earth is actually moving. While we go on with the little things that make up our days, the Earth is rotating on its axis, giving us sunrises and sunsets. At the same time, it's spinning so fast that it grounds us. Yet, it still orbits around the sun, a journey that takes a full year. And the sun—" He turned his face to it. "—it's large and full of magma, but we're so far away from it that it looks like nothing more than an orb. And yet, it's still powerful enough to burn us. Although it's motionless compared to earth, the sun orbits around the center of the Milky Way."

Beth sighed. "Makes me feel so small."

"But we're part of the puzzle."

Beth tilted her head to him. "We're part of the mystery." She smiled and then added softly, "I think we should face the ocean. In case he's waiting to sneak up on us."

"Good idea."

While facing the waves, he kissed her temple, and she lay her head on his shoulder. They sat like that for several minutes. Oranges, yellows, and thin streaks of purple filled the sky to their left. With Beth at his hip, the soft sand beneath him, frothy ocean water creeping closer, he forgot why they were there.

Beth picked up a shell and held it up for him to see. "My first shell from Hawaii. In San Fran, you said the shells I collected could've come from anywhere in the world and washed up there for me to find. Do you remember that?"

"How could I forget?"

She tucked her new shell into the breast pocket of her shirt. "I could be wrong," she whispered. "We've been here a long time. Maybe he's not—"

Something slammed into Donovan's back with such force his head went back. *Bullet!* That one word was a scream in his head. He collapsed onto the sand. The scream in his head turned into Beth's scream in his ear.

Chapter Twenty Four

Beth draped herself over Donovan and tapped his cheek. "Donovan?"

His eyes stayed sealed.

"Donovan?" She pushed his shoulder off the sand so she could slip her hand underneath him. Wetness touched her skin. She pulled her hand back and choked on a sob at the sight of red tainting her fingers.

"No! Donovan!" Tears blurred his face.

He wasn't moving, wasn't breathing.

She lay her forehead to his chest. "You promised me forever."

Sand shot into the air a foot from where Beth knelt. She lifted her head to see Mr. Gun a few yards away. He looked more menacing than she remembered, the gun in his hand larger.

"Hello, Beth."

Her mouth went dry. Her tongue stuck to the roof of her mouth. The moisture in her body collected in her eyes and leaked down her cheeks.

"Get up," he ordered with a jab of the gun in her direction.

She rose onto wobbling knees. Her hands shook.

Next to her feet, Donovan lay lifelessly.

"You killed him," she gasped.

Mr. Gun cocked his head to the side. "You always knew I would. I said from the beginning I'd kill him."

"You also said you'd kill me, so why didn't you shoot me in the back, too? Why didn't you take me out? Put me out of my misery?"

"After I told Jackson how wounded you were, how fragile you became, he realized you weren't as much of a threat as he first thought. Donovan was always the main objective. Not you."

"But I want to die," she shouted. "I don't want to live without him."

"Ah, but that would be a waste of a good bullet."

Anger edged out her sorrow. "You already put a bullet in me. Using another one won't be much of a loss."

Mr. Gun shrugged. "I'm not fond of unnecessary bloodshed."

Beth sputtered. "You live for bloodshed. You work for Jackson Storm for God's sake!"

"And I have orders from Jackson to let you live. You should be happy."

"Happy?" Her body vibrated with a million swarming emotions. "Happy? My husband is lying dead at my feet. You've taken everything from me—my husband, my sanity, my happiness. Now take my fucking life. End this once and for all!"

"Beth, Beth, Beth—"

"Don't say my name like you know me," she shouted. "You're scum. You don't know anything about me, and I don't want to know a damn thing about you."

"Ouch!" He rubbed a hand over his heart. "You're hurting my feelings." He had the nerve to pout. "I'm gonna go." He flicked the muzzle of his gun at Donovan. "Enjoy your dead husband."

His comment was like a blow to her heart. She bent forward as breath punched out of her body.

Mr. Gun strutted away, whistling. The bastard was whistling! All the anger she ever felt during her life didn't compare to the rage she had at that moment. Red flashes stole her vision. Her heart rate was so erratic it was all she could feel—a thousand hearts beating at once with the force to shatter her body. Her chest heaved. She dug into her shirt's pocket and threw the shell at Mr. Gun. His head jerked forward, and she knew it had cracked into his skull. She hoped it had cut him.

"I'm not weak," she shouted. Her voice spat venom. "I'm not broken! You can lock me in a closet, starve me, shoot me, beat me. You can do your worst, and I will still survive. I will still be a bigger *man* than you'll ever be."

Mr. Gun charged at her, but she stood her ground. Not so much as taking a step back in retreat. "You don't think I'm a threat?" she said. "You don't know the meaning of the word." Her voice had taken on an edge she had never heard come out of her vocal chords. It was deep and raw.

Mr. Gun stopped a foot from her and jabbed the muzzle of the gun between her brows. She could smell the metal, the grease, the gun powder. She pressed her forehead to it and glared into his black-hole eyes.

"If you don't kill me, I will become a threat bigger than Jackson Storm. I've studied stalkers, wife beaters and murderers, and I will use that knowledge to hunt you down and kill you. So, shoot me or be a hunted bitch."

Mr. Gun seethed. Stale alcohol burned her nostrils.

"You have a death wish, is that it?"

Beth grinned, splitting her face. It felt manic. It felt awesome!

"Oh yes," she said. "I do have a death wish. But it's not for me…it's for you."

His upper lip curled back, exposing pale gums. "You think you have the power to take me down?"

"I know I do."

He shook his head and let out a whoop of laughter. "Are you still delusional, Beth? You should get that checked out." He lowered the gun to his side. "I'm going to walk off this beach and live a life of wealth, once I get my money for killing your husband. And I won't ever have to worry about you."

"I wouldn't be so sure about that," she said with a hint of smugness. She had more resources at her disposal than he could ever imagine. She had a whole police department backing her up.

Mr. Gun tucked his gun in the back of his jeans. "I hope you enjoy the rest of your life, Beth." He turned his back on her. "I know I'll enjoy mine."

"I wouldn't bet on it," she muttered.

Movement at her feet.

The muffled sound of shoes crunching into stiff, wet sand.

Fingers brushed hers; she clutched the hand that was offered.

Donovan stood beside her, unharmed thanks to the bulletproof vest with exploding dye packs.

She lifted her chin and called out to Mr. Gun. "One more thing…"

He laughed. "What? Have another shell to throw at me?"

She waited until he turned to her before saying, "We aren't so easy to kill."

"No," Mr. Gun whispered. And then on a scream, "No! I killed you. I fucking killed you!" He reached behind his back. "You're going to stay dead this time." He surged toward them. Rage came off him in waves. The rabid look in his eyes was like that of a shark with the scent of blood.

Beth stumbled into the surf, dragging Donovan with her.

Mr. Gun pulled out his weapon. As he leveled it at them, terror slammed into Beth's chest. Her heart ceased beating and plummeted to her bowels. *Oh no.* Panic made her hyperventilate.

Where's Thorn? Why isn't he shooting? Why isn't he shooting?!

She closed her eyes, not wanting to see the bullet coming, and gripped Donovan's hand. Her mind was impossibly blank. She didn't think about the things she wished she could've done. No flashbacks dominated her thoughts. No regrets. She was empty, as if she already was a corpse, a skeleton, ashes in an urn. Then she heard a grunt. Her eyelids flipped open. Mr. Gun dropped to his knees. A foot away from his body, his gun lay in the sand. He face-planted, revealing a patch of red on the back of his white T-shirt.

Thorn and several other undercover officers burst out of their hiding places and stormed the beach with their weapons drawn. Their mouths were moving, but she couldn't hear their shouts.

Beth stood in shock as they rolled Mr. Gun onto his back and checked his vitals.

Thorn approached them. "It's okay. Everything's

going to be okay."

Beth nodded. Her gaze flitted to Mr. Gun—unmoving and unable to cause any more harm—then back to Thorn. "Thank you."

He squeezed her chin with his thumb and forefinger before joining the other agents.

Strong hands turned her. Donovan cupped her face and peered into her eyes. "You were brilliant." She smiled although her knees hadn't stopped shaking. "But..." His eyes darkened. "Would you really want to die if I wasn't alive?"

She nodded as tears filled her eyes.

Donovan pressed his lips to her forehead. "So would I," he whispered.

"It was smart of Thorn to think of putting the exploding dye packs under our shirts," she said when she finally found her voice. "Does it hurt?" Her hand molded around his side, wanting to feel his bruises and aches.

"A little," he admitted. "The bullet hit the vest but knocked the wind out of me. I'll be bruised and sore, but I've dealt with worse."

She recalled his fractured ribs from a year ago and knew he was right. He could barely move then, but he took the pain like a gladiator.

My gladiator.

"Can you hug me?"

His gaze softened. "I'm not that hurt, Beth." He slipped an arm around her waist and brought her close with a hand at the back of her head. She hid her face in the crook of his neck and breathed in his scent. The feel of his solid body and the smell of his skin were comforts she could wallow in forever. She wanted him.

She wanted their home. She wanted their life together.

"Can we go home?"

Donovan kissed the top of her head. "Yeah, we can go home." He steered her around the officers.

Several feet away, she scooped up the shell she had chucked at Mr. Gun's head. "I think we should frame this."

Epilogue

Beth's favorite spot on a plane was always the window seat, but she gave it to Donovan for their flight home. During the takeoff, she closed her eyes, and Donovan knew why. She didn't want to risk seeing any of the tsunami's aftermath from a bird's eye view. She wanted to put what happened on the island behind her. Starting immediately.

He picked up her hand and pressed his lips to it when the clouds obscured the land. "It's okay to look."

She opened her eyes and looked straight ahead for a few seconds before turning a weak smile to him. Her gaze briefly drifted to the window; her curiosity too great. When she couldn't see anything, she relaxed into her seat.

During the flight, Donovan's excitement grew. They were returning to Florida, and he was taking them to their new home. He had thought about this moment for months, and it was finally happening. His happiness was brimming to the top, like the froth atop a good mug of beer.

Beth gently poked him in the cheek. "Your dimples are showing. Why are you smiling for no reason at all?"

"Oh, I have a reason." He kissed her cheek. "And it's a good one."

She arched a brow, a sign that he had her hooked. "Care to share?"

"You'll see. It's a surprise."

Her eyes widened. "A Donovan Goldwyn surprise? I'm even more curious. Tell me," she begged.

"Patience."

She gasped. "That's cruel. You know that's the one thing I don't have." She gave him a teasing smile. "So, I don't get a hint?"

"It's my wedding gift to you. You'll get it once we land."

"But *you* are my wedding gift, Donovan. I don't need anything else. I'm just happy to be going home, and that we're both alive."

Her words warmed him. "So am I. You're all I'll ever want or need, but this gift is something I've been wanting to give to you since Hurricane Sabrina."

She grinned. "Floaties?"

"An inner tube."

She laughed. "All right. I guess I'll have to wait."

When they landed, they met Thorn at baggage claim. "I'm going to go home, take a shower, and then I have to talk to Chief Cormac. But I wanted to tell you something, Beth, before I go. It's about Mr. Gun."

Beth stiffened.

Donovan wanted to deck Thorn for dredging up bad memories within minutes of being home.

"His real name was Bruce Grosswiener."

Donovan felt a chuckle rising up his chest. He peered at Beth. Her face twitched.

She mashed her lips together in an effort to keep her laughter at bay, but it was too strong. A closed-mouth giggle escaped. She fought hard to keep her face placid, but her shoulders bobbed up and down. Another sound came out. Her face contorted. Then she threw back her head and released the laughter beating inside her.

"Oh my gosh." She pressed her hand to her chest. "Seriously? His name was Bruce…Gross…wiener." She could barely get his name out.

Thorn grinned. "I knew that would make your day. See you around." He gave them a two-finger salute before wandering off.

Beth wiped away figurative tears. "That is great. I feel so much better."

Donovan smirked. "I'm glad. Let's go home."

In his truck, he stole glances at Beth. When they went in the opposite direction of their apartment, she returned the stare but didn't say anything. She even kept her questions stifled when they entered the old city where she grew up. But the second he turned down the street where she lived when Hurricane Sabrina hit, she faced him.

Curiosity bloomed across her eyes. "Donovan, what are we doing here?"

"This is your gift."

She shook her head, not understanding. "What is?"

He slowed in front of the lot where her childhood home used to be. Except it wasn't an empty lot anymore. A two-story house of brick and wood sat on the lot with a large covered porch and an extra-wide garage and driveway.

He pulled his truck into the driveway and cut the engine. "This…" He gestured to the house. "I'm bringing you home, Beth."

She shook her head. "No, Donovan, I sold the land."

"I know." He smiled as he took her hand. "I bought

it."

Her mouth peeled open. She stared at the house through the windshield. "So, the money we got was your money all along?" He nodded. "The money you got from your grandfather's will paid for this?"

"Every last penny."

"Donovan..." Her voice was a breath. "I can't believe you did this."

Her words confused him. "Do you want to look at it?" He pulled the keys from the ignition and selected a silver key. "I have the key."

She followed him to the front door. He inserted the key, unlocked the door, and let her in ahead of him. She moved through the first floor, which he had designed specifically to look like the home she used to know, but with some adjustments like the fireplace where he imagined setting up a fire during the rare, cold Florida days. And the two downstairs bedrooms had been transformed into a gym and a guest room. Upstairs was a master suite with a vaulted bath and walk-in closet. Two extra rooms shared an adjacent bathroom.

Beth paused in the middle of the master suite. When she looked at Donovan, he felt giddy, like a boy at Christmas. At the same time, he was apprehensive. She hadn't said a word since stepping over the threshold.

"What do you think?"

Her mouth cracked open. A tiny sound came out. She closed her mouth, swallowed, and tried again. "I think you're the best husband in the universe. I already feel at home here." She shook her head. "I love you with all my heart."

Donovan went to her, framed her face with his

hands, and kissed her with all the feelings he had pent up inside—excitement, anxiety, happiness, and fear.

"You're too good for me," she murmured between his lips.

He shook his head and lifted her face so she'd look into his eyes. "I'm as good as you've made me, Beth. This…" He lifted his gaze to the ceiling. "This is what I pictured when I proposed to you. My money was collecting dust anyway, so don't for one second feel guilty or undeserving." He looped an arm around her and brought her closer. "We met in this very spot. It only makes sense to spend our forever here. This house is going to be where we raise our children and tell them about their grandparents and the hurricane that brought us together. We're going to grow old together here, and then, we'll pass it on to our kids. It's going to be an heirloom of our love."

Tears coursed down Beth's cheeks. He swiped them away with his thumbs. "Will you live here with me, Beth? Love here with me? Grow old here with me?"

She nodded as more tears ran down her cheeks. "One hundred times yes."

Donovan's fear and anxiety dissolved with her words. His shoulders lowered. He kissed her as he did on their wedding day, with promises, hopes, and dreams on his lips.

"Just one thing…" Beth inched back and peered up at him. "Did you make this house disaster proof?"

A word about the author...

Chrys Fey is the author of the *Disaster Crimes* series, a unique concept blending romance, crimes, and disasters. She's partnered with the Insecure Writer's Support Group and runs their Goodreads book club. She's also an editor for Dancing Lemur Press.

Fey realized she wanted to write by watching her mother pursue publication. At the age of twelve, she started her first novel, which flourished into a series she later rewrote at seventeen.

Fey lives in Florida and is always on the lookout for hurricanes. She has four cats and three nephews; both keep her entertained with their antics.

Get your free copy of LIGHTNING CRIMES on Amazon!

Thank you for purchasing
this publication of The Wild Rose Press, Inc.

If you enjoyed the story, we would appreciate your
letting others know by leaving a review.

For other wonderful stories,
please visit our on-line bookstore at
www.thewildrosepress.com.

For questions or more information
contact us at
info@thewildrosepress.com.

The Wild Rose Press, Inc.
www.thewildrosepress.com

Stay current with The Wild Rose Press, Inc.

Like us on Facebook

https://www.facebook.com/TheWildRosePress

And Follow us on Twitter
https://twitter.com/WildRosePress